WHEN
I
WAS
DEATH

ALEXIS HENDERSON

PENGUIN BOOKS

PENGUIN BOOKS

UK | USA | Canada | Ireland | Australia
India | New Zealand | South Africa

Penguin Books is part of the Penguin Random House group of companies whose addresses can be found at global.penguinrandomhouse.com.

www.penguin.co.uk   www.puffin.co.uk   www.ladybird.co.uk

First published in the USA by G. P. Putnam's Sons,
an imprint of Penguin Random House LLC 2026
First published in Great Britain by Penguin Books, 2026

001

Copyright © Alexis Henderson, 2026

The moral right of the author has been asserted

Penguin Random House values and supports copyright.
Copyright fuels creativity, encourages diverse voices, promotes freedom
of expression and supports a vibrant culture. Thank you for purchasing
an authorized edition of this book and for respecting intellectual property
laws by not reproducing, scanning or distributing any part of it by any
means without permission. You are supporting authors and enabling
Penguin Random House to continue to publish books for everyone.
No part of this book may be used or reproduced in any manner for the
purpose of training artificial intelligence technologies or systems. In accordance
with Article 4(3) of the DSM Directive 2019/790, Penguin Random House
expressly reserves this work from the text and data mining exception.

Printed and bound in Great Britain by Clays Ltd, Elcograf S.p.A.

The authorized representative in the EEA is Penguin Random House Ireland,
Morrison Chambers, 32 Nassau Street, Dublin D02 YH68

A CIP catalogue record for this book is available from the British Library

ISBN: 978-0-241-71627-4

All correspondence to:
Penguin Books
Penguin Random House Children's
One Embassy Gardens, 8 Viaduct Gardens, London SW11 7BW

Penguin Random House is committed to a sustainable future for our business, our readers and our planet. This book is made from Forest Stewardship Council® certified paper.

For my sister

Chapter 1

The girls arrived on a bleak morning in May, eight months after my sister's death. I first saw them through my bedroom window, three vehicles—a rust-eaten pickup truck, an old station wagon, and an Airstream RV—crawling down the street and around the bend of the cul-de-sac. There were three teenage girls sitting in the bed of the pickup truck, all of them staring at my house as though it were a landmark. I stared back, and I swore one of them—a pale girl with hair like fire—looked up at my window and smiled. But by the time I scrambled downstairs and burst through the front door, they were gone. I might've thought I'd dreamed them if not for the smell of diesel hanging like a ghost in the cool morning air.

A few hours later, I left my house and walked down the sorry little main street of my hometown in Michigan. But calling it a town at all is generous. Towns are comprised of people, and once emptied of them, they lose their respective designations and become something else. The something else is what I walked through that day. Cracked streets licked with heat waves, a thin trickle of traffic passing by. The dusty storefronts of antique shops and jewelry stores that never had any customers. The remnants of a place that barely existed.

I scanned the streets, half hoping to spot the girls who had driven past my house that morning, but they seemed to have disappeared without a trace.

Still, I couldn't stop thinking about them.

It was a two-mile walk from my house to Conny's Coney Dogs, the twenty-four-hour diner where I worked as a waitress. The diner's owner and namesake, Conny—a tall, grave woman who smelled perpetually of patchouli and pot smoke—had hired me, probably out of pity, because I'd never waited a table in my life. By that time, the whole town knew about my sister and had closed ranks around my family the way small towns are supposed to when something tragic and terrible happens to one of their own.

But Conny had offered something others hadn't: distraction. In the long months that followed my sister's death, she taught me the rhythms of the diner—how to flirt tips from begrudging patrons who had next to nothing in their pockets, how to anticipate their needs with no more than a passing glance. In the grimy staff bathroom, I gathered my curls into a fat braid, scrubbed at my armpits with hand soap and a soggy wad of paper towels (I'd slept through my alarm and hadn't had the chance to shower) before changing into my uniform. It was a peach-pink dress—the color of a newborn baby's flush—with snagged stockings and a paper-pale apron so small it didn't cover much of anything. Once dressed, I pinned on my name tag just a few inches below my starched collar. It read *Roslyn Volk* in smudged Sharpie, because Conny liked it when her servers introduced themselves by their first and last names. Something about the importance of family, of knowing where a person was from and, in her words, exactly what stuff they were made of.

My sneakers squelched on the sticky tile floors as I carried steaming plates of pancakes and scrambled eggs, biscuits half submerged in gravy, and burnt triangles of toast to their respective tables. I refilled coffeepots and chatted with the regulars, trying my best to keep up with the breakfast rush.

On a staticky TV screen above the bar, the news was playing, though the sound was partly drowned out by the clamor of the kitchen—pots and pans clattering, slabs of bacon sizzling on the grill, cooks shouting orders above the din. The headline of the day was a string of violent storms that had washed across the Midwest the night before, spawning a series of tornadoes, one of which flattened a small town in Ohio, claiming the lives of more than a dozen people. It was the first bad storm of the year, and the meteorologist predicted more would follow.

There was a congressman on TV crying about the devastation when the girls entered the diner, the five of them streaming in single file.

One of the girls wore a long fur-collared coat despite the thickening heat. Another swept past in a heavy peasant skirt paired with a cropped and pilled flannel shirt. A third wore heavy boots and ripped men's jeans that looked like they were fished from the bowels of a Salvation Army bin and attacked with a razor.

They were around my age, but they dressed the way sixth

graders imagined themselves dressing at twenty, without the smothering supervision of their parents or the pressure of their peers. Their hair was wild, as if none of them owned a brush. And they were all pretty, but in the way that girls find each other pretty. Which is to say, unkempt and decidedly intimidating, like a boy's idea of a dream girl gone ragged at the edges.

I hoped they wouldn't sit in my section—groups of girls my age made me anxious—but the five of them did just that, occupying a small booth at the back of the diner, sitting crushed together hip-to-hip on the same side as if there wasn't another empty bench right in front of them.

I recognized the redhead immediately. She was the same fire-haired girl who I thought might've smiled at me that morning when the caravan drove past the house. Her bony hands were covered in faded stick-and-poke tattoos that looked like doodles drawn with pen, and she had wedding rings on every finger. She wore hoop earrings so large I could've slid one halfway up my arm, and she was impeccably dressed in wide-cut patchwork jeans and a lace top that looked like vintage lingerie with its vaguely cone-shaped bra cups.

Sitting close beside the redhead was the youngest of the five—maybe thirteen, give or take a year. She fixed her brilliant blue eyes on me and smiled at my approach. She had downy blond hair and wore lipstick, cracked and smeared and bleeding at the edges of her mouth like she'd applied and reapplied it with a heavy hand several days prior. She slipped a vape pen from the pocket of her coat and held it like a cigarette, pinched between two knuckles.

One of the older girls—she had dark eyes and hair the color of sand, which hung down her back in long microbraids—leaned across the table, snatched the vape pen from the blonde's hand, and turned it off despite the younger girl's protests.

None of them were locals, of that much I was certain. My graduating class would be comprised of fewer than a dozen students. I could rattle off their names, first and last, and some of their parents' too. These girls were newcomers, which was strange for a small town devoid of tourism where things never really changed.

The young girl kept smiling at me, mouth wide and bloody from the lipstick. "I like your dress. I've been looking for one just like that for ages. Do they sell them here?"

"Um . . . afraid not, b-but thank you?" I fumbled with my pen and notepad and nearly dropped both. "What would you like to drink?"

"Pink lemonade," said the girl. She kicked off her sandals, cork platforms with leather straps as thin as strings, and swapped them with the sneakers of the girl to her left. "They're a better match. Don't you think?"

"Um, yeah. We don't have pink lemonade. Is regular lemonade okay? It's house made."

She bobbed her head. "Sounds good. You can just bring it by the pitcher, and we'd like coffee, or better yet, hot chocolate if you have it. And we'll order the rest now too. Assuming you're ready?"

I nodded down at my notepad, my pen poised. Together, they ordered what seemed like half the menu—several stacks of pancakes, French toast, hash browns smothered with cheese and onions, six sunny-side up eggs, a plate of bacon, two chili dogs from the lunch menu, a ham and cheese omelet, as well as fresh fruit in a to-go box.

"For Shiloh," said a different, more sullen girl with a shifting gaze and the golden sliver of a nose ring pierced through her left nostril. Her hair was dark and cut in a ragged jaw-length bob, and her eyes were large and gray.

Conny, overhearing their lengthy order, got suspicious and made the girls pay for the meal up front. An older girl with blunt black bangs and blue eyeshadow lifted a large purse that looked like a carpetbag and set it on the table with a heavy *thud* that made the silverware jump and clatter. From it, she produced several fistfuls of wrinkled bills (I put them in the pocket of my apron to count later) and a small mason jar filled with silver change. She slid it to Conny with a smile. "Keep the change."

Whenever I returned to their table, their conversation seemed to die into silence or abruptly change subjects. They were enviably self-contained and entirely unbothered despite the curious gazes of the other diners, particularly the male ones who watched them with rapt, too-sharp interest.

The girls weren't naive or otherwise oblivious to the attention they received. Nor were they distant in the heavy-lidded, theatrical way girls often are when they're trying to appear pointedly aloof. They were merely... impassive. Perhaps they were too consumed by their own conversation. At times, their discussion grew so intense it appeared they were arguing about something. The same name kept coming up repeatedly; I'd hear it—a hot, hissing whisper—as I passed their table: *Shiloh*. The one the fruit was for.

I watched them eat with furtive glances cast over my shoulder or from across the diner behind the bar. The redhead shoveled large forkfuls of French toast into her mouth as if this were the last meal she'd ever eat and she had only minutes left to finish it.

Beside her sat the girl with the braids. I was tempted to call her the pretty one, because even among the girls she stood out as particularly stunning. Her skin was deep and dewy, utterly flawless, though she didn't look like she was wearing any concealer. She had full lips and high cheekbones that would've been the envy of any model. I stared as she popped the yolks of all six eggs on her plate—one after the other—with the tip of a steak knife and watched the yellow bleed into the white with dead eyes before licking the blade clean. The blonde emptied a small ramekin of maple syrup into the dregs of her coffee and drank the sludgy remnants in a single gulp.

"Slow down or you'll choke," said the older girl, the one with the powdery blue eyeshadow who'd paid for the food. When the youngest did, in fact, begin to choke just minutes later, the older girl patted her back until the coughing fit subsided.

It was a strange and intimate gesture, so maternal and natural that I wondered for a moment if the two were family. But they couldn't have looked any less alike. Different races—one white, the other Asian. Different hair. Different demeanor. All five girls had a distinct way of being. I didn't know how to describe it exactly, but it was both familiar and distinctly unusual.

They had a kind of confidence that came easily to them. The redhead kicked her feet out into the aisle that ran between tables, oblivious to the way she was taking up space. Bold in a way that boys are usually, and even then, only the most self-assured among them. The varsity athletes or that one overeager theater kid who lands all the lead roles in school plays.

After the girls finished their feast, I brought them a copy of the receipt. I doubted they'd want it. They'd refused to accept their change and seemed to have no care for cost, but I wanted another excuse to return to their table—curiosity surmounting my initial anxiety—to examine them up close one more time. "Can I interest you in something else? Maybe some dessert?"

"I'll take a hot fudge sundae," said the girl with the long braids. "No peanuts, with extra whip and maraschino cherries if you have them. And can you box it up so we can take it for the road?"

I nodded and was leaving to make it when the youngest of the group, the little blond girl, called me back. "Do you like to swim?"

"Sure," I said. "I guess so."

The young one nodded to the blue-eyeshadow girl, whom I took to be the leader of this strange flock. She reached into the other girl's carpetbag purse, found a pen, and scrawled an address on the back of the receipt I'd supplied them with, then folded it and put it into the pocket of my apron without asking whether or not I wanted it.

"Tonight." She slipped out of the booth. "Show up anytime after nine."

I made the sundae as the girls wolfed down their final bites of food. When I delivered it to the booth, they were already on their feet, laughing and talking among themselves.

"See you tonight," said the blonde. And then they were gone into the white brilliance of the day.

Chapter 2

I was a person once. I had friends and hobbies and a boyfriend, crowned homecoming king, who liked me enough to text me every morning and night. Back then, I was on the track team, and my coach thought I was good enough to get a scholarship at the kind of college that would maybe make my parents want to brag to their friends. I posted online semiregularly: selfies with the camera blurred out of focus, the smears of sunsets, my sister's face behind a rain-streaked window, a black squirrel rummaging through the contents of a dumpster. I'd write these long captions because I liked the thrill of stashing little pieces of myself in those posts. I guess some part of me believed that my life as I lived it was worth witnessing through a screen.

But even back then, when I was still a person, Adeline was something else. Something more. I was fairly well liked, approaching popular, even. But Adeline, one year my senior, was adored. Not just by her friends and our family, but by people she had never even spoken to. Everything that made me different and weird in the eyes of my classmates—like the fact that we were the only two biracial students at our small-town private school (our dad white and our mom Black)—just made Adeline all the more alluring. It helped that she was beautiful, and not in a pedestrian way. She was tall and bronze skinned like our mom but with our dad's blond hair and hazel eyes. Heads swiveled when she came down the hall at school, people turning to look no matter how many times they'd seen her before.

She didn't need an algorithm forcing her to the tops of people's feeds to get attention. Wherever she went, people watched and listened, and she never once had to ask for it.

But it wasn't just beauty that drew people to Adeline, it was something more. Adeline was capricious in a way that kept people on their toes. Her emotions were sharp and intense. Her happiness, at its height, was like the sun glaring sharply off a blanket of freshly fallen snow, and I'd find myself squinting at the sight of her smile. But when Adeline was sad—and she was often sad—the storms of her deep depressions swallowed her up, and me along with her. I told myself that this was because we were so close, but my emotions never affected Adeline the way hers did me. When Adeline was happy, I was happy. When she was sad, I was sad. And when she died, I became nothing at all.

Maybe I was nothing to begin with.

Adeline disappeared on a Thursday morning in late September, when I was preparing for school. She was in our shared bathroom with the door locked. She always woke earlier than I did, and I was used to waiting for her to finish her morning routine, but on that day, she was taking a lot longer than usual. I stood in the hall, with my towel and school uniform folded in a tight bundle against my chest, listening with an ear pressed to the door. I could hear the faucet running on the other side, but nothing more than that. "Addie?"

No answer.

I knocked twice. I needed to shave my legs and shower, brush my teeth and fix my hair, comb mascara through my lashes (which I always took pains to do in those early weeks of the semester, before the stress beat the intent to make a good impression right out of me). I banged on the door, open handed, until my palms stung. "Adeline, hurry the hell up."

Nothing.

I began to worry then, less because I was certain there was something wrong and more because Adeline was the sort of girl one worried about. She liked to disappear. She'd run away from home several times and, on weekends, made a sport of wriggling out of basement windows to attend college parties in the next town over. She'd kept a roster of secret boyfriends and, in the eighth grade, had snuck out to meet one under the guise of a weekend field trip (the man, a twenty-year-old, was later arrested). Adeline was so good at disappearances that sometimes she did it while still present, escaping the cage of her own body and drifting someplace else. I'd seen her do it sitting right in front of me. She'd just empty herself of all thought and sensibility, her eyes like those of someone who'd fallen asleep without shutting them. I'd envied that talent, her innate ability to escape herself at will.

Exasperated, I'd pushed into the bathroom. The faucet was on, the sink flooded almost up to the top, like it had been on for hours. As if she'd left in a hurry without bothering to shut it off. There was an open container of whipped moisturizer on the countertop, the same cream she applied every night, working it into the bags beneath her eyes. As I edged up to the counter, I suppressed the compulsion to dip my index finger into the soft peaks of the cream and lick it clean. The window above the toilet was just ajar. There was no sign of Adeline.

We looked for her, of course. First, just my parents and me. And then, twelve hours into a fruitless search, we got the police involved. Search parties were organized by local churches and the high school, and they combed through the woods around the town. Police dogs paced the fields of nearby farms with their noses to the ground. They dusted our shared bathroom for fingerprints but found only mine and Adeline's. Everyone who knew Adeline—family, friends, ex-boyfriends and flings—were questioned. Then questioned again. They dredged the pond behind our house down to the muck of its bottom, looking for a body. Helicopters circled the sky, trying to find what the search parties might've missed. Fundraisers cropped up online (I don't know what they were funding, exactly, as we never saw any of the pledged donations). My parents promised reward money they didn't have to spare, planning to draw from our college funds if anyone turned up with answers.

When Adeline was finally discovered, some eight weeks had passed. They found her body folded into one of those pastel plastic playhouses—half-overgrown with black mold and ivy—in the middle of the woods, four miles from the nearest road, nine from our house. No one understood how all those search parties and police dogs had neglected to find it, or why there was a random playhouse in the middle of the woods at all. It defied all logic, as if someone had hidden her away in the pocket of another reality, out of space and time. Like her body and the house that contained it had just spawned at random.

Why Adeline died there was another question unanswered. There was nothing sentimental about the place, and it had nothing to recommend it except, perhaps, that it was rather remote and quiet, and Adeline liked quiet places.

A hiker found her there, rotting but otherwise undisturbed, as if she'd simply fallen asleep and hadn't bothered to wake up again.

That same day, I found a short letter in the drafts of her email, something I'd missed when I'd searched her computer before because, amid the chaos of the search for her, I'd never thought to comb through what she hadn't sent or received. The email had been written a few weeks before she went missing. Not a suicide letter, per se, but something like one. As if she somehow knew what was coming and wanted to get ahead of it, have her say.

The letter was brief and confessional, the shorthand of an excuse (as if one's own death were a thing that could be excused away). Things didn't taste the same, she'd said. The sky was a duller blue. The air was thinner and drier than she remembered. Fall, her favorite season, was shorter than it used to be, the winters were longer, and she swore the snow fell gray instead of white, tainted before it ever even touched the ground, and she couldn't bear it.

They removed her body from the playhouse, ferried her to the coroner's office, where they ran toxicology reports and opened her up like the rats we'd dissected in biology class. I pondered over these gruesome details and had harbored some thin hope that, upon slitting open her stomach, the mortician might find a second letter, the paper soaked through with bile and acid, addressed to me in her cramped and messy handwriting. In this one, Adeline would apologize to me properly and assure me that I meant something to her, that she loved me, and that even death couldn't change that. But, of course, there was no letter. The contents of her stomach, as outlined by the autopsy, consisted of gin and the remnants of her dinner the night before she disappeared, confirming that she died just hours later. Because there was nothing in her blood or belly that could've caused her death and no wounds or signs of struggle, her official cause of death was deemed inconclusive.

Adeline's death remade me into something I never chose to be. Every hope I'd had for a future, every dream, had gone with her. I withdrew. Eventually, my friends stopped calling. I had a boyfriend at the time, and I broke up with him in a two-line text. We had a fight, in person, where he cried a lot (I found that strange, given that I'd caught him texting other girls behind my back the day before Adeline went missing), and I said very little at all, apart from the fact that I was sorry and tired and that my mom would be concerned if I didn't get home soon. I deleted all my social media, made myself disappear.

But even after all of that, it took me a few months to realize I wasn't really a person anymore. That somewhere along the way I'd become my grief. A glass cup filled to the brim with it so that everyone who saw me—all my friends, my family, my teammates, my coach—just saw the loss of Adeline. I began to suspect that I was unbearable to be around. That it hurt too much for people to exist in close proximity with someone who wore their pain so transparently.

Social interactions became painful and awkward. I had to think about things that other people didn't—like how to smile or when to nod. My performance was less than convincing. Halfway through the spring semester, my grades slipped so low that the chances of being accepted to any decent colleges were next to zero.

I even forgot how to run. Every time I stepped out onto the track, it was like I was sprinting through syrup. I went from one of the fastest runners in the state to the slowest on the team. But I didn't get kicked off until I refused to race. At least, that's what I told my coach right before he benched me. The truth was, after a few months, my legs just gave out on me, my knees buckling every time I tried to push off the starting block. I formally quit the team soon after the benching, a decision that should've been devastating, but I felt little more than relief. Shortly after, I got my parents and therapist to co-sign my absence for the last few weeks of school, on account of bereavement. Free of distractions, I had more time to devote to the only thing I really cared about: figuring out what happened to my sister. Why she died.

I never accepted the coroner's conclusion, mostly because it wasn't one. I didn't believe that my sister's heart had just given out that night, at random, the way everyone else seemed content to. But in the absence of any compelling possibilities—fingerprints at the crime scene, DNA traces, suicide letters, or grainy CCTV footage—I had nothing to grab hold of, nothing to bolster my belief that my sister didn't just die in a cruel stroke of misfortune except for the gut feeling, this unshakable instinct, that there was more to the story. I knew it not because of the way Adeline died, but because of how strange she'd acted in the last weeks of her life.

At the end of the last semester of her junior year, Adeline had been in a bad way. She started skipping classes, just how she was apt to do when her depression took a turn for the worse. There was talk of truancy and emergency meetings with therapists and guidance counselors. None of it worried me much; Adeline's moods came and went. It was all normal for her.

What was abnormal, though, was my aunt's intervention. At the end of that semester, as spring tipped into summer, she offered to let Adeline stay with her in a cabin on the lake in a rural part of northern Michigan, telling my parents that the nature and lack of cell service would do her good. Adeline, who was at that point choosing between an involuntary psych hold and a few long months on the lake, wisely opted for the latter.

The rest was rather fuzzy on my end. At the time, I was at a track camp several states away, but I know that, two weeks into her stay with my aunt, she made some friends—good influences, my aunt had called them, though she didn't seem to know very much about them. Which was why I found it so surprising that my aunt and parents allowed her to leave with them that summer.

I returned home just a few days after Adeline did, and what I discovered rattled me. My beautiful storm of a sister—defiant and contemptuous, sharp toothed and wicked smart, mean sometimes just for the sport of it—was utterly and completely subdued, all the life gone out of her. Like she'd cut her own tongue out of her mouth and offered it up with a smile.

I was the only one who noticed, the only one who seemed to care. My parents were so relieved to have their daughter back, whole and healed and as obedient as they'd always wanted her to be, that they never seemed curious to discover what had prompted her turn for the better.

Adeline, for her part, was convincing enough. She went to church on Sundays and attended school without complaint, never skipping any classes, never late to the bus stop. When I picked fights with her, stealing her favorite T-shirt to wear for a track meet, taking more than my share of time in the bathroom, she never voiced the smallest complaint. She came home from school on time every day, never sullen or smelling of smoke. She did her homework and made pleasant conversation at the dinner table with my parents, nodding at all the right times.

There were no house parties or secret college boyfriends. No sneaking in through the basement windows after nights out. No fights with my parents or panic attacks. No bouts of depression that kept her in bed for days at a time.

To put it simply, she wasn't the sister I knew.

In the short weeks of that summer away, she'd become a stranger to me.

When I finally questioned her about it, cornering her one night in her bedroom after my parents were asleep, demanding to know what happened to her over the summer that had changed her into a person I didn't even know anymore, she just smiled at me. And I saw it then, something horrible in her eyes. Something ugly.

I named it, called it what it was. I pleaded with her to snap out of it, begged her to come back to me. The anger set in then, and I made sure she knew that, while she might've fooled everyone else, she couldn't hide from me.

And I was suffering because of it. We both were.

What followed was the worst fight we'd ever had. A fight so terrible I had never been able to bring myself to revisit it, except one time. The night of my questioning at the police station, when I turned my memories inside out making sure I told the officers every detail—Adeline's false smile, the deadness in her eyes, the way she seemed like a stranger, the way what seemed like a turn for the better was really just her giving up. But in the end, it didn't matter. The police, my parents, the people in our town—they had all decided what they wanted to believe.

A girl goes out into the forest alone.

She falls asleep.

She doesn't wake up.

These things do happen, after all.

I tried to confide in my parents, but they wouldn't hear me. The most they offered were soft and pitying glances, thin platitudes about acceptance and letting go. They shuttled me to teen grief groups and therapy sessions, but none of it helped. If I couldn't have the truth about what happened to my sister, then I didn't want much of anything at all.

Alone in my search for the truth, I grew numb and stony and despondent. Not unlike Adeline in the last days of her short life, but without the fakeness and the pleasantries. I had become so accustomed to feeling nothing but the weight of my grief that, when those five girls walked into the diner, so fully alive in the way Adeline was—the way she had been before she'd changed—I couldn't stop thinking about them, even after they left. I had to know more about them. I was desperate to, if only because I wanted to keep feeling that... alive.

"Well, I don't like them," said Conny, after I'd told her about their party and my intention to attend. "Those girls have a hungry look about them. Like they'd eat their own if it came down to it."

This didn't surprise me. Conny, while kind to me, had never taken to girls who did things like apply blush to the tips of their noses or bleach-dye their jeans. Girls like Adeline. Their kind of, sure, *garish* beauty was intolerable to her, and I now saw it was because it made her feel plain and perhaps a little small. I couldn't entirely blame her. Sometimes I felt the same way, standing next to Adeline.

After my shift, I changed out of my uniform and examined the receipt with the party address. The girl's handwriting was lacy and ragged like a tattered cobweb: *585 Grove Street*. Just reading it sent an illicit little thrill down my spine like a trickle of ice water. I knew that I had to go, that there was no alternate reality where I didn't. Those girls reminded me of Adeline, and I would've done anything—gone anywhere—to get closer to my sister or the next best thing, those five girls who were so much like her that it scared me.

Grove Street was within walking distance of the diner, and it was easily the most expensive street in town, the last place I'd expected to find them. All the houses were large and quaint. Around Christmastime, they strung up the most beautiful lights, and people came from all over town—bundled up in hats and scarves—and walked hand in hand, house to house, admiring the decorations: the lights strung between the trees, the electric reindeer, and the animatronic Santa Claus that waved, yelling "Ho ho ho!" at groups of teenage girls who erupted into fits of laughter.

That night, there were next to no lights on. Even the lampposts were dead thanks to a routine blackout. No one on the sidewalks but me. I made my way through the neighborhood, head down, hands in my pockets, glancing over my shoulder every minute or so to make sure I wasn't being followed. This was one of the nicest parts of town, but it wasn't a particularly good idea for a girl to walk alone at night in any town anywhere.

I kept going east until I found the address, a large two-story house, tastefully renovated, with a lime-green door and dark windows. It was the largest one on the cul-de-sac. There was a for sale sign staked in the yard that read FORECLOSURE in thick red letters.

I swallowed dry.

There were just two cars parked in the driveway: the rusty pickup truck and the station wagon that had crawled past my house that morning. Just down the street, parked flush with the curb, was the Airstream RV, one of those silver sleeper vans that looked a lot like a soup can with a sticker stripped off. There were patterned curtains drawn over most of its porthole windows, light shining out through them. Someone inside, maybe? Watching TV or perhaps getting ready for bed.

I edged past the vehicles, started toward the front door, and knocked once, then again more loudly when there was no answer.

A full minute later, a girl answered the door. The same one from the diner, with the eerie gray eyes, the nose ring, and the shaggy bob, dead ends brushing along a sharp-cut jaw. She wore flared pants, low slung, hipbones jutting above the waist, and a cropped leather vest for a shirt.

Behind her was a dark and empty foyer. For a house party, it was awfully quiet. No lights or music. I wondered, at the sight of that empty house, if I was about to be murdered or sex trafficked or something equally terrible. But even that fear wasn't enough to deter me. I had to see this through. I didn't realize until that moment just how desperate and reckless my grief had made me. I didn't feel much of anything anymore, and so even my suspicions felt... dampened and insignificant. Like my life was a small thing to risk if it meant that I had the chance to really feel something again. Something real and bright.

The girl took me in with a slow pass of her gaze, no warmth or recognition, as if she didn't even remember me from the diner just hours before. "Naomi invited you?" When I didn't immediately respond, she said, "Tall? Long hair, blue eyeshadow?"

I realized, only then, that I didn't know any of the girls' names. With a flush of shame warming the back of my neck, I held out the wrinkled and greasy scrap of receipt paper onto which the blond girl had written the address.

"No, not her. The girl who invited me was blond and youngish?"

The girl didn't step out of the doorway.

Just then, one of the other girls from the diner, the one with the long sandy braids, appeared in the foyer. "Jesus Christ, Riley. Stop being such a hard-ass and let her in, will you?"

Riley frowned but moved out of the way. "Guess that's your ticket in."

I stepped into the foyer tentatively, feeling like an intruder to this not-party that I'd been invited to. Riley turned on her heel. She was wearing cowboy boots, and the spurs rattled as she strode into the living room and disappeared out the back door.

The other girl turned to me. She had flakes of gold leaf stuck to her cheeks. "Sorry about her. She's . . . not great with being social or, like, people in general."

"It's okay, I get it." An awkward silence ensued, made worse when I thrust out my hand, a motion so sudden the girl flinched a little. "I'm Roslyn."

God. I'd become something of a hermit after Adeline's death, but my own awkwardness still surprised me. How long had it been since I'd attempted small talk? Or even had a proper conversation with someone who wasn't Conny or my parents or someone else who was obligated to talk to me?

The girl extended her hand to mine, and we shook, a slightly stilted introduction, but her warm smile made the gesture feel less awkward than it was. "I'm Iona. Glad you came."

"I wasn't sure I would." Which was to say, I wasn't entirely sure I was brave enough until the moment Riley answered the door.

Iona seemed to understand without my having to elaborate. She was quick, I realized, perceptive in a way that made me feel like I couldn't hide anything from her. "You're brave to show up anyway. Skye was starting to think you wouldn't."

"Skye?"

"From the diner? You know, fourteen, scrawny, blond, talkative, too nosy for her own good." Iona meant the blond girl who'd first spoken to me. The youngest one. She'd ordered the drinks for the table and asked me if I liked to swim. "She's fond of you."

Iona took me by the hand again, me startling a bit at her touch but holding on anyway. Without a word, she guided me through the empty living room, devoid of furniture, and past the equally empty kitchen to a large patio overlooking the backyard. There was a pool there, filled with murky greenish water, and two girls in it, wearing soggy bras and underwear, three more sitting around it with their feet dangling in the dirty water.

I recognized the two in the pool from the diner. There was the oldest one, Naomi, with the sleek black hair and blue eyeshadow, sitting on a slimy stair in the shallows. And then the youngest, Skye, sprawled out on an inflatable pizza slice, staring listlessly at the stars.

The girls sitting outside the pool, on its far end, included Riley, the rude one who'd answered the door, and the redhead, who waved as we approached, making all the diamonds on her various engagement rings flicker in the porch light. Her name, I later learned, was Chloe.

Beside Riley and Chloe was the only girl who hadn't been at the diner. She had high-cut cheekbones, freckles scattered across her nose, a downturned mouth stuck through with the mouthpiece of a vape pen. She tipped her head to the stars and parted her lips, loosing pale whorls of smoke that hung, wraithlike, in the cool night air.

Her hair was somewhere between dark blond and light brown, and it was sun dyed and tangled. She wore it in a low and messy bun at the nape of her neck. But when the wind blew, a few strands came loose and clung to her parted lips.

Skye called out to us, waving frantically, almost falling off the inflatable like she was trying to make sure we spotted her in a crowd. But it was just the seven of us. No loud music, or music at all, really, except for a few faint chords streaming from a cell phone on the side of the pool, so quiet I could barely hear the song over the lapping water. It should've come as a relief. I'd always preferred parties that were more . . . chill, nothing too rowdy, no drinking or drugs so I didn't have to worry about the cops getting involved. But this was different. Subdued, yes, but somehow tense, and I was more nervous than I'd ever been at any party I'd ever attended.

Iona moved to join Naomi and Skye in the pool. She took her dress by the hem and pulled it up over her head in one fluid motion. Had I attempted that, my arms would've tangled in the sleeves. Her underwear was mismatched, a tightly crocheted top paired with plain white briefs. She turned back to look at me, caught me staring. "Well? Come on, then. The night won't wait for you."

It was one of those chilly summer evenings that felt like autumn; the air was a bit too cold and the water far too dirty for swimming. It smelled sulfurous, and a scattering of leaves floated on its surface, a fleet of ships on the ocean sailing to nowhere. But in spite of this, I never considered saying no.

The girls had a hold on me. I couldn't admit it then, but it was nonetheless true. I wanted so badly to be like them, girls who could draw gazes and keep them. I had never been able to harness that power. But what if this was my chance to try? To pretend to be like them, if only for a little while?

"We've never bitten, mugged, or kidnapped anyone," said Skye. "If that's what you're worried about."

Naomi cast Skye a sharp look. "You can't just say stuff like that—"

"What?" Skye demanded, looking a little affronted. "I was just trying to be hospitable."

"You were trying to be hospitable by telling her we're not going to *kidnap* her?" Iona demanded. "That's the first impression you want us to make?"

"When you say it like that, it sounds bad," said Skye. "But it wasn't a creepy 'we're not going to kidnap you.' It was meant to be like, you know, a *welcoming* 'we're not going to kidnap you.' I just wanted to clear the air."

Iona stared at the sky like she hoped to find help up there. She muttered something, a silent prayer, maybe, if the small gold cross on her choker was any indication at all.

Naomi issued a low warning. "Skye."

"I was just trying to be nice," said Skye, her voice high-pitched and wheedling. "It's her first time, and she's obviously scared."

"I'm not, actually," I said, a blatant lie. But to back it up, I kicked off my sneakers and started to undress. I was aware of all the eyes on me as I stepped out of my jeans, fumbling and hopping on one foot when my toes snared in the gaping rip at the knee. I managed to pull them off and kicked them away from me. I left my T-shirt on and slipped into the pool. The water was so cold my stomach suctioned into a tight knot behind my ribs. It was almost unendurable, but I pushed through, trying to keep my teeth from chattering. As I waded out of the shallows and toward the deep end, the water grew even colder. I dipped beneath the surface and swam a bit, diving low to the bottom of the pool.

When I surfaced again, through the distortion of my wet eyelashes, I saw my sister, Adeline.

She was sitting at the far end of the pool beside Chloe. I froze there, in the middle of the pool, but when I wiped my eyes on my wrist, I saw that it wasn't Adeline at all. It was the same quiet girl with the vape, watching me from across the dark and shimmering water.

This was a frequent occurrence. After she disappeared, I began to slot Adeline into every place I supposed she should be—Christmas dinners, homeroom classes, the booth at the back of the diner, the passenger seats of cars I spotted on the highway.

A man loses a leg and wakes in the night to feel it aching. A girl loses her sister and begins to see her everywhere. Even in the faces of strangers.

The girl who wasn't Adeline stared at me from across the water, frowning, as if she too had mistaken me for someone I wasn't. Up close, I saw that her eyes were wide and raw like she'd been crying, but there was a hardness to her expression, the set of her mouth, that made me think otherwise. Her lashes were wet and long enough to appear tangled. But her clothes were dry; it was clear she hadn't been swimming.

I'm not sure why I mistook her for Adeline; there was nothing about her that was even vaguely reminiscent of my sister except for, perhaps, an ephemeral quality that made me feel like, if the light struck her just so, I would be able to stare straight through her.

What I did know, though, was that she was Shiloh, the one the girls had mentioned back at the diner, holding her name in their mouths like a stone they were taking great pains not to swallow. All the girls were strange and striking in their own ways, but she was the only one who commanded that kind of . . . respect without ever saying a word. Whatever this situation was, I knew that she sat close to the heart of it.

"Are you all right?"

I snapped to attention, my trance breaking, gaze shifting from Shiloh to Skye, who lay supine and motionless—her soft white belly exposed—buoyed by the inflatable pizza slice, one leg dangling limply in the water. She held a Styrofoam cup, the smeared crescent of her lipstick on the rim. She extended it to me as she drifted nearer, straining a little with the effort of it, her arm stretched stiff, drink sloshing over the rim of the cup and into the pool water below. "Here," she said, extending it. "Your lips are blue."

I took the cup and stared at its contents. The liquid inside it looked a bit like tea.

Skye stared at me, expectant. "Well, go on, then. Drink up. You'll freeze if you don't."

Obediently, I raised the cup, turning it to avoid the bright smear of Skye's lip print, and took a big sip. The drink tasted a bit like Red Bull mixed with licorice and bitter ginger, and it burned my throat on the way down. I swallowed hard, staring at Shiloh above the rim, and Shiloh stared back at me, her gaze alone enough to make the hairs on the back of my neck bristle.

I wasn't an idiot. I knew myself well enough to identify what I was feeling, even though it had been months since I'd felt it, well before Adeline's death. In the wake of that loss, I'd begun to think that maybe grief demanded so much I didn't have it in me to feel anything else. Certainly not the pointless intensity of passing crushes or even just the curiosity piqued by someone new and particularly intriguing. But the girls had proved me wrong, and Shiloh's presence on the other end of the pool only further confirmed that. When I met her gaze, I could feel something stirring to life within my chest. If not attraction, then maybe just fear. Like she knew she had the power to break me if she wanted to and I was worried that I might let her.

Maybe the other girls felt it too. Was that why they said her name with that strange reverence? Even back at the diner, before I'd put a face to her name, I could sense her through them, see the shape of her in the spaces between them.

Skye took the cup out of my hand and downed the last of it in a single swallow. She slid off her pizza slice with a rubbery squelch. The empty cup floated slowly past me, bobbing on the water.

I tried to pass it back to her, but she was gone in pursuit of something I couldn't see in the far corner of the pool. I watched in horror as she slipped a hand into the scummy filtration system—a decision that seemed about as brave as it was stupid.

"There's a frog!" Skye fished it out and held its gelatinous body cradled in her cupped hands. When she pressed on its stomach with her finger, the way you would ring a doorbell, a bit of water bubbled from its open mouth. "And it's dead. Does CPR work on frogs? Do you think it's too late?"

The mean one who'd answered the door, Riley, rolled her eyes. "Jesus Christ, Skye, could you be normal for like two seconds? You should put that thing down before you get some sort of skin disease."

But the redhead beside her, Chloe, slipped into the water and waded to Skye. She peered down at the frog. "Do you think they have souls?" Chloe's voice was surprisingly deep, and she had a thick Southern accent that seemed to sand every word she spoke round and smooth.

"Only if they have a sense of self," said Naomi. She was still sitting on the stairs, serene and watchful. Her long hair formed dark spirals on the surface of the water. "And I think they do."

"We should give it a proper burial." Skye waded closer, cradling the frog to her face like she was seriously considering whether or not she should attempt to kiss it back to life. "I have a shoebox we could use. We could set it on fire. You know, the Viking way?"

"I want to go out like that." Riley leaned back to lie on the concrete. "Me, dead in a canoe filled with gasoline. A tossed match."

"Can I be the one to toss it?" Skye asked.

"Let's see how you do with the frog first," said Riley, and even though she was speaking to Skye, her gaze shifted left to Shiloh sitting on the edge of the pool. "Then we'll talk."

"Fair enough."

Their chatter took on the faraway quality of someone speaking in another room or across the street, and I felt a little ignored. I did my best to keep up, but the rhythm of their conversation was too fast. I knew they weren't trying to ice me out the way that Adeline and her friends sometimes did. It was the opposite with these girls. They just seemed to forget that I hadn't always been there.

But I noticed they were hyperaware of Shiloh, even though she wasn't even trying to nod along. I watched as their gazes shifted toward her after they spoke in anticipation of a response that never came, their every word a test of her approval. I realized then that Shiloh was to them what Adeline had been to me. The prime number that remained, whole and indivisible, after all the social arithmetic was finished. In every group of girls, there's always that one.

"What about you, Roslyn?" Iona turned to me now, as if she'd only just remembered I was there. "How do you want to go out?"

"Um . . . dunno. Cremation, I guess? Better for the environment." It sounded pathetic even to my own ears. I winced, grasped for something cooler. "I've heard of these places that'll break your body down into compost, turn you into a tree. But I think it's pretty expensive."

"What about before that?" Riley sat up to look me in the eye. Every time she leveled her gaze at me, I felt like I was failing a test I'd only just realized I was taking.

"Before that?" I asked, confused.

"Like, how do you want to die?" said the redhead, Chloe.

"I mean, does anyone really want to die? When it comes down to it?" I realized then that of course people did. There was suicide and euthanasia, old widows eager to be reunited with their past loves. "I mean, obviously I know some people want to, but for the rest of us . . . I don't know. It doesn't seem like the sort of thing you really plan out. It happens the way it happens."

Riley looked unimpressed.

Skye pulled her gaze off the frog to look up at me. "But if you could choose, how would you want it to go?"

I saw a flash of the plastic playhouse in the middle of the woods. "Filthy rich, eighty years old, and in my sleep, I guess?"

"*Boring*," said Riley, and I flushed with embarrassment. Riley, for her part, didn't seem to notice. She reached out to Shiloh. "Pass me the vape?"

I saw it then, as Shiloh complied, extending her hand to Riley. A bracelet—high up on her forearm, hidden beneath her sleeve—slid down to her wrist. A chain of pale mismatched river pearls, salvaged from earrings and broken bits of thrift shop jewelry. I knew because I'd strung it together myself. It had been a birthday gift for my sister.

Shiloh caught me staring. Her gaze dropped to the bracelet around her wrist, then back up to me. She said something—my name, maybe—but I couldn't hear her over the rush of blood in my ears.

I drew back toward the stairs, feet scrabbling for purchase on the scummy bottom of the pool. The water, cold to begin with, turned suddenly freezing. "How did you get that? How did you know my sister?"

Chapter 3

Shiloh stripped the bracelet off her wrist. "We were friends," she said, extending it to me across the water.

I didn't take the bracelet. Didn't move. My ears began to ring again, and things slowed after that. Or maybe I just departed. I had the disorienting sensation of being pulled backward out of my own body. Everyone else seemed to shrink away, becoming small and indistinct, their voices soft and distant.

I vaguely registered Skye placing a hand on my shoulder. "Roslyn—"

I might've shaken her off. I don't know. I looked to Shiloh again, my eyes so full of tears that I could barely see her. When I finally spoke, my voice sounded strange and stilted, like the recording of a recording. "What do you mean by friends?"

Which was to say, *What do you know? What are you keeping from me about the person I thought I knew better than anyone else?*

A few feet away, feet that felt like miles, Naomi gingerly took the frog from Skye's cupped hands, placed it on the edge of the pool, and wiped her hands together as if she were cleaning them instead of just smearing frog goop between them. "Shiloh." She was the only girl who said the name with anything less than reverence. "Be gentle with her."

Shiloh tried. I could tell because she softened her tone just a bit. "We met last summer. She traveled with us."

"Where?" I asked.

"Let's talk," she said, and slipped her feet from the pool, stood up, and made for the house.

Cold and chattering, I trailed Shiloh through the living room and into the kitchen. Shiloh stepped outside the house again, walked down the driveway, and ducked through the door of the soup-can RV parked on the street. It looked like a dollhouse on the inside. There were couches on either side of the space draped with quilts and cowhides and the great webworks of what appeared to be finger-knit blankets, a few of them only half-finished and affixed, as if with an umbilical cord, to spools of yarn the size of toddlers. I tripped over them as I stepped inside and drew the door shut. On every available surface—windowsills and fold-down tables, the tops of cabinets and the countertops in the kitchenette—were melted candles, fused where they stood in hardened puddles of wax. The entire place smelled like a vintage store or the inside of an old leather purse.

Shiloh stood in the cramped kitchenette, hunched over the countertop, staring at a nothing spot on the cabinet in front of her as if she intended to bore a hole through the laminate with the power of her gaze alone. Like Adeline, Shiloh had the eyes of someone who'd looked upon what shouldn't be seen. I could call it despair, and in Adeline perhaps it was that, especially in those last days before the end. But in this girl it was something different entirely.

"So how do you know my sister?" I said, and I had the stark and sudden feeling that this was the most important question I had ever asked.

"We met up north."

I faltered, realizing after a long beat who she was, who they all were. Those strange and faceless friends my mom had, defying all logic, allowed Adeline to spend the bulk of her summer with. I hadn't been able to find any trace of them in her call logs or old text messages, or in any of those emails I'd combed through. When I'd grilled my aunt, she hadn't even known their names. All I'd had to go on were those two strange words: *good influences*.

But one look at Shiloh and it was obvious she was far from that.

"What did you say to get my aunt to let Adeline spend so much time with you?" I asked, because it made no sense to me. That these girls had been the ones who'd whisked my sister away, that they were the ones who had changed her so drastically, watching—or maybe even responsible for—that horrible metamorphosis she'd undergone between the start of that summer and its tragic end.

Shiloh was looking at the floor now, frowning. Instead of an answer to my question, she gave me this: "There's a place for you here, with us, if you want one. We'll be leaving town in the morning, and I think you should come with us."

"Come with you and go where? What do you guys even do?"

"This and that," said Shiloh, intentionally cryptic. "A lot of it's just travel. You know, seeing the world through new eyes. It's kind of hard to explain, but I know Adeline would want you to experience it."

"What do you know about what Adeline wanted?" I snapped, angry at this stranger who was speaking to me as if she could possibly know Adeline better than me.

"More than you know."

I wanted to challenge that, to tell her she had no idea what my sister would've wanted. But a part of me wondered if perhaps she was right about me and what Adeline would've wanted. There were gaps in the story of her last months on earth, parts of herself she hadn't shared with me, ways she'd changed without my knowing. Looking at Shiloh standing there in the kitchen, I saw that there was something kindred about the two of them, as if my sister had been dragged up from the grave and brought to me in the form of the girl who stood before me.

It hurt that she seemed to know my sister—or if not that, then some part of her—better than I did. But the pain made me feel closer to my sister than I had since she'd gone missing. I'd never felt as haunted by her as I did in that moment in the RV with Shiloh. I realized that she was what I had been waiting for—the letter I'd never received from Adeline, the person who could tell me what had happened to her that summer before her death, the answer to all the questions that had plagued me through my grief. This was my chance to uncover the truth. Maybe the only one that I would ever get.

"I know a fair bit about Adeline," said Shiloh gently, like she was trying to break some bad news. "Maybe more than I should."

I believed her and hated her for it.

"We leave at eight in the morning." Shiloh stepped past me on her way out of the RV. "Don't be late."

Chapter 4

I dragged myself home, shivering, my clothes soaking wet, legs like dead weight beneath me, as though I had cinder blocks for shoes. My house sat at the bend of the cul-de-sac, redbrick with big bay windows and a whitewashed porch crowded with dusty rocking chairs. I staggered inside to find my dad sitting in front of the TV, watching *Jeopardy!* reruns the way he usually did at night when Mom was away at work. There was a plastic tray balanced in his lap. On it, one of those tasteless frozen TV meals that almost no one eats anymore. Tonight's feast was a gnarly piece of half-thawed Salisbury steak submerged in dark gravy, a mix of peas and carrots, and instant mashed potatoes topped with a pat of melting butter, which he mechanically ushered into his mouth. "What is the ring-tailed lemur," he said in unison with the contestant on TV.

I kicked my shoes off by the door. A few of Adeline's pairs were still there; no one had the heart to donate them. "I'm thinking about going on a trip this weekend."

Dad didn't take his eyes off the TV. "Where to?"

I hadn't had the chance to come up with a decent lie, and I floundered for a moment, sifting through possible options and ultimately seizing on something that sounded more like Adeline's antics than mine.

"Um, the lake?" Guilt made my voice thin and pitchy. "A couple of my friends want to go camping over the weekend—"

"Friends?" He peeled his eyes from the TV for the first time since I walked in. "What friends?"

"Just a couple of girls I know. One of them invited me."

I watched as my father digested this information, spooning soupy potatoes into his mouth, swallowing without bothering to chew the mush. "Have you talked to your mom?"

"You and I both know she won't be around to say anything." This wasn't a testament to how good, or present, of a mom she was or wasn't. In fact, in the scheme of moms, I think I got a good one. But after Adeline disappeared, she became only half herself. And I didn't begrudge her that. Because it was the same with me, and with Dad too. None of us knew how to function without her. "If she even notices I'm gone, she'll just think I'm at Conny's. Let her."

But Dad shook his head. "You should tell her. Give her a chance. She might surprise you."

"Fine, but if she freaks out, I expect you to have my back."

He made no promises. Turned back to the TV. "This girl, the one who invited you, what's her name?"

"Shiloh," I said to him, and I watched closely to see if the name sparked recognition in his eyes. Before Adeline died, my dad had been the household's secret keeper. The one we confided in with the things we were too scared to tell Mom, who was shrewder. I could see Adeline confiding in him instead of me, given how suspicious I was in the days after she returned.

"Never heard of her."

Upstairs, I showered and got ready for bed, thinking about the girls and Shiloh and who Adeline was when she traveled with them. I returned to my bedroom, and was halfway through packing—stuffing clothes into the duffel I used to take to track meets—when my mom knocked on my door. She was still dressed in her nurse's scrubs, her braids gathered into a loose bun at the back of her head. She was home earlier than expected.

Adeline joked that our parents made us make sense. When we were alone, despite how close we were in age, we couldn't pass for sisters unless you really squinted and searched for the resemblance. While Adeline was all big hazel eyes, firm nose, wild curly hair, and deeply bronzed skin, I was paler like our dad but with my mom's black hair and blunt eyebrows, her sharp cheekbones, and eyes the color of ink.

My mom and I had the same demeanor—shy and a little reclusive—with none of the charisma that came so easily to Adeline. Even at her lowest, when she was most depressed, people liked being around my sister. But the same couldn't be said for me and Mom. Maybe that's why we were both closer to Adeline than we'd ever been to each other. We just liked her better, though neither of us was willing to admit it out loud.

"Your dad said you wanted to talk?"

I straightened, faltered. I hadn't expected to talk with her tonight, and my story was only half-baked. "Yeah. I got invited to go up north, on a camping trip with some of my friends. We'll leave tomorrow morning, probably before you get up. That is . . . if you let me go?" I told myself I could explain everything to her later, over the phone if I had to. I'd often found that the truth was best taken in small doses. But my efforts to lessen the blow didn't change the fact that this was a cruel thing to do to a woman who had just lost her first, and arguably favorite, daughter.

"Which friends are these?"

"They're some girls I know from the diner. Don't worry, they're my age."

To my surprise, Mom started to smile. She smothered it quickly, schooling her face firm and expressionless, but it was still more than I'd expected. Perhaps it wasn't lost on her that this was the first social event that I'd asked to attend since Adeline died. If it hadn't been for that fact, I don't think she would've let me go, at least not without putting faces to the names of my friends, making sure they were trustworthy. Mom didn't mind if I went to the occasional house party or even on the odd overnight trip. But she was always picky about *who* I hung out with. Her preference, her demand, was that I spend my time with *good girls*, like the ones on my track team. Honors students, positive influences, girls who had something to lose if they got caught drinking or doing drugs.

But grief, mine and hers, must have lowered her defenses, made her more desperate. Instead of the expected suspicion, she just seemed relieved that I was getting out of the house at all. "When will you be coming back?"

I realized that I didn't know. Shiloh never said. "Um, next week? I think."

Mom knew I was lying about how long I'd be away. I could tell by the small wrinkle that formed over the bridge of her nose when she frowned.

I knew she worried about me being alone and at home most of the time. She'd pressed me to get the job at the diner so that I'd have a reason to leave the house and function like a normal person. But I also think it was easier for her when I was away. It was bad enough that she had to grieve over her own daughter. I got the impression that watching me mourn was like doubling the pain. In that way, the trip was good for both of us. We needed the time apart from each other.

Mom stepped closer, brushed my curls away, and kissed me just above the arch of my eyebrow. "Have fun."

I packed the last of my things and spent half the night tossing and turning fitfully in my bed before I gave up on trying to sleep, grabbed my duffel bag, and made for the woods behind our house. I didn't dress for the occasion—I wore nothing more than my thin pajamas and a pair of well-worn ballet flats that Adeline had bought at a vintage shop years before—but it was still surprisingly easy for me to find my way to the playhouse. The path was well trod, my having tamped it down so many times in the months after Adeline's death, and it wasn't that far from our house to begin with, a few miles through the forest.

The playhouse emerged from the trees, moonlit and green with moss. It was still sun-stained pink when they'd found Adeline, but the forest had hastily subsumed it in the months that followed, as if to erase all traces of her. I nudged open the door and ducked inside. There were weeds and mushrooms sprouting up from the dirt. A canopy of silver spiderwebs hung from the low ceiling; a few snared on my hair as I settled myself and spread my comforter across the floor.

In the wake of Adeline's death, I would come here and nestle myself in the right corner of the window, trying to arrange myself in the way that I imagined Adeline had the night she'd died here. She had a particular way of sitting, slumped and boneless, with her legs bent and spread wide apart. When she was a child, my mother had called this her rag doll pose, but once she became a teenager, Mom had scolded her for it, claimed that it was rude and unseemly and invited the wrong kind of attention. Adeline, stubborn as all hell, had never stopped.

"What happened to you?" I asked aloud into the dark. "What secrets were you keeping from me?"

Of course, there was no answer.

Chapter 5

I woke that morning in the playhouse to the sound of birds in the trees and the sharp trilling of my phone alarm. I checked the time. It was almost 9:00 a.m., nearly an hour past the time that Shiloh said they'd be leaving town.

I'd slept through my alarm. Shit.

I took off through the forest at full speed, cutting east past the high school, running until my legs weakened and ached, my duffel bag slamming against my hip, heart pounding with so much violence I feared it would give out. I kept going until my lungs burned badly enough to bring tears to my eyes.

By some miracle, I spotted them at a busy intersection in the heart of town, approaching a stoplight. Between us were several lanes of fast-moving traffic, each going a different direction, semis storming past with a roar. I can call it nothing less than a stupid act of faith, my throwing myself into the oncoming traffic, racing the red light as I sprinted after them. A car slammed on its brakes, a semi blasted its horn, and I stumbled into the deep gouge of a median between traffic, wading through the biting high grass and waist-high thistles as fast as I could. But I was too slow, out of shape, and even though I waved my arms and screamed at the top of my lungs, the rush of passing traffic drowned me out.

The RV rolled forward, the pickup truck and station wagon close behind, me still a few yards back. Panicked, I lunged so fast I almost stumbled out of my shoes and just barely managed to catch the lip of the pickup truck. It rolled forward, oblivious to my presence, and as I held on, my shoe skimmed the asphalt, the friction burning through the leather of my flat, down to my bare toe. By the skin of my teeth, I managed to scramble up into the truck bed to safety. I lay there on my back, panting and laughing and staring up at the sky for some time before I collected myself and sat up. The wind tore at my hair, and the green scenes of rural Michigan smeared past in a sick blur.

I turned, tapped the glass on the back of the truck, and saw Shiloh's gaze flicker up to the rearview mirror. She didn't look remotely surprised, and I would wonder later if she'd known I was there all along, spotted my reflection, and said nothing.

Shiloh reached behind her to slide open the window. I pulled myself through with some difficulty and climbed into the passenger seat. "Where are we—"

"None of that," said Shiloh. "You'll know when we get there."

"And when will that be?" I inquired, slipping my phone from my pocket to fire off a quick text to my mom letting her know I was on my way.

"Like I said, you'll figure that out when we get there," said Shiloh, impatient now. "What phone numbers do you know by heart?"

"What?"

"Phone numbers. Which ones do you know? Off the top of your head?"

"Um . . . my mom's. I know 911. Everyone knows that one, I guess. And I think I know my dad's number. I mean, he changed carriers recently, so—"

"Good enough," said Shiloh, and she snatched my cell phone out of my hand and tossed it into the back seat with a jerk of her wrist.

"What the fuck?"

"It's a distraction," she said. "You'll get sucked into whatever content is pushed through your screen, and you won't be able to focus."

I couldn't even argue with that. The months after Adeline died had been, in large part, a bright blur of me scrolling through the posts of people whose lives were better than mine. "Focus on what?"

But Shiloh didn't answer the question. It was like she hadn't heard it at all. "We always have a few phones charged. You can ask Naomi for one if you need to call home. You should keep some contact with your family. You know, for appearances."

I bristled at the idea of asking anyone for permission to use my own phone when I wanted to. Especially because that phone held some of the last photos Adeline had ever taken, the last texts she'd ever sent. "Well, that seems strangely cultlike and controlling. You do know you're supposed to ease people into these things, right? Frog in a pot of boiling water, that sort of thing?"

Shiloh smiled, a deep dimple formed in her right cheek, and I had the abrupt and alarming compulsion to touch it, fitting my index finger into the divot. She braked at another red light, peeled her gaze off the road to look at me, and caught me staring. "If you don't like it, you can leave. Door's unlocked, Roslyn."

I didn't move.

We kept driving for hours, through the green-gray smear of the Indiana suburbs, bumper to bumper, never weaving in and out of traffic or allowing other cars to merge into the lane, driving west against the sun at a steady clip. We didn't talk much during that time on the road, but the silence between us felt easy, and I liked the fact that Shiloh didn't feel compelled to fill it with small talk or indirect questions about Adeline—or worse yet, my grief.

At sunset, the vehicles ahead veered toward an exit in the middle of nowhere, to the parking lot of a by-the-hour motel overlooking the great gash of a quarry, its cliffside wrapped tight with a tall fence topped with whorls of barbed wire.

Shiloh parked the truck, and I stepped out into the soupy heat of the evening. Riley followed suit, sliding out from behind the wheel of the RV with a stretch and a yawn. She twisted at the waist, and her back gave a gnarly crack that was so loud I thought she might've actually broken her spine.

"It freaks me out when you do that," Iona grumbled, hopping out after her.

"I've got the bones of a fifty-year-old with osteoporosis. I can't help it if I—" Riley stopped short at the sight of me and frowned.

The other girls noticed me at the same time. Skye came stumbling out of the station wagon, airborne, lunging for me, her arms wrapping tight around my neck. "I knew it! I knew you'd come."

The other girls joined—sans Riley, who stood scowling at a distance—Naomi, Chloe, and Iona drawing me into a group hug.

"We were betting on whether or not you'd show." Chloe pulled away to look at me but grabbed one of my hands as she did. "Riley over there bet twenty bucks that you'd bail."

Skye caught hold of my other hand, and her fingers were about as cold as a corpse's despite the thick summer heat. "Well, I knew you'd come. Never once doubted you."

We unloaded the bags all together. Despite what Riley called her *old bones*, she made a point to carry all the heaviest items, slinging a backpack over each of her frail shoulders, dragging not one, but two suitcases across the parking lot with gritted teeth, pulling hard when the wheels caught on cracks in the pavement.

I moved to help her, but she just shouldered past me. "I can do it myself."

Shiloh made for the front desk of the motel, where she appeased a bewildered clerk with a credit card and that dimpled smile of hers that seemed to have the same effect on the clerk as it did me. I realized how it must've seemed, to be on the other side of us. This band of teenage girls checking into a motel, no parents or guardians in sight. The motel clerk, for his part, seemed conflicted. Scanning us in search of someone who looked . . . older—and in charge. I thought for a moment he wasn't going to give us the room Shiloh'd requested, but that smile of hers won out in the end.

With some reluctance, he passed the keys over the countertop. "You girls have a good night. Stay out of trouble."

Shiloh's smile dropped the moment she took the keys. "We will."

On the floor of a large motel suite, we ate a buffet spread of gas station snacks—hot dogs and honey buns and overlarge bottles of blue Gatorade, a bag of wrinkled oranges and strips of beef jerky, steaming cups of ramen boiled in the pot of a coffee maker. Skye talked rapidly through mouthfuls of Doritos as if against a running clock.

"Jesus Christ, this is delicious." She licked the orange dust off her fingertips. "Nothing beats it. Swear to god, I could live on Doritos alone. I don't know why they don't sell the dust as, like, a shake-on seasoning. Million-dollar idea, I'm telling you guys right now."

Someone turned the TV on, maybe to drown Skye out, and flipped to a nature channel, where a reality survival show was playing. A handful of contestants dumped naked in the middle of the wilderness, scrounging for grubs under rotten logs.

Riley sneered and gestured to the screen with a stick of jerky. "It's so fucking weird how people choose to suffer—not for money or any real clout, just to prove that they can."

Chloe nodded in agreement. "I think I'd rather die than be stuck out there. Like, if it came down to it, and I had to drink boiled giardia water and shit in a hole to live? That's it for me. I'm out."

Iona struggled to twist open a jar of Nutella. Shiloh took it from her, twisted the top off, and passed it back. Iona, barely even registering the gesture, stuck a spoon right into the jar and began to eat it, speaking thickly through a sticky mouthful. "You're saying that, after everything we've been through, *camping* would do you in?"

"Easily," said Chloe. "Hell, two nights and no hot showers would be enough to do me in. I'd just keel over in the middle of the woods, and they'd find me weeks later rotting out there." Her eyes flashed wide when she realized what she'd just said. She looked at me, appalled. "I am so, so sorry—"

"No, it's fine," I said, and to my surprise, I really meant it. "It's nice, actually. You know, to talk openly about death and stuff like that."

Naomi looked less skeptical than concerned. "It doesn't bring up bad memories of . . . her?"

I had the sudden urge to tell her to—to demand that she—say my sister's name. I hated it when people talked around her. I knew it wasn't fair, but it felt like they were giving her a second death. There was her first death in the forest, and then her second, longer and more drawn out, as the world learned to forget her. A kind of erasure that occurred every time someone refused to say her name or steered a conversation away from the mention of her.

Iona offered me the jar of Nutella in what I realized was meant to be a comforting gesture. I took it, mostly so that I had something to look at that wasn't them when I spoke. "It's the opposite, actually. Usually, people try to talk around Adeline and death and anything that could possibly remind me of what happened. But the thing is, everything reminds me of her. I see her everywhere, and people can tell, so they tiptoe around me, treading so lightly, like if they say the wrong thing, I'm just going to completely fall apart."

Shiloh gazed at me from her place sitting perched on the desk, one leg drawn to her chest and the other dangling. I wondered when I would stop feeling so small and unsettled whenever she looked at me. If I would ever get used to her. "And will you?" she asked. "Fall apart, I mean."

I sensed that the question was a test, but I didn't know how to pass it. I could bluff, say I was strong enough to endure anything, but that wasn't quite true. The truth was I did fall apart. Often. But not completely, or if I did, I knew how to put myself back together again. "It's not that I don't have bad days. It's that I've learned how to figure my shit out despite them. That's half of grief, I think. Figuring it out."

It came out less certain than I'd hoped—more a question than a statement—but somehow I knew, from the silence that ensued, the expression that passed over Shiloh's face like a shadow, that I'd passed her test. The girls seemed to sense it too. Naomi reached out to squeeze my hand, and Skye gave Riley a smug smile. "See. I told you she'd fit in."

Naomi and Shiloh began to pick up the trash from dinner—the wreckage of crushed soda cans and beef jerky wrappers. I did my part, but I was dead tired and achy after the long drive.

All I wanted was to crash, sprawl out in bed (the girls had been kind enough to offer me a queen mattress to myself). But I knew my mom was waiting to hear from me, so I asked Chloe for my phone—annoyed that I even had to—and called her. When she didn't pick up, I decided to call the house. The ringer gave six long peals. And then Adeline spoke:

"This is the Volk residence. If you want, you can leave a message, and we'll think about calling you back."

The phone gave a long beep, and I sat there, frozen. I listened to static on the line, reeling from the sound of Adeline's voice (I hadn't been expecting her; I didn't often call the house) and unsure of what to say. "Um . . . hi, Mom, it's Roslyn," I said, once I managed to speak. My throat was so tight and pinched it was hard to get the words out. "We stopped at a motel for the night somewhere in . . ."

Shit. I couldn't even remember exactly where we were.

"*Lemont, Illinois,*" Iona mouthed from across the room, trying to help me out.

"Lemont," I repeated, trying my best to sound like I knew what we were talking about. I realized then that I'd made a horrible mistake. I'd told my mom we were going north, to camp on the lake. "I, um . . . We decided to camp on the Wisconsin side of the lake. I got it wrong before. Anyway, we'll be driving up tomorrow, and we're having fun." Skye and Chloe giggling in the background probably made that part convincing, at least. "Not too much fun, though. Everyone's, you know, wearing their seat belts and being good. We'll hit Wisconsin tomorrow, I think. If you get the chance, could you drop by the diner and tell Conny I'll be gone for a few days? She'll be pissed, but she'll take it better from you, in person. I don't want her to worry. Well, um, love you. Text when you can. Or call. The service might be a bit spotty near the campground, but yeah. I'll be around."

I put the phone down, feeling a little dejected. I didn't want my mom to worry about me, but I did want to be missed.

Naomi looked to me. "You all right?"

"Yeah," I said, and even to my own ears it sounded high-pitched, painfully chirpy, and utterly unconvincing. "It's just weird, you know. Being away from home. I'm probably too old to be homesick, but I never went to camp or did any of that sort of stuff, really. And I haven't really been out much since Adeline." I realized only after this embarrassing admittance how pathetic I sounded. "So this is different. But in a good way."

Naomi smiled at me, and I could tell she was trying to be kind even though the light didn't reach her eyes. I wondered if she was just tired, or maybe sad about something she was trying to set aside. "I was so carsick after my first day with the group that Shiloh had to pull over twice so I could throw up on the side of the highway. I was so embarrassed I thought about making a break for it, then and there, running through the trees to god knows where. I think I just wanted to escape."

Iona, who I hadn't realized was listening, added her own story. "I cried myself to sleep every night for the first week after I joined. I missed my mom so much I thought it would actually kill me. But it does get easier—you'll see."

The idea of things getting easier implied that things were . . . difficult. But why? Just what were the girls doing out on the road that had kept them away from their homes and families for what I sensed was more than just a few weeks? Maybe more than a few months, even.

Naomi, perhaps sensing my anxiety, gave my hand a small squeeze. "Don't worry. You'll adapt, and we'll be here to help you every step of the way."

"Adapt to what?" I didn't mean for the question to come out as bluntly as it did. But the moment it landed, I knew I'd struck something. I could tell from the glances Chloe and Skye exchanged, the way Iona stiffened.

Naomi, however, didn't miss a beat. "Adapt to leaving your life behind, your family, your home. It's not an easy thing."

"Well, I mean, it's just a couple weeks. Right? Kids go to summer camp. I'm pretty sure I can handle this."

Riley smirked from across the room.

The conversation dissolved with that, the girls dispersing themselves to get ready for bed, crowding the bathroom all at once, sharing face creams and lip balms, sorting through a suitcase that didn't seem to belong to anyone in particular, pulling on oversized T-shirts, merch from bands I'd never heard of, and silky vintage nightgowns to sleep in. At one point, I was fairly certain I caught Skye using the same lime-green toothbrush that Chloe had used just minutes before. She didn't realize her mistake, or didn't care.

Amid the chaos, across the suite, Shiloh stood unmoving by the window, gazing through the slit between drawn curtains. Naomi dragged a desk chair to the side of the window and tried to persuade her to sit. But Shiloh waved her off.

"You can rest," said Naomi in a low tone. "I don't think we have anything to worry about tonight."

Shiloh kept her arms folded tight over her chest, her eyes on the window. "You don't know that. Better to be prepared."

"I can keep watch tonight," Skye offered.

"Please," said Iona. "The last three times you kept watch, you fell dead asleep, and we had to pick up the slack."

"What are we watching for?" I asked, because it seemed the most obvious question, and for a long beat, it went unanswered.

All the girls' gazes turned sharply to Shiloh, who said, "Girls traveling alone on the road tend to draw the wrong kind of attention. So we like to stay alert. But we'll be all right. You should get some rest."

I climbed into one of the two queen-size beds in the suite. Skye and Iona sandwiched themselves into the other. Naomi claimed the pullout couch, and Chloe slept on a narrow folding bed by the door. Riley somehow made herself comfortable in the bathroom with an armful of spare blankets and pillows. Shiloh was the only girl to opt for the RV. She left the motel room right before Naomi cut the lights.

"Sleep well," she said, and was gone into the night.

Chapter 6

I closed my eyes, but sleep didn't come. Even though Chloe cranked up the AC as high as it would go, it was stuffy in the room, and the walls were so thin I could hear people tramping around in the suite overhead or down the hall, their suitcases rattling behind them.

Sometime in the middle of the night, I headed to the bathroom and saw that the light was on. I raised my hand to knock on the door but stopped short when I heard two voices on the other side.

"You do realize she's going to fuck us all over," I heard someone say. Riley, maybe. "This is how it begins. Shiloh goes rogue, and the whole thing unravels. We should've just kept driving like we were supposed to."

"You're being dramatic," said Chloe. I knew it was her from that gravelly Southern drawl. "If she doesn't shape up, she's out, and the rest of us will carry on. It's that simple."

"Nothing is ever that simple," said Riley. I was certain it was her now. It was the delivery that gave her away—that jadedness and anger that set her apart from the rest of the girls in the group. "He's going to make one of us do it when the time comes."

He? The group was only girls. What boy or man could they possibly be referring to? Someone's dad, maybe? A guardian of some kind?

"*If* it comes to that." Chloe's voice was so soft I could barely hear her.

"It will. Even Adeline couldn't hack it. There's no way she'll make it through."

My breath hitched at the mention of my sister's name.

"That's harsh."

"But true."

There was a long beat before Chloe spoke again. "How long do you think she's going to last?"

Another pause, as Riley considered the question. "If she's even allowed to stay, I give her about a month, max."

A month? I'd told my mom I was going to go on a week-long camping trip, and mentally, I hadn't prepared to be gone for anything more than three weeks, max. The length of a longish road trip. But Chloe and Riley were talking like this was something more permanent. As if I was going to be like them, on the road indefinitely. It made me want to burst into the bathroom, let them know that I had a home and family to return to. I wasn't just going to leave everything behind.

I bit my tongue to keep from speaking.

"She's been lucky so far," said Riley. "Shiloh's gone easy on her, given everything that happened to her sister. And Skye likes her, which counts for a lot, unfortunately. They'll make sure she gets the clean dispatches. But it won't stay that way forever, and I don't think she has the stomach for the gnarly stuff."

I wondered what they meant by dispatches; some kind of job, maybe? How else could a handful of girls fund their road trips? Gas was expensive, and food wasn't cheap either. The money had to be coming from somewhere. But what made a job clean versus gnarly? I couldn't imagine the girls scrubbing floors or being suited to any hard labor. With the exception of Riley and Shiloh, who seemed to favor men's jeans and button-downs, the girls certainly didn't dress for it.

"I think you might be underestimating her. She's already been through a lot."

"Please," said Riley, and I could practically see her rolling her eyes. "Her sister was a force, and even she folded in the end. Roslyn seems . . . softer. And that's me being generous."

"Don't be generous. Say what you mean. It's just you and me. The others are asleep."

"She's average at best, weak at worst," said Riley. "If it wasn't for her sister, you and I both know she wouldn't even be here. She's lucky Shiloh likes a pretty face."

I flushed at the implication, my cheeks burning. Was Riley right? I'd assumed that my . . . *reaction* to Shiloh was one-sided. But was it possible that Shiloh had taken notice of me in the same way? I couldn't imagine it, a girl like that finding anything to notice about someone like me.

"There are a lot of pretty faces around here," said Chloe, and she sounded a little dejected. Jealous, even, though there was no real fire behind it.

"None quite like hers, though. And you know Shiloh. She always knows what she wants, and she has a way of getting it."

Riley sounded so convinced, and she seemed to know Shiloh well, as well as anyone could know someone as withdrawn as Shiloh, anyway. Maybe there was truth to it, to the beginnings of whatever this was that I was feeling. Something between us, something different and perhaps more dangerous than what Shiloh shared with the other girls in the group.

I liked the idea of that, for reasons I wasn't brave enough to confront.

"It wasn't just Shiloh. Adeline wanted her here too."

I froze, my heart trilling a fast rhythm against my sternum. Adeline had wanted me here? But why? I strained toward the door, wanting to make sure I caught every word that came next.

"For whatever that's worth. Adeline couldn't make it herself."

"Yeah," said Chloe. "But we both know what that was about."

It was all I could do not to burst into the bathroom and demand that she elaborate and, in doing so, reveal I'd been eavesdropping. I couldn't imagine that going over well, especially with Riley, who clearly had some sort of grudge against me for reasons I didn't yet understand.

"Adeline always had to win," said Riley. "Must've been hard for her to lose for once. She couldn't have been expecting it."

A pit formed in my stomach. Who did Adeline lose to? And while playing what game?

I heard the faucet running, and I lunged away from the door, back to bed. I managed to slide under the covers and squeeze my eyes shut just as the bathroom door opened and Chloe stepped out into the suite, returning to the cot. I lay there frozen for some time before I worked up the courage to get up and go back to the bathroom, the pressure in my bladder making it impossible to sleep.

I didn't knock before entering, on principle mostly. It wasn't fair that Riley got dibs on the bathroom when there was a pullout couch and an RV she could be sleeping in.

When I opened the door, I saw her sound asleep in the tub. She had her boots on, crusted with mud and braced above the rusty faucet. I wondered how she could sleep comfortably, folded nearly in half, with all the blood rushing down from her legs.

I edged up to the toilet, drew the shower curtain closed for privacy, and attempted to pee as quietly as I could. But I'd barely started when Riley spoke.

"You know you can still go home," she said, as if we'd already been talking. She drew the curtain back to look at me, her eyes narrow and cloudy with sleep. "You don't have to stay with us."

I flinched, a little hurt. It was obvious Riley didn't want me here, but her opinion clearly wasn't the one that mattered. So why did I feel so much pressure to win her over, to prove that I was worthy of being here just like everyone else?

"Naomi and Iona were lying earlier." Riley shifted her weight with a slight wince. That was the first time I noticed the scar on her knee, surgically straight, thick, and silvered over the way scars do with enough time. I wondered how she'd gotten it. "It doesn't get any easier with time," she said, eyeing me from the tub. "It just gets hard in a different way. That's what your sister used to say."

With that, Riley shifted in the tub, turning her back to me, and promptly fell back asleep.

I didn't have the guts to wake her up, to ask more questions about Adeline and what she did with the girls that summer. I hated myself for that. I was here to find out what happened to my sister, but I couldn't even work up the courage to demand the truth.

On my way back to bed, I looked out the window. There, standing on the other side of the fence, right at the edge of the quarry, was a figure.

Shiloh. Awake and alone outside despite the fact that it was past midnight.

I went to her, stealing out of the suite and traversing the long walkways of the motel, without really knowing why except that I was too wired to sleep—my mind reeling with theories about Adeline and these strange girls that she'd traveled with. I didn't want to be alone with my thoughts and questions, especially when there was someone awake who could answer them.

Outside, it was unseasonably cold and quiet. There was a hole in the fence that encircled the parking lot, and I ducked through it. A few of my curls tangled painfully in the cut chain links, and I had to untangle them before starting toward Shiloh, who stood right on the cliff's edge.

"Can't sleep?" Even though I spoke softly, the words carried over the gash of the quarry in a series of long echoes.

Shiloh didn't answer or even pull her gaze from the quarry. I had the eerie suspicion that she'd known it was me from the moment I'd left the motel. Maybe even before that.

I noticed, as I came to stand alongside her, just how close she was to the cliff. She gazed over its edge, tense and expectant, and I wondered who or what she could've been waiting for at that hour, alone in the dark. "You should know that I don't have what you're looking for. All that stuff that happened with Adeline, that storm she was caught up in. We were only privy to it for a while, and in the end, I—*we*—couldn't save her from it. Believe me, we tried."

It was a nonanswer. A diversion. But I didn't call her on it then. "I just want to know what happened to her. She changed that summer when she was with you. She must have, because she came back so . . ." I trailed off, grasping for the right word.

"Different?"

"So wrong," I corrected her firmly. I had tolerated my parents and therapists poking holes in my theories with their Socratic questioning and gentle appeals. But I wouldn't, couldn't, take it from her. "I know something happened."

"And you've come here to find out exactly what that is?"

I didn't deny it. No point being coy when she clearly knew what I was after. "What happened to her when she was traveling with you? And why was she even with you in the first place? What do you guys even do? You never really answered that question when I asked yesterday, and I know there's more that you're not telling me. I heard Riley and Chloe talking earlier."

"What did they say?" she asked, without the barest hint of curiosity. Like she was just trying to humor me, to say the right thing at the right time.

Just then, a cold wind dragged across the quarry. I shivered, folding my arms tight over my chest, and Shiloh turned to look at me for the first time. "What the hell, Roslyn? It's freezing out here."

She shrugged off her coat—a denim trucker jacket with patches at both elbows. I tried to wave her away, but she set it down over my shoulders anyway. It was heavy and warm, and it smelled like her—clean and earthen, like a forest after it rains. "You should go inside. Warm up."

But I didn't move. I thought about what Riley said earlier, about Shiloh liking a pretty face, and I hated myself for that. I was here for Adeline. I refused to become one of the countless people who allowed themselves to move on and forget her. "You never answered my question about Adeline. What happened when she was with you?"

"I can't answer that," said Shiloh, and then she nodded across the quarry. "But he can."

A man appeared then, as if summoned forth from the mist. A figure across the quarry, on the other side of the barbed wire fence, coming toward us. He walked in a way that was strange and erratic, no rhythm to his steps, a wrenching of his shoulders, a convulsion that bent his arm sharply backward at the joint of the elbow. Even at a distance, he looked like a thing that was not yet used to wearing human skin.

Seeing him, my mouth went dry, and my hands began to shake. The ground felt like it was melting beneath my feet. The only time I'd felt a terror like that was the moment the police showed up on our front porch to tell us they'd found Adeline's corpse in the playhouse. Even before the officer said a word, I knew what he was going to say, could tell from the expression on his face that the mystery of Adeline's disappearance had ended in death.

Now, watching this man approach, I felt that same dread.

It all happened so fast after that. Shiloh took a half step in front of me, angling her body between me and the approaching figure even though he was still a long way off, coming around the bend of the quarry, walking tight against the fence.

"Go wake the girls," she said, in a way that made me want to run. In a way that told me I should. "Let them know our guest is here."

Chapter 7

I scaled the steps up to the second-floor suite two at a time, only to realize when I reached the door that I didn't have the key. I banged, open palmed, and a split moment later, Chloe answered. The other girls were already awake, bleary eyed but tense.

"Is it him?" she asked, as if she'd been expecting some unwanted company.

"I—I don't know. There's a man down by the quarry . . . Shiloh called him a guest—"

That was all it took. The girls were on their feet, getting dressed, stumbling over each other.

Iona stubbed her toe on the corner of the wardrobe and yelped. *"Shit!"*

I didn't understand their panic, and when I asked, no one answered me, but not because they were trying to ignore me. In fact, I'm not even sure that they heard. Panicked and confused in equal part, I peered out the window, but I couldn't see Shiloh or the man she had referred to as her guest. I began to panic. What if he had hurt her? Or was hurting her? Shiloh was alone down there; what if we were too late to save her? What if she ended up like Adeline, young and dead and alone in the dark? The thought was unbearable, and I felt sick with guilt for leaving her to fend for herself.

No one said anything as we took the elevator down to the first floor of the motel. When its doors parted, I turned to look for the motel clerk, but he was gone. The screen of his monitor flashed a series of windows and glitching warning messages before finally shutting off.

Seated comfortably in the empty lobby on a plastic chair near the vending machine was the same man I'd seen from across the quarry. He wore a well-tailored suit, and his shirt was fitted with a priest's collar, although nothing in his demeanor was reminiscent of a clergyman. He sat with one leg crossed over the other, and when he bobbed his foot, his shiny shoes caught the light of the flickering fluorescent bulbs and gleamed brilliantly. Shiloh stood beside him, tense.

"Good evening, girls," said the man.

"Good evening," said the girls in answer, shuffling toward him like a flock of ducklings. I had never seen them look so small. In the wake of this man, they seemed to have lost all their bravado and verve.

I looked to the man again, trying to decide whether he was handsome. He had peculiar features, a prominent nose, skin almost paper pale and so thin you could see the veins beneath it. His hair fell across his furrowed brow in a black slick. No matter how intently I studied him, I couldn't place his age. He almost seemed too young to be called a man, but his demeanor dispelled any notion of boyhood. And there was something decidedly familiar about him, like I might've seen him before, perhaps at Adeline's funeral, seated in one of the pews toward the back, or maybe he was one of the priests at the church, which would have explained his collar.

But what really disturbed me were his eyes. They were large and gray, and as I met his gaze, as I forced myself to hold it, I was reminded of the serial-killer documentaries that Adeline had sometimes made me watch. The men in those films—who beheaded their own mothers and killed cats and stuffed dead girls into the trunks of their cars—had the same flat affect that this man did. The look of someone who had killed once, or maybe many times, and would again. It was less malicious than detached, but I found it more frightening than malice ever could be.

"I'm going to let you begin," said the man, gazing at all of us girls with the look of a father who was less angry than disappointed. He raised an eyebrow. "Well?"

There was a beat of silence, and then all the girls began talking at once, over and under each other. There was a lot of stuttering and hand-waving and ranting, everyone interrupting each other in their haste to plead their case. I heard my name mentioned several times and Adeline's just once, but with everyone talking all at the same time, I couldn't grasp the context or understand what exactly the girls were trying to say.

The man pinched the bridge of his nose, exasperated, and the girls went quiet. "What I'm hearing," he said, "is that you've stepped outside your jurisdiction. Is that so?"

Skye bobbed her head, but Naomi, who was standing just in front of her as if shielding the girl with her own body, didn't move.

"She's one of us," said Shiloh, her voice steady and low. She was the only girl who didn't look scared. "Or at least she can be."

"I'm afraid that isn't possible for her."

"Why?"

"Because Roslyn here doesn't particularly want to live." The man turned to look at me. "Isn't that right, Roslyn?"

My mouth felt so dry I was surprised that I was still able to speak. "Who are you, and how do you know my name?"

"You didn't tell her?" he asked the other girls with mock hurt. "I'm wounded."

Naomi stepped forward, looking sick and drawn and wholly unlike herself. "We thought it would be best to give her time."

"And to let you make your own introductions," said Shiloh.

"Well, I'll get to it, then." He clasped his hands, a gesture that seemed almost professional, like he was about to gesture to a PowerPoint he'd prepared for the occasion. He fixed his gaze on me. "I'm Death."

I looked to the other girls, confused, trying to figure out if I was meant to take this seriously. They met my gaze with blank stares or, in the case of Riley and Iona, didn't look at me at all. I turned back to the man. "Did your parents name you that?"

He laughed aloud, but he was the only one. The other girls, apart from Shiloh, seemed too terrified to speak. "This one has teeth. That's a good quality in a girl."

I stared at him blankly, waiting for him to answer my question—a tactic I'd picked up from Conny during my time at the diner when

I was still learning how to handle the difficult customers. There's power in silence if you can stomach it, she'd once said to me.

When the man realized I wasn't going to speak, he answered. "I don't have any parents or much by way of family. The body you're seeing now is . . . shall we call it *rented*? Something I wear when the occasion demands it, like a good suit."

"I don't understand."

"Well, let me put it this way: When your aunt Veronica died of lung cancer, I was there in the room with her. When your classmate Joel died on his motorcycle, crushed beneath the belly of a semi, I was there with him. And, of course, when our dear Adeline . . ."

I froze at the mention of my sister. "You knew Adeline?"

He nodded. "Quite well, and if you're wondering, then yes, I was there with her at the end. She wasn't alone. No one ever is. Not really."

"So you know what happened to her."

"I *am* what happened to her," he said, and for some reason, it was here that I began to understand. The man before me wasn't a man at all. He was a concept. A great and terrible inevitability bound to a body. He was death.

"What did you do to her?" I asked, my knees going soft beneath me.

When I swayed, it was Iona who sprang forward to steady me with a firm hand at my elbow, whispering nothings into my ear that people usually reserve for the worst of occasions. "Be strong. You can get through this. I know you can."

"I'm afraid I don't give away anything for free," said Death. "All that I offer is earned."

I knew it was bait, but I was desperate to take it anyway. I needed to know. I needed the truth. "How do I earn it?"

"We kill for him," said Skye. "All of us here, that's what we do. What your sister did when traveling with us."

I froze, my mind scrambling to make sense of what she'd just said. My sister killing. My sister a killer. These girls all killers.

Skye's voice softened and quieted. "We were all supposed to die young, but he intervened."

This made no sense to me. The girls were more alive than anyone I had ever known. They were puffy eyes and scraped knees, thin clove cigarettes and morning breath and swallowed apologies and run-on sentences pierced with unnecessary interjections of *like* and *um* and *sorry*. They were bitten nails and super tampons passed under the walls of bathroom stalls. They were more alive than anyone I had ever known before, with all the time in the world to do anything they wanted to do, become whoever they wanted to be.

Or so I thought.

Another idea occurred to me then: If Death only recruited girls who were destined to die, and if these girls worked on his behalf killing people . . . is that why they'd first come to me? Had they come to kill me?

"It's not what you think," said Shiloh, doing that thing again, like she was reading my mind. "I wouldn't have hurt you. It was the opposite, actually. We came to Michigan to check on you. We were passing through Ohio when I made the call, decided to take a short detour up north, to you."

"Why?" My voice cracked. "Why would you drag me into this?"

"Adeline asked us to," said Shiloh. "She wanted us to make sure you were okay, and . . . you clearly weren't. If you were, if you had accepted what happened, processed a bit, you wouldn't have left your life behind so quickly. Wouldn't have dropped everything just to chase the ghost of her."

Shiloh was right, and I hated that she knew, on first meeting, that I was nothing more than a vessel of grief. I'd wanted to believe that there was something more that she was drawn to, a vestige of the girl that I used to be. But that was me deluding myself. Shiloh was making good on a promise to Adeline, taking care of her weak little sister who floundered, helpless, without her.

I turned back to Death. "Did you make her kill for you?"

"I don't make anyone do anything," said Death. "I give these girls a choice. Everyone here was destined to die young. They would have, if not for my interference. I offered them a deal. If they kill on my behalf, their lives are spared."

"So Adeline was supposed to die?" I turned to look at the other girls for confirmation.

It was Iona who spoke up. "There was . . . an accident on the lake. Adeline swam too deep or maybe got caught up in a current. It was hard to see from the shoreline."

"She was drowning," said Death, stepping in. "Or at least, she would have drowned if not for my offer. That day on the lake was meant to be her last."

"So she accepted your offer and started killing for you?" I could barely bring myself to say it.

Death gave a grim nod.

"But at the end of that summer, she came home. So what happened then?" I searched Death's face, and then the faces of the other girls, for an answer that didn't come. Iona, Chloe, and Skye looked about as confused as I felt. But Shiloh and Riley, I noticed, pointedly avoided my gaze. They knew something. Naomi, too, if her pained expression was any indication at all.

"At that time, my agreement with Adeline was . . . in a state of transition." It was as close to an answer as he was willing to give me that night. I hated how bureaucratic it all sounded, like he had a secret contract with Adeline drawn up, locked away in a file cabinet somewhere. "In the end, though, she made her own choices."

It was reminiscent of what Shiloh had said when we were standing on the quarry. Adeline choosing her own fate, conjuring a storm of her own making. "I know she didn't kill herself, if that's what you're trying to imply."

Death held up his hands, a small gesture of surrender. "I never said that she did."

I looked to the girls again, still waiting for some explanation from them. They were the ones who dragged me into this, after all. "So, what? This is like the Twenty-Seven Club or something? A deal with the devil?" I'd always thought that stuff was all conspiracy, Satanic Panic, Illuminati bullshit. But I wasn't so sure anymore.

Death looked a little offended. "I'm far from the devil."

"And we don't sell our souls in exchange for fame or money. We don't sell our souls at all." I wasn't sure if Shiloh was trying to defend herself or Death. "We act on his behalf, ushering people into the afterlife when it's their time to go, and in return, he spares us from our would-be tragic and early deaths. It's not easy work, but . . . we get to live because of it. It's a matter of survival."

"Which is precisely why you're not fit for this job," said Death, like an interviewer who was trying to break the bad news as gently as he could. "Even if I were willing to bend the rules, induct someone who isn't currently under threat of imminent demise, Roslyn here isn't the type. A girl who isn't particularly attached to the idea of life doesn't have enough motivation to stomach the work of death."

Riley nodded, looking smug. "That's exactly what I've been saying. She doesn't fit."

"You're wrong," said Shiloh. "Both of you. I know she can—"

Death held up a hand for silence. "There's no help to be had for it. Even if I threatened her life here and now, she lacks the motivation. I can see it in her eyes. All she wants, deep down, is to be with her sister."

"There is something else that I want." Everyone turned to look at me.

"And what is that?"

"The truth. The truth about what happened to her that night. The night she—" I couldn't finish. "The autopsy was inconclusive. Two coroners cut her open, and they still couldn't figure out what happened to her. But I know that, after she traveled with you guys and came home, she was *changed*. And there was a letter that made it seem like she knew something was wrong, but she never told me.

Never said anything before she left for that playhouse in the night, and I—" My voice breaks. "I just want to know. I want to know what she knew and how she died and why."

Death smiled, and when he did, I realized he was two steps ahead of me. That he'd orchestrated this conclusion, guided me to it, without my even realizing it.

"Well, that is something, isn't it? A strange circumstance, but . . . interesting in its own way. You serve me, and I give you an answer you value more than life itself. I have to admit it's very compelling. But, at the same time, it wouldn't be fair if you didn't offer me something in return for the information you seek about your sister."

"What do you want, exactly?"

Death paused, considering, but I sensed it was just theatrics. He knew exactly what he wanted. "You could kill for me, like they do."

I felt the floor shift a little beneath my feet, or maybe it was just my own mind reeling. "That's cruel," I heard myself say in a flat monotone that didn't even sound like me.

"Yes, well, that's sort of the old MO, isn't it? I am what I am. Honestly, you're one of the lucky ones. It's not often that I bargain." He narrowed his eyes at me as if he were trying to see through my skin. "I'll admit you've surprised me, Roslyn. But do you really think you have the stomach for it? I wasn't particularly impressed with the performance of your sister."

"She's stronger than Adeline," said Shiloh, vouching for me. "She has a stomach for this work. You can trust me. You've always said I have a good eye."

"Fair enough." The man pressed to his feet. He was, to put it politely, freakishly tall. "How about this? You kill for me, and I'll show you everything, answer every question you have about your sister."

It was a tempting proposition, too good to be true. "How would you do that?"

"Give me your hand," he said, extending his. It was large and pale, and there were strange faint markings across his knuckles that vaguely reminded me of Chloe's stick-and-poke tattoos.

Immediately, I recoiled, fear spiking through me. "Why would I do that?"

One of the girls—Skye, I think—laughed aloud at this. Someone shushed her.

Death pressed his lips into a tight irritated smile. "This isn't a negotiation."

"Do it," said Shiloh.

Still I didn't give the man my hand. Every animal instinct—that primal part of yourself that acts before your brain has the chance to think—told me not to do it, told me to run away. Even the thought of Adeline wasn't enough to make me raise my hand. Another long beat passed, and when I still didn't move, he snatched it. His hand was very cold.

He pressed his thumb into the meat of my palm, deep enough to hurt, to bruise, even. I tried to pull away, but he caught me by the wrist. The pain of his finger intensified, became like a nail piercing through the soft flesh of my palm and between the tendons. My knees buckled, I screamed, and when I crumpled to the ground, the man went with me, crouching there beside me, my hand still clutched in his.

I heard myself pleading. Adeline's name tangled behind my teeth. I squeezed my eyes shut, and when I opened them again, I was in the playhouse with her and the man, Death.

It seemed impossible . . . because there was no room for the three of us within its plastic walls. But we dwelled there together just the same. Adeline was folded fetal against the far wall, still alive, her hand pressed to her chest.

"Go on, then," said the man, and his breath hung like a ghost in the cold air. "Do it."

Adeline gazed at me. Smiled through tears. She peeled the hand off her chest and extended it to me. "Please," she said. "Roslyn, please."

Terrified, I recoiled, lost my balance, fell back through the door of the playhouse and through what felt like time itself until I returned to the floor of the motel with the man who held my hands and all the girls crowded tight around us. I sat up, and they drew away.

Death released my hand. It struck the floor, limp and throbbing. I tried to move it but couldn't.

He gazed down at me, less concerned than vaguely disgusted. "Not sure your eyes are quite as sharp as they used to be, Shiloh."

"Give her time." I heard Shiloh speak and realized that my head was in her lap, her calloused hand clasped over my brow like she was trying to feel for a fever. "If she's not ready when the time comes, I'll handle her myself."

"That's not good enough," said Death. "I need collateral. Your decision to welcome her into this group was a collective one, yes?"

Riley rubbed the back of her neck. "I mean, I didn't want—"

Shiloh silenced her with a single look, then turned back to the man. She started to speak, but Naomi cut her off. "It was a collective decision."

Death turned to her with a knowing smile. "You know, sometimes I forget how young you really are. But then there are nights like this one, where you make me remember."

Naomi paled and began to shake, her hands shuddering. She clutched them into fists, her long painted nails driving deep into her palms, drawing a bead of blood. She didn't seem to notice the pain, or if she did, she didn't care.

Death took both of her fists—within his hands they seemed so small—and gently unfurled her fingers.

Naomi stiffened at his touch, her eyes glassing over, and I wondered what visions Death's touch had conjured. What was he making her see?

The man's gaze returned to me again, appraising. "I'm going to put you on a trial run with this group. You have three weeks to prove your worth. After the three weeks are over, I'll return with one last task to finalize our arrangement. If you carry it out successfully, I'll take you back to your sister, and every question you've ever asked yourself about her undoing will be answered in turn." He leaned a little closer. "So, what will it be, Roslyn? Do we have a deal or not?"

I faltered, thinking about those faceless people, their lives at stake. But were they really? If this man was to be believed, if he was really Death, they would die anyway, with or without my participation. No one lived forever. And if I wanted to find out what really happened to Adeline, this man was the only one who could tell me.

I knew that the moment he touched me, when I fell through time back to the day of Adeline's death. Or maybe I'd known it well before, when I first saw him at the quarry, or further back, when the girls first appeared outside my house.

There was no reality where I refused him.

"Okay," I said. "I'm in."

"Lovely," said Death with a broad smile, but his eyes remained flat as stones. He turned to the other girls. "As for the rest of you, as I mentioned before, a collective decision to welcome Roslyn into the group, defying the terms of our agreement to do so, warrants a collective punishment if this little experiment fails. Therefore, if Roslyn isn't able to keep up her end of the deal, if she fails this experiment, the consequences of that failure will fall on you as well. Which is to say, if she fails to pull her own weight, then our little agreement is null and void."

"Wait, that's not fair," said Riley, unable to contain herself any longer. "I shouldn't be punished when I don't even want her here—"

The man turned on her, and his expression was unlike that of any man I had ever met or seen before. It was a serenity so complete it seemed devoid of both emotion and morality. He became, in that moment, more phenomenon than man. A star collapsing in on itself. "If it's your desire to leave this group, then no one is keeping you here. Is that what you want?"

Riley recoiled. Shook her head.

"Then it's settled," said the man, and he smiled graciously, like an actor accepting an award. "We'll give Roslyn a few hours to collect herself. Then you'll show her the ropes?" The man's eyes flickered over the girls as if waiting for confirmation that his plan was a good one. I hated the way he spoke about me as if I weren't even there. I had half a mind to say something, but when I tried to speak, I couldn't find the words or the courage to say them.

"Who is it this time?" Iona inquired, staring up at the man.

"Stewart Gavin. Aneurysm. His residence is in Wisconsin. I've given Shiloh all the details. After visiting him, you'll travel west. Then we'll reconvene in Las Vegas three weeks from today." Death made for the doors of the motel. As he passed me by, I caught a whiff of musky cologne and mildew. "Good luck."

Chapter 8

We left the motel in the middle of the night, just after Death departed, driving north up the highway to a lake house owned by Stewart Gavin. I sat curled fetal on the RV's built-in couch, ignoring the girls. I pretended that I didn't hear Skye's whispered apologies for not telling me the truth sooner, for not letting me know what they were before inviting me to join them. I pushed away the cups of tea Naomi coaxed into my hands. Chloe's questions—about whether or not I was okay and if I wanted to call my mom in the morning or maybe speak with someone who wasn't them, like a parent or a friend or perhaps a therapist—went unanswered, like I hadn't heard her at all.

We were well past the Wisconsin border when Naomi put a hand on my shoulder and kept it there, a firm pressure. "Hey. Shiloh wants to talk."

I pushed to my feet, off-balance. The RV was moving fast and the asphalt was pocked with potholes. I made my way to the back of the RV, where I found Shiloh sitting cross-legged on the Murphy bed. "How's your hand?"

"Fine." I flexed my fingers. The pain had disappeared soon after Death departed, and when it did, my mobility returned. My hand bore no mark or scar, nothing indicative of the agony I'd suffered. I felt like I was being pranked or gaslit by Death or the girls, and I kept toying with the idea that it was all in my head. If the girls hadn't been there, I might've thought I was going insane.

"Sit with me," Shiloh said, and I obliged her, claiming a corner of the mattress, drawing one leg up to my chest just to have something to hold on to. "I owe you an apology. We all do. We kept things from you, and that wasn't fair."

My hand, the one Death had touched, spasmed painlessly, the muscle pulling tight, then releasing.

Shiloh saw, watched me clench my hand into a tight and bloodless fist. "It's called the touch of Death. It's a gift that lends us the ability to kill with a single touch."

I got off the bed. It was all too much, but the RV hit another pothole, and I lost my balance and barely managed to catch myself on the wall. I felt suddenly carsick, my mind reeling.

"Roslyn, it's okay—"

I wheeled on her. "No, it's not."

Shiloh went silent.

"That man—or thing—back at the motel, it showed me my sister dying in the woods. How did he do that?"

"He's Death. He can do a lot of things."

"Did my sister kill people for him?" I already knew the answer;

I'd heard it straight from Death. But I wanted to hear her say it anyway.

"She did."

I thought about the man I'd have to kill if I wanted to discover what happened to Adeline that night in the playhouse. His life the price of the truth.

My knees buckled. I fell back onto the bed.

"Hey," said Shiloh, and she cupped me by the chin. "I want you to look at me."

I looked. It hurt to meet her eyes.

"We're going to take care of you, all right?"

"And what if I can't do this?" I said, and I hated her then for dragging me into this. Almost as much as I hated the man called Death. "How will you take care of me then?"

Shiloh dropped my chin. "I don't want it to come to that."

I picked at a fraying thread on the cuff of a jacket I'd only just remembered was Shiloh's. I'd never taken it off. I had half a mind to give it back to her, but the weight around my shoulders was comforting. It kept me grounded when everything else felt like it was spiraling wildly out of control.

"Look, I know it's a lot—"

"A lot?" I laughed out loud, but it came out shaky and hysterical. "That's an underestimate. I've been coerced—some might argue kidnapped—by a cult of teenage girls that worship a deranged man who calls himself Death—"

"We don't worship anyone."

I kept going as if I hadn't heard her. "And now you're telling me

I have to kill people or you're going to kill me? That doesn't sound insane to you?"

"You're just going to have to trust us on this."

"Trust you? I don't even *know* you—"

"Adeline did," said Shiloh, her expression unchanged. "And she trusted me."

"Adeline is dead," I snapped. "Clearly, trusting you didn't get her very far."

Shiloh flinched like I'd hit her. "Before she . . . left us that summer, she asked us to make sure that you were okay if anything happened to her. I went to Michigan wanting to keep that promise, but when I saw you, I realized you weren't okay at all. You were . . ."

I braced myself, but Shiloh stayed quiet. "What? Just say it."

"Lost. Hollow. Death was right when he said you don't have an attachment to your life. And maybe it was an overstep, but I wanted—I want—to help you. Adeline wanted me to help you. Begged me to."

That sounded like Adeline, sticking her nose where it didn't belong, trying to take care of me from beyond the grave because even in death she didn't believe I was capable of taking care of myself.

"You think you're helping me?" A harsh peal of laughter stripped my throat raw. "This isn't help, Shiloh. This is twisted, and the only reason I'm still here is because that man—that thing back there proclaiming to be Death—is dangling the truth about my sister's death above my head just out of reach, forcing me to participate in this sick game you're playing."

Shiloh was quiet for a long time at that; we both were.

She looked down at her hands. There was black beneath some of her nails. Dirt, maybe. Or blood. "I'm sorry. I'm not good at this part. I never have been. I always try to explain things as best I can, but I never get it right. Naomi's always telling me my bedside manner needs work—"

"That's an understatement."

Shiloh almost smiled, caught herself, as if remembering the seriousness of our conversation. "Look, I know there's nothing I can say that is going to make you believe or trust me, and that's fair. I'm not sure that what we do can be explained in words. You just have to live it."

"Living the deaths of other people." I shook my head, disgusted with Shiloh and moreover myself for not throwing open the door of the RV, then and there, demanding that they let me out, take me home. Just how far was I willing to go to discover the truth?

We drove north through the last of the night, up to the northernmost part of Wisconsin. The rising sun was just pulling clear of the pines when I first caught sight of Stewart Gavin's house, flashing between the trees as we came up the road. It was a cabin with a sharply slanted roof and a crude stone chimney listing to the left. There was a wide gravel clearing in front of the house, and the caravan encircled it. Riley parked Shiloh's truck just a few feet from the porch but didn't get out. Iona pulled up in the station wagon. Shiloh emerged from the bedroom of the RV, and as she did, Chloe and Skye, who had been sitting with me in the kitchen, stood up.

"Well?" said Shiloh, looking down at me. "What's it going to be?"

"I'm not ready." My voice was hoarse from the effort of holding back tears. I didn't want to hurt anyone, much less kill them. Hell,

I couldn't even bring myself to stomp on spiders, even though they absolutely terrified me. I always made Adeline do the dirty work, but she wasn't here to stand in for me now. I was on my own. Maybe that's what she'd wanted all along, a trial by fire, to make me as strong as she was. "I need time. Just a day or two—"

"We don't have it to spare," said Shiloh. "Are you going in or not?"

I was terrified and torn. Had Adeline felt the same way when faced with this choice? Did she feel as helpless and guilt-sick as I did? The thought brought me some comfort. This was a nightmare, but at least it was one that my sister had once lived. Just the thought of that made me feel closer to her, in a way that I hadn't since she'd first disappeared. I closed my eyes, caught the briefest glimpse of her dying alone in that playhouse. The vision Death had given me.

It was enough. "Okay. I'll do it."

Shiloh, for her part, didn't seem surprised. She turned to the other girls. "Wait here. This'll be quick." Then she held open the door of the RV for me. "After you."

I had assumed there'd be some vital element of surprise at play. That we'd ditch the vehicles at some secluded location, a mile or so from the house, and approach on foot to avoid announcing our arrival. Maybe we'd slip inside through a cracked window like burglars in the night. But Shiloh's approach lacked that theatricality. She walked up the steps of the porch as though it was her own home. I felt like I was about to pass out again.

"Before we go in, a few ground rules." We were just inches from the front door, but Shiloh didn't even bother to whisper. "The first thing you need to understand is that we're not here to kill him. This is a *dispatch*," said Shiloh. "We're here because he has to die.

Mind the difference between the two. The second is that, when you try the door, it'll be unlocked for you. It always is. The third is that, once our mark lays eyes on us, things will change. You'll feel it. We'll be in another reality, adjacent to this one but different. It's almost like time stops for a little while, until the dispatch is complete." It bothered me that she called killing someone a dispatch, like something to cross off a to-do list. "Got all that?"

I didn't, but I nodded anyway, ready to get this over with before I lost my nerve.

Shiloh waved me forward. "After you."

The door was unlocked, like Shiloh promised it would be, and we stepped into a large cathedral living room with wood-paneled walls and big windows gone green with moss. Stewart Gavin sat in an armchair in front of the TV. He only turned to look at us when the door closed, its screen snapping shut loudly. He was small and pale. Something about him reminded me of a porcelain doll—if porcelain dolls had thick bifocals and wore red gingham flannels.

He craned to look at us over the top of his recliner, waved us into the living room with a shaking hand. "I didn't expect there to be two of you."

I was stunned. "Y-you know why we're here?"

"Course I know," said the man, affronted. "I'm eighty-five years old and you think I don't know death when it comes through my own front door?"

Bewildered, I looked to Shiloh, who seemed impressed but not surprised. "It happens sometimes," she said. "People—the older ones, especially—know when it's coming. They see us for what we are even if we don't tell them."

"My wife went on ahead of me," said Stewart, as if to explain himself. "I was waiting for my turn. Things got boring around here anyway. All they seem to play on TV these days is reruns and new shows so bad they're not worth watching twice."

I didn't know what to do or say. I felt the moment warranted something grave and reverent, but I came up with nothing, and Shiloh didn't offer any condolences or apologies. She watched me, waiting to see what I would do.

"I—I'm so sorry," I sputtered, choking on tears.

Stewart just waved me off with a flap of his hand. But he looked, for the briefest moment, afraid. And I could tell, from the way his chin wrinkled, that he was struggling to hold back tears. "There's nothing for it. Let's just get on with it."

Those were his last words.

Shiloh came to stand behind the man, a motion so fluid I didn't even see her move. "Come here," she said. "Stand with me."

I walked to her, my legs leaden, and came to stand behind the recliner next to Shiloh. Stewart gazed very pointedly at the TV.

"Give me your hand," said Shiloh. "The one Death touched."

I gave her my left hand. I had long fingers—piano hands, my mom always said, wasted on my lack of music talent—but Shiloh's were longer still, her palm warm and calloused. When she touched me, small shocks raced up my arms, spreading through me in a series of soft chills, and I had to fight not to shudder.

Shiloh turned my palm over in her hands and guided it gently to the base of Stewart's neck. His nape was covered in downy wisps of white hair, and his skin was warm to the touch. I felt the animal of him then—the organic aspects of his body separate from humanity and sentience and all the other qualities we believe set us apart from other living things. I thought, in passing, that if I'd touched him with my eyes closed, I wouldn't have known him from a dog or a pig.

"I want you to think about the gift that Death gave you last night," Shiloh told me, pressing my palm flush to Stewart's neck. "Let it carry through you into him."

At first, I felt nothing, but then my hand began to throb, and that throb turned into a sharp pull, as if my mind, my soul, was being drawn out through my palm. I closed my eyes, and when I opened them again, I was in a different body. Smaller, younger... softer. The body of a little boy. I could see myself in the window of the car I was sitting in, my round face, cheeks flushed red with rosacea, eyes narrowed against the sun. In the driver's seat, behind the wheel, was a tanned man with deep smile lines and crow's-feet creases at the edges of his eyes.

A father. *My* father.

He was singing along to a song on the radio. A country ballad I didn't remember hearing before, and yet, somehow, I sang along with him as we drove.

I closed my eyes against the sun, and when I opened them again, I was older and taller, standing in a sea of high grass. In the distance, there was a mountain, washed blue with fog, a wedding unfolding at the foot of it. There were flowers strewn across a narrow aisle shorn right through the high grass. A woman in white stood at its end, a hand extended to me. I took it, and we promised that we would never let go of each other.

The memory changed again. I saw the same woman walking

ahead of me. Her hair had turned white, and she had hiking sticks in both hands. She seemed frail, squatting under the weight of an overlarge backpack, but even in her weakened state, I couldn't keep up with her, no matter how fast I went or how hard I tried. She was always just ahead of me.

There was the white flash of a hospital waiting room. And then I was back in the cabin with the woman, my wife. Her hair was gone, and she was shivering despite the heavy quilt draped around her shoulders. I took her cold hands in mine and worked ointment into her rough calluses and swollen knuckles. She told me, with tears in her eyes, that it was time for her to go.

This time, I could follow her.

I was pulled backward out of Stewart's body, and all at once, I returned to my own. Hot tears slicked my cheeks as I peered down at Stewart. He lay dead in his chair, eyes open. Maybe with the woman from his memories, following her wherever she went.

Or maybe he was nowhere at all.

One with nothing.

"You see?" said Shiloh, eyes not on the dead man but me. "It's not so bad, is it?"

I needed to sit down after that, and did on the recliner beside Stewart's. It was slightly smaller than his, and I wondered if it had belonged to his wife. I cried for a long time, out of guilt and maybe grief, though I didn't know Stewart well enough to mourn him properly.

Shiloh took a seat on the brick hearth of the fireplace, legs braced apart, staring at the floor.

She startled me when she stood abruptly and made for the

kitchen. When she pulled open the fridge, I saw that there was nothing much in it apart from frozen bricks of meat and energy drinks. I wondered, in passing, who had attended to Stewart in his final days. Who, if anyone, had made him warm meals and made sure he'd had enough to eat. I hoped he'd had someone, a nurse or a daughter, or perhaps a son.

"Do you want anything to drink?" She held up a Red Bull.

I must've said yes, because she put it in my hand. The can was so cold it hurt to hold, but I didn't flinch. The pain was grounding. It brought me back to myself.

I peered up at Shiloh, who loomed over me, silent and watchful, as if waiting for me to break. I decided only then that I wouldn't, swallowing down my tears, squaring my shoulders. They thought I was weak, but I intended to show them all just how tough I really was. "How did all of this begin, anyway? With you and Death?"

Shiloh shrugged, like it wasn't a story worth telling. "He appeared to me one night when I was still a kid and told me things no one else could've ever known—things about me and my friends and family, when they were going to die and how. I guess he wanted to prove to me that he was the real deal, and when I was thoroughly convinced, he told me he wanted me to help him with a project. And that project was this, us, all these girls he enlisted."

"Why girls?" I asked, because, frankly, I feared Death was a bit of a pervert.

"Death never really said, and I never asked. I think it's less a boys-versus-girls thing and more that he happened to find us interesting. I mean, you try being immortal, living through the eons all alone. It gets old after a while, I bet."

"Speak of the devil." Shiloh got up then and walked to the door and ducked her head outside. Against her wishes, the girls had made their way out of the RV and were milling around in the front yard. Naomi and Riley were splitting a vape by the vegetable patch. Skye was holding what appeared to be a very well-fed farm cat, her face buried in its fur.

"I thought I told you all to wait in the RV," said Shiloh, but she waved them inside anyway. The girls cut off the vape, and Skye put down the cat, checking its tags first to make sure it didn't belong to Stewart. They streamed into the living room, quiet and grave, gathering around Stewart's body.

Skye stroked his cheek, which still had a bit of color in it. "Poor thing. He seems like a sweetheart."

"Should we bury him?" I asked, feeling uneasy. There had been a sense of sacredness when it was just me and Shiloh keeping vigil over Stewart. But with the rest of the girls filling the room, his corpse seemed more like a spectacle.

"No," said Shiloh. "That's against the rules. We leave them be. Always."

I swallowed dry. "B-but what if no one knows he's dead?"

"So?" Riley snatched the energy drink from my hand, pried back the tab, and downed it. "Dead is as dead does. What difference does it make?"

"Show some respect," said Shiloh with an edge. And then, to me: "We don't interfere after a death. It's not just against the rules; it's distasteful. The people we assist don't belong to us just because we spent a few moments with them at the end of their lives. We don't have the right to decide how the news of their death is distributed. We let the people they've chosen to allow into their lives handle that."

"But what if someone finds out we're here?" I asked. It was the question that had been eating at me since we'd first stepped onto Stewart's porch.

Naomi traced her fingertips along the mantel of the fireplace, checked them for dust. There was none. "They won't. We leave no finger- or footprints. No hair. No DNA. Nothing."

"We're invisible." Skye waved her fingers for dramatic effect. I wondered how a girl as young as her could be so cavalier, so comfortable with a dead man sitting in his recliner just a few feet from where she stood.

I looked to Shiloh. "How can you be sure of that?"

"It's Death's doing," said Naomi. "The work we do is important, and he makes sure it's protected."

"He makes sure that *we're* protected," said Shiloh, not looking at me or anyone. "As long as we keep up our end of the deal."

Chapter 9

Later that day, at a pizza buffet on the border between Wisconsin and Minnesota, Shiloh informed me that my next kill would take place at a music festival in the salt flats of Nevada. She wouldn't give me a name when I asked, or tell me how the person would die, just that it was coming. Another chance to prove that I could keep up my end of the bargain and find out what had really happened to my sister the night she died.

The buffet was a little seedy. The pizza was stale and dry under the red glare of the heat lamps, and the lettuce in the salad bar was brown and wilting. The girls claimed a booth, all of us sliding into the benches on either side of the table.

I looked to Shiloh. "How many people do I have to kill, anyway?"

"There is no set number," said Shiloh, and she caught Iona's eye across the table, then nodded to a lone woman sitting at the bar. She was a box-blonde in a tailored suit, looked to be in her forties.

She sat hunched over several empty shot glasses. "It's about how you kill, not how many."

Iona slid out of the booth, crossing the restaurant in a few long strides. She perched herself on an unclaimed stool beside the woman, gave her a wide and dazzling smile and said something, a joke, maybe, or a compliment; I couldn't hear them from so far away. But whatever it was brought a smile to the woman's face.

It was only then that I realized Iona was going to kill her.

Shiloh kept her gaze trained on Iona. "Watch her work. You see how she stays present? That's crucial. You need to live their last moments with them. Ease them through it."

I watched with a pit in my stomach as Iona slid a hand across the sticky bar top. She touched the woman's fingers, and that was all it took. The woman slumped forward out of her stool and hit the ground.

Riley tossed a crumpled napkin on a half-eaten slice of pizza and slid out of the booth. "Welp. Guess that's our cue."

The other girls followed suit, trailing her out of the restaurant, Iona close at their heels. But I stayed, alone in the booth, staring at the woman lying dead on the ground until Shiloh caught me by the arm and dragged me away.

Outside the buffet, as ambulance sirens wailed in the distance, Shiloh spread a paper map across the hood of her truck and developed a plan. From eastern Minnesota to the Nevada salt flats where the music festival would take place was nearly a twenty-three-hour drive. She estimated it would take us about three days of driving, and only if we didn't make too many pit stops.

To stay on time, we agreed to stop every two or three hours for pee breaks at gas stations, rest stops, or, in particularly rural areas, on the shoulder of the road, hidden by the high grass. We'd drive during the daylight hours and spend our nights in campsites or desolate stretches owned by the Bureau of Land Management, where anyone could stay as long as they wanted to.

An ambulance pulled into the parking lot, help for a woman who was already dead. The lights flashed and the sirens howled. Iona watched on, expressionless, as paramedics rushed into the restaurant.

Shiloh, for her part, didn't even register them. She was already focused on the next dispatch, tracing a finger along the map, following the path of a highway. "If we stay on target, we should make it to Nevada on Friday, give or take. Just as the festival begins." Her gaze flickered up to me, eyes sharp in the flashing lights of the ambulance. "That'll give you plenty of time to find your mark."

I swallowed what felt like a stone. I hadn't let myself think of Stewart much in the wake of his death. Every time I thought of him—alone in that cabin, dead—I just . . . shut down. But now, faced with the impending reality of my second kill, all the memories came flooding back. The feel of him under my hand, the visions of his life, the life I'd taken.

I wasn't sure I had it in me to do it again.

If not for Adeline, I don't even think I would've had the strength to try.

The paramedics burst from the restaurant with the woman, the corpse, strapped to the gurney. They ushered her into the ambulance and pulled out onto the street. No sirens this time, just the lights flashing silently.

THAT FIRST DAY on the open road, driving through the grassy plains of South Dakota, was like the dream of a dream. The empty highways were licked with heat waves. The prairies were flat and featureless, stretching endlessly toward the distant horizon. Sometimes we went what felt like hours without seeing a single other car on the road and it was safe enough for Skye and Naomi to ride in the bed of Shiloh's truck, the wind whipping their hair wild and weightless, Skye with her arms raised *Titanic*-style and Naomi bracing her to keep her from falling.

That night, we camped on BLM land. The whole scene was fast and frantic. It reminded me of an overstuffed closet bursting open and spilling out onto the empty plains. Chloe, one of the taller girls in the group, strung Christmas lights across the fold-down awning over the RV's door. Iona unfurled a large and dusty Persian rug and pried open a series of rusting lounge chairs, padding the seats with tasseled pillows in a variety of sizes and colors. Naomi turned on music, and the rasping vocals of Fleetwood Mac's Stevie Nicks crackled from an old speaker that Skye had set up in the bed of Shiloh's truck.

As darkness fell, Iona strung a sheet up on the side of the RV, a makeshift screen. Riley made popcorn in a pan over the open fire while Naomi and Iona fussed with a tangled knot of extension cords until—wheezing and overheated—a projector finally spit grainy black-and-white footage at the sheet. Skye, Iona, and Chloe piled into the trunk of the station wagon, and the rest of us dragged up folding chairs and pillows, clutching bowls of warm popcorn to our chests as the opening credits reeled. I was surprised when Shiloh bypassed the other girls and sat down on a pillow beside me, so close our knees very nearly touched. When the wind blew just so, I could feel her hair skim across my cheek.

And I wondered what it meant that I wanted her closer still.

THE NEXT DAY, we got up before dawn, packed up camp in the blue dark, and hit the highway hoping to make it across the better part of Wyoming and into Utah before nightfall. We were a good four hours into our drive and, as far as I could tell, roughly in the middle of nowhere when Chloe convinced Shiloh to pull over at Flower Children, a vintage shop that had been announcing itself in a series of sun-faded billboards posted at intervals along the side of the road.

"We have nothing to wear to the music festival." Chloe leaned forward from the back seat of the truck to make sure that Shiloh heard her. "You always say we need to keep a low profile; how are we going to do that if we don't even look the part?" She then gestured to me with a jab of her thumb, and I was grateful that Shiloh didn't take her eyes off the road to look at me. "I mean, Roslyn's wardrobe is almost entirely comprised of gym shorts and hand-me-down Catholic camp T-shirts. No offense."

"None taken," I said, though in truth, I was a little embarrassed, because I knew my wardrobe was sorely lacking. When Adeline was alive, I'd dressed better, because she coaxed me into borrowing her clothes—thrifted cotton maxi skirts and tiny crop tops stolen from our local strip mall and bleach-dyed in our parents' deep Jacuzzi tub.

Adeline was always adventurous with what she wore, and I had always followed suit. But after she died, I lost the heart to wear her clothes. They still smelled like her, and I worried that the scent would fade with wear. So I left her clothes in her closet untouched.

My personal wardrobe was mostly comprised of stuff that Adeline wouldn't even wear to bed: sweat-wicking shorts, baggy T-shirts, and neon sports bras that Adeline had once called *garish and tasteless*.

"If I don't stretch my legs a bit, I'm going to get a blood clot," Skye whined, backing Chloe up. "Please can we just have a look?"

Shiloh didn't answer her, but when the antique shop appeared on the roadside—it was a warehouse painted red to look like a barn—she steered her truck into the parking lot with an exasperated sigh. "You have thirty minutes."

Flower Children was as big as a department store, and it was packed to capacity with so many antiques that, upon entering, my brain briefly overloaded. There were two floors. The bottom was reserved mostly for furniture and other antiques. The second floor was all vintage clothes.

The girls immediately raced upstairs and began to sort through the selections, the hangers screeching along the racks as they clawed their way through a bevy of wedding gowns gone yellow with age, fur-trimmed coats, and long silken nightgowns, among other finds.

Chloe, perhaps feeling guilty for her choice comments about my wardrobe, designated herself as my personal stylist. "I'm not trying to change your wardrobe, per se, just expand it so that it's more . . . you."

I gestured to my outfit: dirty Converse, athletic shorts, an old T-shirt from a Catholic summer camp I'd been forced to attend years ago. The only redeemable element of the outfit was Shiloh's coat, which . . . I'd been wearing a lot for no reason I was willing to admit out loud. "What if this *is* me?"

Chloe glanced at me up and down. The neon-pink running shorts, the ratty T-shirt, Shiloh's coat over it. She wrinkled her nose. "I find that highly unlikely. The goal is to pick pieces that call to you, not just whatever is around. Everything has to go . . . except that coat. It's Shiloh's, right?"

I flushed hot. "She let me borrow it."

That wasn't exactly true. She'd put it on me that night at the motel, the night I met Death, and just . . . never asked for it back. And I'd never offered.

"You must be a special case. Shiloh never lets anyone wear that coat. I've tried." Chloe eyed the coat a beat longer, and I still don't know if I imagined the flicker of jealousy that crossed her face like a shadow. Whatever it was, it passed quickly. She turned on her heel and began to comb through the rack in front of her, pulling things I would've never even considered wearing: creamy silk camis that pooled like melted butter in my hands, cardigans with leather elbow patches, and knee-high military boots that looked like they'd been pulled from the feet of a fallen soldier.

I realized only after she'd herded me into the fitting room that she'd never asked my shoe size. But the boots fit perfectly, like almost everything else that Chloe had selected for me. And it wasn't just the size that she'd gotten right, it was the way I felt in the clothes. They were so . . . comfortable, and I was surprised by how much I liked the way I looked in them.

Whenever I'd worn Adeline's clothes—whenever she'd dressed me—I'd always felt like I was in costume, and I acted in turn, awkward and sheepish, never quite feeling like myself, as if I needed to pretend to be someone else so her clothes would fit me right. But it wasn't the same in the outfits that Chloe had selected for me.

"What do you think?" Chloe asked, and I could tell that she really wanted to know.

I squinted at my reflection in the mirror, didn't hate what I saw. "I like the top. But the skirt's a bit frilly, I guess?"

"Swap it out with this one." She handed me another. This one was sleek, silky, and so light that all I could feel was the weight of the hanger when I took it.

I checked the price tag and winced. "Can't afford it."

"Don't worry about that," said Chloe. "Clothes are complimentary."

"What do you mean?"

"It's part of our agreement," she explained, whispering now. "We do Death's bidding, and Death provides. I mean, in moderation, of course."

The skirt was one hundred fifty bucks. The cardigan eighty. I couldn't find a price tag on the cami, but I noticed that the yellowing tag at the back read, in wispy black thread, MISS DIOR, so it had to be expensive too. "This is moderation?"

Chloe snatched it back. "It's *quality*. Everyone needs statement pieces."

The girls finished their shopping and loaded their selections onto the countertop. It seemed that everyone had found something. Skye clung to a beaver-skin muffler, insisting that, when they traveled north in the winter, it would spare her fingers from frostbite. Iona wanted an old rotary phone that we didn't have any room for in the RV. Riley had discovered a tarnished Japanese chef's knife, which she was convinced she could restore with a little bit of oil and elbow grease.

Naomi found a bracelet of bluish river pearls. Chloe had procured what appeared to be a monster romance novel from the seventies that featured a swooning woman beside some sort of bulky swamp humanoid. To accompany the book, several long nightgowns that matched the one the woman was wearing on the cover.

It took the shopkeeper a full thirty minutes to check us out, and the total came to over a thousand dollars.

I felt sick.

Shiloh sidled up to the register, sensing my unease as if I'd voiced it aloud. "Don't worry about the money." She pulled a few hundred-dollar bills from a fold-over wallet. "It's yours to spend."

But I shook my head. "It's too much. I can't accept all this—"

"Why not?" Shiloh's gaze passed over me. She took in my new outfit, her coat that I had yet to return. "You got the clothes you needed, and . . . they suit you."

I tried not to read into the compliment, but it was hard when she looked at me like that, with a question in her eyes that I didn't know how to answer.

We got back into our cars and drove another two hours, into a nearby town to break camp for the night. We made a pit stop at the first pharmacy we saw, and the girls stocked up on necessities—dessert-flavored lip balms, tubes of mascara, eyeliners, and craft glitter glue to be smeared over bare arms and shoulders.

"We have to look the part," said Skye, chucking a couple of eyeshadow palettes into her cart. One of them cracked on impact, but she didn't seem to notice or care.

"And what part are we trying to look like, exactly?" I asked.

"Pretty and interesting," said Skye, very matter-of-fact. "If we're going to be one of the last things people see before they die, we should attempt to be something worth looking at."

Chloe nodded in agreement and said, "This one guy, Jordan, heart attack." I was surprised that they could even remember the names and deaths of the people they'd killed. "He told me I looked like his wife before he died. Said she used to wear the same lipstick and then he *named* the exact shade and brand I was wearing at the time. Felt serendipitous."

"There's nothing serendipitous about it. They're just nervous and stalling," said Riley, tossing a box of tampons into her cart. "Trying to find something to hold on to to prolong their lives, talk their way out of death."

Skye nodded enthusiastically. "It's like when you come to the conclusion of a paper you wrote the night before it was due, and you don't know how to tie all your batshit crazy ideas together, as if you can talk your way into an A if you ramble long enough."

"Or maybe they're just grasping for the right moment to end on," said Iona.

"I think it's just a distraction," said Naomi. She held a basket in the crook of her arm, only a few things in it: a small round of blue eyeshadow—her signature—a carton of eggs, a bag of tangerines, and a small pack of toilet paper. "They talk to reassure themselves. The sound of their own voice reminds them they're still alive. The memories of people they loved bring them comfort. I think they're all just desperate bids for connection. I think that's all anyone really wants in the end."

"Or maybe they don't want it to end at all," said Iona in a soft voice, and I wondered if she was thinking about the woman at the bar. "I mean, can you blame them for wanting things to go on forever? If their lives suck, they want to live long enough to remedy that. And if their lives are great, then why would they want them to end?"

Chapter 10

We made camp in a Walmart parking lot that evening. The location was less . . . idyllic than the campgrounds we'd passed along the way. And arguably a lot sketchier. But as soon as we parked, the girls got out and began to unpack, the way they did every time they camped, much to the amusement of our nearby neighbors, a group of men smoking around their muscle cars, showing them off to each other. But none of the girls seemed to care . . . or even notice them. Nor were they particularly concerned about being chased out of the parking lot by Walmart staff, claiming that no one ever disturbed them. Another perk of working on behalf of Death.

As usual, the girls channeled their energy into making a home of the parking lot, which, as far as I knew, we were only supposed to stay in for one night. I couldn't help but feel like their efforts to nest and decorate were wasted on a place as seedy as this one. It was one thing to set up in an RV park, where others were doing the same, or empty expanses of BLM land, where everyone was, more or less, left to their own devices. But I wondered how they could be so relaxed in the parking lot of a rundown town with a leering group of men just a few yards away. I was beginning to think I was the only one who noticed them staring, but I saw that Chloe was watching them, too, her gaze hard and unblinking.

Next to Shiloh—who kept her cards close to her chest, never talking about the circumstances of her near-death experience—Chloe was the most withholding girl in the group. But I didn't realize this at first, mostly because she liked to spin stories, strange scenarios and wild tales that became increasingly ridiculous until you realized they were lies.

"I don't tell this to just anyone, but . . . my near-death experience was a bouncy house caught in a windstorm," she'd said to me the day that I joined the group. "I had a good grip on the netting, but my mom fell out. It's the nails that did her in, acrylics. They were so long she couldn't close her hand into a proper fist. That's why I get gel sets. They remind me of her."

Gullible as I was, I'd offered her my most sincere condolences, only for her to change the story the next day, citing a bank robbery gone wrong, a gun pressed to her temple.

I quickly learned to save my sympathies. Chloe didn't want my pity, anyway.

Still, the mystery of her near-death was a source of perpetual curiosity, especially as I learned the other girls' first brushes with mortality. There was Riley, diagnosed with a rare and aggressive bone cancer at just three years old that she'd fought for her entire childhood. During her sophomore year of high school, after three years of remission, it metastasized. Her oncologists tried and failed to kill it, first with bouts of radiation and then with bone saws, removing the cancer from the femur, replacing it with steel. The doctors told her there was nothing more they could do, and that same night, Shiloh appeared at the foot of her bed with an offer from Death.

Naomi's story was similarly tragic. She'd found herself homeless in the dead of winter after fleeing the last of a series of horrible foster homes. She was sleeping in a playground, half-dead with cold, when Shiloh appeared and offered her a way out, a warm car to sleep in.

Iona's was a car accident, two days after she passed her driver's exam. "I wasn't the one at fault," she'd assured me the first time I rode in the station wagon with her.

Skye didn't even know, or seem to care, about the circumstances of her near-death. The girls had just turned up at her home in Palm Springs, laid out their terms, and made her an offer that sounded not only better than death, but better than spending the long months of summer at home with her mother and the bevy of her pretentious D-list socialite friends who flocked from LA every summer.

"I think I was just really, really bored," she'd said to me just yesterday, at a gas station in the middle of the prairie. "Maybe that was how I was supposed to go. Death by ennui."

The girls seemed to bond through these near-death experiences, trading stories and showing off their battle scars around the fire. But I sensed that Chloe's story was decidedly different and darker than that of the other girls. I could tell by the way the girls exempted her from all their grim discussions and posturing. If they referred to Chloe's near-death at all, they did it in vague whispers when she wasn't around. But I didn't need the details to understand. It was a story I'd heard before, one I feared.

A girl walks home alone at night, and a car slows to a stop beside her.

A door opens, and a man emerges, stepping onto the sidewalk.

There's a snatching and a scream. Flailing limbs and nails dragged through thick flesh.

None of it enough in the end.

Chloe's story would have ended the way the stories of so many before her had, but Death intervened with an offer that she took. I'm not sure when the offer came, if it was before the worst or after. No one knew how long she'd had to wait to be rescued, if she ever was. Maybe she'd freed herself, fighting off her attacker and fleeing into the night.

It was hard to believe what she'd been through, looking at her then as she stared down those leering men across the parking lot. Most girls have a way of shrinking themselves under the gazes of the men that want them, the fear compacting them into these tiny, hunched versions of themselves. At least, that's what I used to do, having read all the statistics and digested copious amounts of true crime. I knew all the grisly ways that men like to hurt girls like me, and I'd spent the bulk of my teenage life trying to avoid a series of tragic and gruesome ends. I walked home with a small canister of pepper spray in the front pocket of my backpack. I wedged my keys between my knuckles and gripped them tight. I used to keep a tracking app on my phone so that my parents (and ex-boyfriend) always knew where I was, so that even if the worst happened, they had a better chance of finding whatever was left of me.

But Chloe wasn't like that.

She was unafraid. Defiant, even.

The men took notice of the way she seemed to grow taller under the weight of their gazes . . . instead of shrinking like she was supposed to. At first, they were perplexed, laughing awkwardly, milling about in circles, dragging on their cigarettes with a kind of agitated franticness. One of them even pointed at her with a quick jab of his thumb as if to say *Get a load of this.*

But their awkwardness and good humor quickly became something else the longer that Chloe held them in her unflagging gaze.

The men could stomach, with some unease, the disregard of the other girls. But they resented Chloe, as if she'd taken something from them.

When one of them spit a bloody dip of chewing tobacco in Chloe's general direction, Shiloh stood up. And I realized that she'd been watching them all along, tracking their every move from her periphery.

In fact, all the girls had.

They stopped what they were doing—conversations dying into silence, peals of laughter cut abruptly short—and stood with Chloe, unflinching.

I saw the moment the men realized they were in danger, some quiet instinct within them cuing them into the truth. It was as if they saw us for what we were. Small deaths incarnate. The power to kill in the palms of our hands. As they retreated to their respective muscle cars, a kind of smugness came over me, a small and sweet taste of what it must've felt like to be fearless.

To be like them.

To be Death himself.

Chapter 11

That night, I decided to go for a run. My first in many months. I didn't ask for my phone or even tell anyone I was leaving. I didn't change into a more modest outfit—an oversized sweatshirt with the hood up, baggy pants so that no one could tell if I was a girl or a boy—or keep to the well-lit sidewalks along the busier streets. I just stepped out of the RV, stretched my hamstrings, and sprinted through the parking lot and into the dark of the town.

I ran with my back to oncoming traffic, my legs strong and sure beneath me. I pressed on, cutting past abandoned buildings and the lit plastic tents of homeless encampments and through what I imagined was a rough part of town—small homes with overgrown lawns and broken windows, chained dogs snapping their jaws at me as I passed them by.

But I thought of Chloe. And I didn't flinch.

I kept running, never once looking over my shoulder to see who might be tailing me. When the odd man caught my eye—and a few of them did, made a point to—I held their gazes the way Chloe had. I didn't sidestep to make room for them on the sidewalk, clipping shoulders with one man that I passed. He might've called me a bitch, but whatever he said, the accusation or empty threat, it meant nothing to me.

It was 2:00 a.m. by the time I returned to the Walmart parking lot. My eyes were raw and streaming tears, though I felt no sadness, just relief. I broke, falling to my knees there in the middle of the parking lot, my lungs on fire, laughing breathlessly until I panicked and began to hyperventilate. But it wasn't fear that sent me reeling. It was its absence. The vast expanse of my own new freedom.

It was the first time that I'd ever run without fear. I held the power of Death in my palm, carried with me the promise of my own survival. Nothing could touch or hurt me that I couldn't hurt worse.

I sat down in one of the folding chairs by the fire to catch my breath, massaged my calves to keep them from cramping. That was when I saw them, way out on the other side of the parking lot.

Shiloh and Death.

They were sitting on the curb, in a cone of light from the streetlamp shining overhead, the burning bulb swarmed with moths and flies. They sat the same way: half-hunched, arms braced on their knees. I couldn't hear them or even read their lips for the distance, but their conversation seemed intense. Death was talking more than Shiloh, her nodding as she listened, interjecting only once or twice with what seemed like a question . . . or concern.

They talked for several minutes. Then Death put a heavy hand on Shiloh's shoulder and stood up, stepping past her and disappearing into the pine forest.

Shiloh sat frozen there on the curb long after he left, her gaze boring down into the asphalt. When she finally pressed to her feet, I thought she might follow Death into the trees or that maybe she would notice me and come over to talk. But if she did notice me sitting there by the dying fire, she gave no indication. I watched as she slipped her hands into the pockets of her jeans and started across the parking lot, her back turned to me, walking toward the same seedy neighborhood that I'd just run through. Her strides were long and purposeful, like she was late for something important.

Another death.

Death must've given her a name.

The thought of another dispatch made me sick with guilt. But despite that, I had the strange urge to follow her, to make sure she was okay. Shiloh could handle herself, I knew that. But it didn't quell the growing urge I had to protect her, as if that was something I was capable of doing.

Instead of acting on that instinct, I leaned back into the folding chair, watched the midges swarm the streetlight overhead. I closed my eyes, and then, what felt like moments later, I was in the past with Adeline, the two of us racing down our street barefoot, the asphalt chafing our heels. We were laughing, but the sound was warped and slowed. Adeline pulled ahead of me—strange, because I was always the faster of the two of us—and when she turned to look at me, her hair wrapped around her face so I couldn't see anything but her eyes through the curtain of her curls.

I woke hours later to Shiloh looming over me. She was wearing the same flannel shirt and jeans from last night when I'd spotted her with Death. But I could see the exhaustion in her eyes, the bags beneath them. Her sandy hair was dark with grease at the roots, and she'd pulled it back out of her face with a clip. She looked like she'd been up all night. "Did you sleep well?"

I hadn't realized I'd been sleeping at all. Had I spent the night alone, outside, in the middle of a Walmart parking lot? I could've been kidnapped or killed.

I sat up, stunned I'd slept outside, and so late into the morning. The run the night before must've really tired me out.

"Festival's still an eight-hour drive from here, ten with traffic. We should get on the road as quick as we can. We don't want to miss your dispatch."

I nodded. Squinting against the sunlight, I saw what appeared to be a viciously competitive shopping cart drag race across the mostly empty parking lot. The carts were loaded with groceries and shrieking teenage girls and they drifted across the asphalt, threatening to topple over. Chloe steered one of them, pushing hard, racing against Riley to make it to the finish line, which appeared to be the stop sign that marked the end of the parking lot.

Shiloh watched them with a grim shake of her head. "I swear I don't know where they get it from. All that energy."

"They got it from you," I said, the sun so bright it made it hard to look up at her. "Death gave them a second chance, and they're making the most of it."

Shiloh frowned, fishing her vape from her back pocket, and sheathed the mouthpiece between her lips.

The girls, I'd noticed, were rather reckless with their health, a natural result of their conditional immortality, Death tipping the scales of reality in their favor, protecting them from the consequences of their vices and bad habits. Shiloh's vaping was really no different from my jogging alone at night. It was a risk we could now most certainly afford to take. But I did wonder what would happen if we were cut loose from our deal with Death. Would all the years of risky decisions catch up to us all at once? The moment Death set us free, if he ever set us free, would the girls who smoked immediately be stricken with a racking cough and the promise of lung cancer? Were we going to be made to pay for this someday?

I almost asked the question, but Shiloh strode toward the girls before I had the chance, putting an end to the shopping cart race with a simple raise of her hand. "Time to head out."

We piled into our vehicles of choice and made our way west, through the last of Utah, where the mountains gave way to the salt flats of Nevada. From there, the drive to the festival proper should have been relatively short. But there was a three-hour-long line of traffic through the salt plains just to get to the campground. Chloe immediately capitalized on this occasion and began to plan what she called our *festival looks*. She enlisted Iona to paint our faces. But there was some debate about theming, none of the girls able to agree on a look that would suit all of us.

"What about fallen angels?" Skye waved her hands by her head, trying to mimic angel wings. "Like biblically accurate ones. We could paint eyeballs all over our faces."

Chloe wrinkled her nose. "Ew."

"I like the idea," said Iona encouragingly. "But it would take twelve hours to do that on all of you. I'll need something I can paint quicker."

"We could go for skulls?" Chloe suggested.

"How original." Riley rolled her eyes. She sat in the driver's seat, steering the RV through the thick of the traffic, a difficult task given she was also towing the station wagon. Of all the girls, she'd been the most vehemently opposed to the idea of costumes, refusing to participate in the antics. "I have an idea. Maybe you should all dress up like clowns. That seems fitting."

It was meant to be an insult, but the idea stuck.

"That's brilliant," said Skye, and she hopped into the passenger seat at the front of the RV, Iona's makeshift makeup chair. "I wanna go first."

Instead of the usual circus clown, Iona opted for a more sophisticated harlequin approach. Faces powdered pale, lips painted downturned at the corners, exaggerated eyebrows flicking upward at the middle, over-blushed cheeks adorned with cartoonishly large teardrops or playing card shapes—diamonds, hearts, spades, and clubs.

When it was my turn to sit in the makeup chair, Iona brushed my hair back from the ends, teasing it large and voluminous so it almost haloed my head. She pressed powder into my face and blushed my cheeks so aggressively I winced a little when I looked in the mirror.

"Trust the process," she said, sensing my mounting anxieties.

"I'm trying."

Iona worked black into my eyeline and carefully smudged it away with her pinkie finger. She worked more blush into the apples of my cheeks and the tip of my nose. "Close your eyes."

I did as I was told, shivering a little as Iona painted over the smudged pencil liner with liquid, tracing crisp black diamonds over my closed eyelids, down to my cheeks.

"Done," said Iona. "You can open your eyes."

I opened them and looked in the mirror she held up to my face, and for the briefest moment, past the makeup or perhaps because of it, I saw Adeline staring back at me. It took me a few blinks to realize I was looking at myself, and it was the first and only time I'd ever thought we'd looked alike. Not because of our features but because I saw in my eyes the light that I only ever found in hers. I saw, when I looked at myself, everything that she was and everything she'd hoped I would be.

We drove for a few hours more. The sun set, and in the blue of the dusk, I spotted the first lights of the festival. It took shape behind a pall of salt dust kicked up by the tires of the trucks and vans that drove alongside us. From a distance, it looked like an overgrown carnival, a mirage of lights winking on the horizon. Someone opened the windows of the RV to let in the sound of music. And I could feel it then, this thrumming energy coming off the festival in waves. All those souls thronging together in the clouds of salt dust. The lives yet to be claimed.

We parked in a camp lit up with achingly bright neon lights.

The girls wore their festival outfits, which could be summarized as a more elaborate, racier iteration of their regular clothes. Peasant skirts with the hems hiked up at the hipbones, held in place with safety pins. Rhinestones affixed with eyelash glue to blushed cheeks. Fishnets and feathers and damp hair spray-dyed into blacks and reds to match Iona's makeup. Skye and Chloe had made us all friendship bracelets to exchange with other festivalgoers that night.

It was so easy to imagine Adeline standing among them. She lived for nights like this one, and I felt sad she wasn't there and guilty because I was. I felt like I'd stolen this life from her, this moment in time that should've been hers.

Shiloh climbed out of her truck. She faltered when she saw me with my painted face, dressed in the clothes Chloe picked for me. She gazed at me with a kind of reluctance—arms folded tight over her chest, eyes narrowed—as if she were staring directly into the sun. Like it hurt to look at me.

I waited for her to say something, and when she didn't, her gaze sliding over me to the other girls, I felt small and stupid. I wanted to backtrack to the RV bathroom, scrub my face clean of the makeup, but instead, I squared my shoulders and resisted the urge.

"It's a big festival, so we need to split up," said Shiloh. She held an old hatbox in one hand, and she pulled off the top to reveal the cell phones within, which she began to distribute. She didn't give me mine, and with some resentment, I wondered if she didn't trust me with it.

Once all the phones had been passed around, Shiloh fired off a text to the group: the selfie of a dark-haired girl our age, her hair drawn up into a tight bun at the top of her head, all the would-be flyaways gelled into place. It was just a headshot, but at the bottom of the picture, I could see that she was wearing some type of white leotard. I guessed she was a dancer.

Jasmine Wu. Our target.

My stomach clenched.

Shiloh slipped her own phone into her pocket. "If you spot her, message the group. Then Roslyn will take her life, per Death's orders."

Skye raised her hand. "What about . . . fun?"

Shiloh looked less than impressed. "Fun?"

Skye nodded, looking a little annoyed. "I mean, we spent hours getting dressed up and Iona did such a good job with our makeup. Shouldn't we at least enjoy ourselves a little bit? See and be seen?"

I couldn't help but think she was right, looking at all of them. Skye wore a monochromatic mod dress from Flower Children, with white platform go-go boots that made her almost as tall as me. Her makeup was like that of a mime: pale face, painted-on brows, and black teardrops beneath both eyes. Chloe had teased her hair at the roots so that it was nearly double its normal size. She wore cotton bloomers for pants with knee-high socks, kitten-heel sandals, and a corset top, which would've looked terrible if I were wearing it. But somehow it was chic on her. Iona was equally breathtaking. Despite the fact that she'd spent the bulk of her time doing makeup for everyone else, her outfit was impeccable: a sequined minidress paired with an oversized pearl choker wrapped all the way up her neck. Naomi—dressed in a long silk skirt that brushed the ground paired with a puff-sleeve blouse that I'm fairly certain was from the Victorian era—sported a darker and more dramatic iteration of her usual makeup look, the blue shadow extending out to her temples and across the bridge of her nose. Iona had drawn black diamonds over both of her eyes, and her lips and cheeks were powdered pale, so she looked almost like a painted corpse.

It seemed a waste of effort, and, frankly, beauty, for them to spend all night searching for someone who was doomed to die anyway.

"I mean, we came all the way here." To my surprise, Naomi, typically one of the more practical girls in the group, backed up Skye. "There's the light shows and a Ferris wheel, performances on the main stage, and—"

"And a really weird tent with a bunch of naked people," said Riley, and after a few horrified glances her way, she added a defensive "Just saying."

Shiloh ignored them. "We're on a deadline. Roslyn has to prove herself in three weeks, or else—"

Skye fished a tube of lip gloss from her pocket, applied it over her black lipstick. "We're screwed?"

"Essentially. So let's try to stay on task for once. We'll split into three groups to cover more ground. Chloe, you stay here at camp and let us know if you see anything."

I immediately gravitated toward Skye and Naomi, but Shiloh called my name before I had the chance to partner with them. "Roslyn, you're with me."

The girls spread out to varying corners of the festival. Skye unsurprisingly made a beeline for the main stage, Naomi trailing after her to make sure she didn't get into too much trouble. Riley and Iona found their way to a ring of lit circus tents on the north edge of the festival, where the crowds were thinner.

Night fell. Shiloh and I walked through the Gallery of Lights, a bright display of sculptures wrapped in neon and fiber optics. There were life-size elephants and a to-scale rendering of Michelangelo's *David* that burned so brightly against the black of the night that my eyes watered a little when I stared up at it.

"How has it been for you?" Shiloh asked as we wove through crowds of concertgoers with wide and dilated eyes, their faces and limbs painted with bright streaks of glowing paint. "Do you regret coming with us? Now that you know what we are?"

"I don't regret anything." I kicked up dust with my boots. They were heavy but comfortable, and I was grateful for whoever it was that had broken them in so thoroughly. I suspected that I had a long night, with lots of walking, ahead of me still. "I thought I might, after Stewart. But . . ." I trailed off, not sure how to put into words what I was thinking. "You were right about me, when you said I was lost."

"Roslyn, I didn't mean to—"

I waved her off. "It's fine. Really. I think I needed to hear that. I knew it already, how dead I felt, but when you said it . . . I don't know. It woke me up a bit, I guess. Made me realize that I have things to do and live for."

Shiloh risked a glance at me, that question apparent in her eyes again. "Like what?"

"Like . . . finding out what happened to Adeline."

Shiloh nodded, and a silence followed that she didn't fill.

So I did. "Why do you think she left the group and came home? If you had to guess."

"I don't know." Shiloh paused to stare up at a fiber optic sculpture of a two-headed woman, her splayed hands grasping at the sky. "Maybe . . . she missed you."

I laughed aloud at that. "Fat chance. She barely even spoke to me that summer."

"Weird. When she was with us, she talked about you all the time."

That came as a surprise. But then . . . Adeline had all these faces she wore around other people. Different facets of herself that she swapped in and out at will. She was good at being whoever she needed to be to win people over. Maybe, with Shiloh and the girls, she'd wanted to play the part of the caring older sister. That made sense, given the nature of their group.

"Did you miss her?"

Shiloh's question was strange enough to make me stop dead. "I mean, she was my sister."

"I know she was your sister. I asked if you missed her when she was traveling with us."

I felt the back of my neck warm with shame. Because the reality was that I hadn't. Secretly, I had been relieved when Adeline had left that summer. She'd been in one of her bad ways prior to going, and she'd cast a long shadow across the house, draped it like a smothering blanket over everyone so that it was almost hard to breathe around her.

What little I deduced, from her sullen silences and her listlessness, was that she felt deprived of the life she was meant to be living. A life that she'd attained upon meeting the girls—perhaps the life she felt she was destined for. Which then begged the question: Why would she ever leave them? Why would she ever come back to the tiny town she hated so much, to a sister who was so unlike her, when she'd found freedom with the girls? I didn't understand it, and Shiloh's half answer hadn't gotten me any closer to the truth.

I couldn't shake the feeling that she was hiding something. They all were.

And I needed to find out what.

We kept walking, searching for Jasmine. Somewhere along the way, Shiloh stopped to buy a beer, stepping into line at a small bar on wheels. It took me by surprise. Of all the girls, Shiloh seemed the most devoted to the work they did for Death. When I'd realized she'd be my partner for the night, I'd given up on any thin hopes of exploring the festival. But Shiloh relaxed during our time together. Maybe being away from the chaos of the other girls had eased her.

As we made our way toward the main stage, the crowds thickened on all sides, and Shiloh grabbed my hand to keep us from being parted. She guided us through the crowd, but when we emerged on the other side of it, she still kept hold of my hand, her fingers slotting into the spaces between mine.

I faltered. "Shiloh, listen, I—"

The crowds parted, and I saw her.

A girl in platform heels, jumping to the music at the risk of breaking her ankles. She was dressed like an angel, in a white fringe dress with feathered wings and a twisted wire halo that slid askew as she danced. She had an upturned nose dotted with rhinestone freckles. Her lips were full and lined dark, and she had purple contacts in her eyes that made them look overlarge and almost eerily doll-like.

Jasmine Wu.

Chapter 12

Shiloh's hand tightened around mine. She led me through the crowds, closing in on Jasmine, even as my legs went weak beneath me. I didn't want to take another step closer to the girl I was supposed to kill, but I let Shiloh guide me anyway, as if I couldn't stop this. As if I were the victim in this scenario rather than the girl who I was about to kill.

We stopped just short of Jasmine, about a yard away. Up close, she resembled the girls in the caravan more than I did, her head thrown back with laughter, a kind of carelessness in her manner, an invincibility. She was dancing with a group of people who were her friends. Friends who could potentially make this dispatch more difficult, or if not that, then all the more heartbreaking.

It hadn't been too terrible to assist in Stewart's death. He'd known who we were as soon as we stepped into his house and had seemed ready to go. He was old, after all, and he was alone, which was in itself a kind of comfort. He hadn't had to contend with anyone's grief or sorrow. His death had been fast and undramatic, and there was no real aftermath. It had been the same with Iona's dispatch back in the diner, that poor woman who'd slumped out of her stool.

But I saw now that Jasmine's passing would be different. Worse.

Jasmine had friends—a boyfriend, maybe, in the man dancing close behind her, his hands at her hips. He was older than everyone else, in his late twenties or early thirties. He was the kind of man a girl would come to regret ever having dated once she had enough time and distance from her teenage years to see the situation for what it was. Or at least that's what I liked to think. But the reality was that Jasmine was not going to live long enough to regret that relationship, or even this night.

These moments were her last, and unlike Stewart, she didn't seem to know it.

How could she?

Gazing at her, I could barely believe it myself. She was just as full of life and verve as any of the girls in the caravan, like she'd also been promised a forever.

I felt tears building in my throat. A pressure, like panic, tamped down on my chest when Shiloh stepped near to me, so close I could hear her voice above the music. "Go on. Do it."

I didn't move. She was the same age as Adeline. I could see my sister in her eyes, like a specter behind glass. "I can't."

"You have to," said Shiloh. "And I think you know that."

"But she's young," I heard myself say, my voice breaking a little on the words.

"Everyone seems that way in the end. There's never a right time or a good age to die."

"But she's *really* young. Adeline's age."

"That's good," said Shiloh. "It means she won't have to live to suffer and learn how shitty the world really is. You're sparing her."

I kept my gaze on Jasmine. "Is that what you tell yourselves?"

"Only when it helps, and sometimes it doesn't. Sometimes . . . you have to just grit your teeth and get through it. Grieve them later."

But I didn't want to grieve anyone else, didn't want to shoulder the guilt of another lost life—replaying all the ways I could've prevented the worst, blaming myself for what I didn't do . . . or what I did. I couldn't bear it, and yet, if I didn't do this, I feared I would never know what happened to Adeline the night of her death. And the repercussions of my cowardice would extend well beyond just me. The girls would be in danger too.

Jasmine stepped back, turned on the heel of her boot, and all at once, we were face-to-face. She had friendship bracelets stacked up her forearms, all the way to the elbows. When she looked at me, she smiled and stripped off one of them, extended it to me.

"Go on," said Shiloh. I could feel her breath, warm against my ear. "Do it."

Jasmine stepped closer, toward her own undoing. She reached for my hand.

I wanted to scream at her—to run, to get away—but I didn't, because I knew deep down that she was dead anyway. If I didn't take her life, then Shiloh would.

So, when Jasmine slipped the bracelet onto my left hand, the one Death had touched just a few days prior, I wrapped my fingers around her wrist. Held on to her.

I slipped off one of my own friendship bracelets, pushed it over her knuckles. "I'm so sorry."

Jasmine's expression fractured, but she looked less upset than confused. She tried to pull free of my grasp, but it was too late. I felt myself dragged into her mind and memories.

Where Stewart's mind had been like an old film reel—cycling through his most pivotal moments, pulling me deep into his psyche—Jasmine's memories hit in flashes and spurts, like paint thrown across a canvas.

I saw myself in a run of mirrors, standing in a dance studio, in a body too small to be mine. I wore a pink leotard, heavy tap shoes on my feet. The mirrors slid away, revealing a roaring audience. In the sea of faces, I spotted a woman—my mother—with tears in her eyes. The curtains fell to the stage, and when they rose again, they revealed the same dance studio, only its mirrors had warped like the ones you'd find in a fun house, my reflection stretched and distorted. I took a deep breath, suctioning my stomach flat behind my ribs.

The memories came faster, layering on top of each other—blurred and triple exposed. There was a screaming match over dinner, plates clattering when my mom struck the table with a closed fist. Dead pointe shoes with glue crusted in the shank. A needle threading through satin.

You have no idea what I do for you. How hard I work. How much it takes.

Bobby pins scattered across a hardwood floor.

I expected more from you.

I felt like I was choking. Could barely speak. "I don't have more to give."

I went dark. From somewhere in the void, I heard the sharp tones of plucked harp strings. Then I was on the stage again, dancing barefoot in the empty theater, pressing up on relevé, my leg snapping through a series of fouetté turns. When the curtains fell, I fell with them, sinking lifeless to the stage floor.

Chapter 13

I tore free of Jasmine's memories with all the violence of a knife ripping from a wound. It took me a moment to realize I was back in my own body, because everything came in flashes.

Sound detached from visuals, like a video played out of sync.

I saw Jasmine lying motionless in the dust. People were screaming for help, but I couldn't hear them over the ringing in my ears. A boy dropped to Jasmine's side, began to pump at her chest with clasped hands, the motion so violent I feared he'd crack her sternum, and I had the sudden urge to spring forward, shove him off her.

And then I realized—with a wave of nausea—that she was dead. I'd killed her.

"You're okay," said Shiloh, her hand on my arm, dragging me away from the scene. "It's over now. I've got you."

The walk back to the campsite was a blur of lights. Halfway

there, it started to rain, hard, and the dust congealed into a thick and grasping mud that sucked my boots right off my feet as I trudged along. I took them off and walked barefoot through the muck, my feet sliding out from under me so that I had to keep catching myself on Shiloh to stay standing.

By the time we made it back to the campsite, both of us were covered in mud. The girls were waiting for us, huddled together under the RV's awning, which bowed badly in the middle, heavy with rain.

"We thought it'd be best to circle back to camp because of the weather," said Naomi. "We can try again in the morning—"

"No need. We're done here," said Shiloh, and the girls, who appeared to have been resting, scrambled to their feet, folding the lawn chairs left in the muck, packing up. "Let's head out when the ground is firm."

I SAT IN the RV, watching rain streak down the windows, as the rest of the girls took down our camp. Naomi draped a blanket over my shoulders, put a cup of tea in my hands that I didn't drink, the steam blooming in my face for a while before it went cold.

I kept thinking about Jasmine dead on the ground. The violence of the CPR, her sternum cracking beneath the pressure. Then, in my warped memory, it was Adeline lying there in the dust, cut open, gloved hands sorting through the contents of her stomach—nudging aside her spleen and liver—opening the dark coils of her intestines with the pass of a scalpel to search for answers they would never find.

My memories dragged me into a dark and dreamless sleep. When I woke again, the rain had stopped and there was sunlight bleeding in through the windows. The rest of the girls were already up, eating breakfast outside. I moved to join them, thinking briefly of Jasmine before I pushed her from my mind the way I knew I had to if I wanted to survive this.

I'd had the night to grieve, but I had to face a new day. Had to keep going if I wanted to know the truth of what happened to Adeline. I'd sacrificed too much—my morals, maybe even my sanity—to give up now.

"You okay?" Shiloh sat in the driver's seat of the RV. She hadn't left all night, keeping vigil over me as if she thought I'd disappear into the night like Adeline if she didn't.

I stretched stiff limbs, stood up. "Honestly? I just want to get out of here."

As soon as the ground firmed up enough for us to drive, we set out. It took us two hours to drive through the salt flats and out onto the road. We pulled off at the first town we saw to top up on gas and eat lunch at a hole-in-the-wall barbecue restaurant. I hadn't eaten since the night before, but I had no appetite, not after everything with Jasmine.

The girls claimed the largest table in the restaurant, a corner booth with cracked red cushions and paper spread over the tabletop. As soon as we sat down, Shiloh pulled a pen from her back pocket and began to draw on the tabletop, sketching out what I thought was a map but then realized was a loose schedule of the days to come, etching names into different parts of the paper, people who needed to die.

It had been four days since I struck my bargain with Death, which meant we had just over two weeks before we'd meet him in Vegas. Two weeks for me to prove my worthiness, and the pressure of that impending deadline was crushing.

A waitress came to the table, young and freckled, with a septum piercing. She smiled at us, her teeth a little blackened, and took down our orders. I opted for a veggie burger, mostly because I couldn't stomach the idea of eating meat. I'd seen enough corpses during my time on the road that the idea of eating one made me feel queasy. But the veggie burger didn't go down easy, and I mostly just picked at my food.

The other girls didn't seem to share in my squeamishness. They ordered a family barbecue meal—sticky ribs and a spatchcocked chicken blackened with grill marks, mustard greens cooked soft in bacon fat.

My stomach turned. But it wasn't just the meat or the guilt over Jasmine.

I looked over my shoulder to the waitress who'd delivered our food. There was something rolling off her, a scent like decay, that mixed with the grease of the meat and made me feel like I was going to be sick. "Do you guys smell that?"

Chloe nodded. She was gnawing on a corncob, her lips slick with butter. "Don't worry, you'll get used to it."

She picked some corn from between her teeth with her pinkie nail, which was long and blue and filed into the shape of a coffin. Somehow, amid the chaos of our trip, she'd procured a full gel set. "I had to guess, she's got about three good weeks left in her. Poor thing."

My stomach clenched at the thought of another death so soon after Jasmine. "So we're supposed to kill her, then? Here?"

But Shiloh shook her head. "She's not one of ours. Death tells me who we're supposed to dispatch, and I tell you. If we were to step outside of that, we'd be no different than murderers. And we'd also open ourselves up to risk. Death doesn't shield us from consequences if we're not doing his work."

The hairs at the back of my neck bristled at the implication. "But if she's not our kill, then whose is she? Are there others like us?"

"A few," said Shiloh, pushing around her mashed potatoes. "But we don't encounter them very often. As you can probably imagine, we're not the kind of people you'd want to bump into. And the others that carry the work of Death are a bit—"

Riley sucked her thumb clean of barbecue sauce. "Fucked-up?"

Iona rolled her eyes. "You say that like we're not."

"Do they travel in groups like you guys?" I asked, forgetting for a moment that I was a part of this too. "I mean like us?"

Skye shoved an entire square of cornbread into her mouth and then talked around it anyway. "Sometimes. But usually they're men and they tend to act alone. They're also . . . a bit more hands-on."

"And by that you mean . . . ?"

Shiloh tossed a bone onto her plate. "They like to get their hands dirty."

"But we're way more fun," said Skye, as if to defend our honor. "Everyone else gives off serial-killer vibes, which is so predictable. It's either that, or they're like state executioners or snipers or something, and to be honest, that's just bureaucratic and boring. I mean, some of them don't even realize that they're working for Death—"

Shiloh's gaze shifted to me. "Speaking of Death, I've got an update from him."

Naomi lowered her fork, looking alarmed. "When did you speak with him?"

"The night before Jasmine."

The night I'd seen her talking to Death in the parking lot.

The vibe abruptly shifted. The whole table fell quiet and bristly. And I saw so clearly then the uncomfortable conceit at the heart of the group. Shiloh was the closest to Death, his convoy and go-between, forever caught at the crossroads. She wasn't just one of his girls. She was *the* girl. The first that Death had chosen. The one, I suspected, that he loved the most. If a thing like him could love.

I wondered what it was about her that made her so different, what made Death choose her in the first place. Something about her air, the way I felt around her, this bristling sense of foreboding. A feeling like standing on the edge of a high drop-off, of looking through an open window at night, wondering what was looking back at you from the dark. I was afraid of her; we all were. I could feel it for the first time as we sat there around the table.

Riley eyed Shiloh across the table, uneasy. "So? What did he say?"

Shiloh wiped her mouth on a napkin, crumpled it, and set it on her plate, which was still full of food. "He wants us to centralize around this area. Well, a hundred-mile radius, servicing the communities in these parts. And when our two weeks are up, we'll meet with Death in Vegas. Whatever he has in store, we'll be ready for it. I'll make sure of it."

Chapter 14

We stopped for the night at a campground not far from the barbecue joint. The place was crawling with other campers—retirees and families in rented RVs with murals of the Grand Canyon emblazoned across the sides, a handful of hikers in hammock tents strung between the trees. There was barely room to accommodate our vehicles, but we managed to squeeze ourselves into a small plot in the middle of the campground, which the girls spruced up with their lawn chairs and string lights.

That night, we slept all together in the overcrowded RV. Around midnight, when the air grew thick and stuffy, someone cracked the windows open, and breaths of wet wind swept through the RV, carrying the scent of rain. I slept in one of the fold-down bunks across from the kitchen, Iona tucked beside me, pressed flush against the metal wall. But when I squeezed my eyes shut, sleep wouldn't come.

I'm not sure if it was my proximity to Iona—I was still getting accustomed to the, at times, suffocating closeness between the girls—or if it was the ghost of Jasmine, still alive in my mind's eye, keeping sleep at bay. But a few hours past midnight, I gave up, kicked off my blankets, and slid down and out of the bunk. There were three girls—Riley, Skye, and Chloe—sleeping on the floor in a nest of quilts and downy pillows.

I picked my way past them on my tiptoes and stepped precariously into the narrow galley of the kitchen, where I made myself a warm cup of milk, my favorite remedy for sleepless nights. It was there that I saw Naomi sitting on the stairs under the awning, the light of her vape winking in the dark. She exhaled mouthfuls of smoke, which rose and floated in a pale halo around her head.

I took my mug of milk and sat down on the stair, beside her. The rain came down hard, but the awning above the RV door kept us mostly dry. Naomi listed to the right, bumping her shoulder with mine in wordless greeting. We just sat there for a long time watching the rain come down. I offered her my mug of milk. "My mom says it helps you sleep. Some chemical in it."

Naomi smiled graciously, took an obligatory sip. "Adeline told me how your mom used to make it for you before bed, with sugar and vanilla."

I was surprised that Adeline had said as much to her. She was never one for nostalgia and always rolled her eyes when my mom recounted her favorite stories from our childhood, as if she was reminding Adeline of something she'd sooner forget. I guess she'd had a change of heart, part of her strange metamorphosis that summer.

Naomi stood up, extended a hand. "Come kill with me."

I didn't take it. "What? Now? Shiloh gave you another name?"

She nodded, gazing off into the alleys that ran between parked RVs. "She does that sometimes, especially with the older girls. Besides, you need to get back in the saddle. If you don't, you'll get scared of it. It's like what they tell you if you get attacked by a dog. The very next day, you need to go to the shelter, play with one before you develop real fear. The kind that grows into a phobia."

I knew she was right. I could already feel the cold fingers of terror seizing around me at the very thought of killing again. I got up, stiff and a little numb. Naomi put her hand in mine and guided me through the dark. She led me to an RV parked a good ways away from the others in the campground.

Naomi showed herself inside. It was a much nicer RV than ours. It was roomy, and it had a flat-screen TV over an electric fireplace, the flames dancing behind slick glass. On the kitchen countertop, an empty bottle of wine and a bottle of pills, also empty. There was a name on its label: ELIZABETH PAULSON.

My heart sank. "Oh my god. They didn't . . . Naomi, did they—"

"We're not investigators," she said, a soft whisper. "We're not here to uncover how or why a person died or judge their decision. Enough people do that already."

"But if they were young and healthy, shouldn't we—"

She stepped past me, through the kitchen and into the back half of the RV. The bedroom. "It's too late."

Naomi opened the door, and I heard it: a horrible rattling, like loose change in a dryer. It was the sound my grandmother had made before she died. There were two people in the bed, under a red quilt that looked handmade. A man and a woman—she was deathly thin, and her head was bald apart from a few stray wisps of hair at her temples. They lay motionless, their breaths slow and labored, mouths wrenched ajar.

If I called 911 now, I wondered if it would be enough to save them. I wondered, too, how long it would take for Death to right my wrong. The woman was gaunt, her skin taut and yellow with jaundice. The man at her side looked barely better. He was painfully skinny just like her, but his hands were red and swollen. Both of them appeared older than Stewart Gavin by a good decade or more. With some relief, I wondered if they were already marked for death no matter what I did.

"She's sick. Cancer, probably, from the looks of it," I said, as if trying to absolve myself of guilt—for not calling for help, for not trying to save them. "Maybe she was tired of suffering and he didn't want to live without her, so he took the pills too. Or maybe he's sick himself in a way that we can't see."

"The good thing about the work we do is that we don't have to rationalize like that," said Naomi, and I could tell she was trying to be gentle with me. "It's not our job to assess the morality of when and how someone dies or whether or not they chose to. They're not our lives or our deaths."

As she said this, Naomi came around the edge of the bed, standing on the man's side. She nodded for me to do the same with the wife. My feet felt leaden and numb beneath me as I stepped up to the bed. I didn't want to look at the woman I was about to kill, but I did it anyway.

Her face was smooth and expressionless, no tension pulling at the corners of her mouth, which probably meant she wasn't in any pain despite how sick she looked. If it wasn't for that horrible rattle every time she breathed, I might've thought she was just asleep.

"You want to know a secret?" Naomi asked, peering down at the husband, a fondness in her eyes that reminded me of the expression mothers wore when they stared down at their newborn babies for the first time. "I love this part."

I froze. I had always assumed that of all the girls, Naomi would be the most averse to what we did. She was warm and gentle. The mother who cared for everyone. And here, by the sides of this couple we were going to dispatch, her manner was no different, but the context was all wrong. I was filled with dread, on the verge of tears, and Naomi was beaming.

"These moments are so precious," she said. "It's an honor to get to see them. To watch a person transition between here and gone. To have some role in that journey."

Naomi put a hand on the man's forehead, and his chest filled with air and just . . . stopped in an eternal inhale. I thought it would be a long time before Naomi moved—the experience of the life montages felt like it stretched on forever for me as I fell through the memories of the dying—but Naomi barely missed a beat. She blinked a few times, as if to clear dust from her eyes. Then she bent down, her long hair sweeping over her shoulder, and pressed a kiss to his brow. When she straightened, her gaze fell to me, expectant. "Go on, then. Don't make him wait for her."

I looked down at the woman. The breaks between each of her rattling breaths grew longer and longer. Her expression bore no signs of pain, but I could tell her body was . . . fighting a futile battle.

"It's necessary," said Naomi, watching me, not the woman.

"Merciful, even, when you think about it. In death, there's so much grief and carnage. Even the expected ones are filled with their share of tragedy. But unlike most, she won't have to suffer for even a moment. She went to bed beside the man she loved, and somewhere between night and morning, she'll just have . . . gone. If only we could all be that lucky."

She made it seem like I was wrong for not doing it. And maybe she was right. I was prolonging the suffering of a worn-out body, poisoned and ailing, all because I was too weak to usher in the inevitable. To give her the mercy of a quiet ending. What if she woke up and saw her husband dead beside her? Her last moments would be filled with horror instead of the peaceful passing I could've given her if I'd just worked up the nerve.

I met Naomi's eyes across the bed. "You can do it," she said. "For her. For Adeline."

So I pressed my hand to the woman's side. She was so thin I could feel the ribbing of her bones beneath her nightgown. I shifted my hand to her arm, and the moment we made contact, skin to skin, I felt the sickening sensation of falling back through time and memory, and I saw her life in a series of bright flashes. Grass blurring beneath pumping legs. A baby's cry. A fish reeled from the water, snapping wildly on the line. Damp and mewling kittens in a cardboard box soaked with rain. A sheet cake stuck through with twenty candles, the wicks black and smoking. A man with kind eyes and broad shoulders, my hand in his.

The memories reeled on, like a roll of film unspooling, until they gave way to a darkness so complete I was lost to it, free-falling through oblivion.

And then, from the nothingness, someone stepped forward. A little girl.

I saw something in the distant dark, a small sun, a living light reaching its fingers through the murk. The little girl started to run toward it, throwing herself forward with a fearlessness that most of us lose somewhere between our first and final breaths.

And then she was gone into the light.

I opened my eyes, and I was back in my own body with Naomi and the two corpses lying on the bed between us.

Naomi smiled at me. "Not so bad, right?"

The room reeled a little when I nodded, but I managed to ground myself. "It was shorter this time. The vision, I mean. All her memories."

"That's good. It means you're not getting dragged too deep. You're adapting, getting good at this."

I followed Naomi out of the RV and into the rain. But instead of heading back to our RV, she settled herself beneath the awning just outside the door. I sat down beside her, and we watched the drizzling rain come down in silence for a little while, as if the deaths hadn't happened. As if we'd been sitting out there the whole time.

I thought about what Naomi said, about my becoming good at this. About whether or not I wanted to be. "Was she any good at this? Adeline, I mean."

"Not at first," said Naomi. "She wasn't particularly squeamish, but I think the closeness bothered her. The memories, being pulled into the mind and life of a stranger. She hated it."

That tracked. Adeline didn't like to involve herself with anyone too deeply.

"But when she found her footing, she took to this like a natural. Killed even quicker than anyone except maybe Riley. It seemed like it came easy to her. And I think, well . . ."

"You think what?"

"I think she liked it. Loved it, maybe even."

Naomi didn't seem like she was lying, but I didn't quite believe her either. Mostly because, that first night with the girls, when I'd overheard Chloe and Riley talking in the bathroom, they made it sound like Adeline had just . . . folded. But Naomi was saying something entirely different. So who was telling the truth? "The first night I was here, I overheard Chloe and Riley talking in the bathroom late at night."

Naomi maintained a flat affect. Suspiciously expressionless. "Those two love to gossip. What did they say this time?"

"They made it seem like Adeline struggled. Couldn't hack it. And they mentioned that she'd lost some kind of game. Do you know anything about that?"

Naomi, for her part, appeared genuinely perplexed. But then . . . she was smart enough to be a good liar. All of them were. "I can't say that I do. But I wouldn't think too much of it, to be honest." She got up, stretched with a stifled yawn. "We all try to be good to each other, as good as we can. But as with all groups, there's . . . competition. Maybe that's what they were talking about?"

I stood up. "What do you compete for?"

"The same things everyone does, I suppose. Recognition,

affection . . . credit for our contributions. I mean, doesn't everyone want to be validated in the end? That's half the work we do on behalf of Death. In those last moments of people's lives, we come to tell them that they mean something, and they're seen, if only by us. You get it. That's why you're here, isn't it? To find that kind of understanding in Adeline, in her death. You want something from her, something she took with her when she crossed over to the other side."

I froze as Naomi put a hand to my cheek, the same one she'd killed the man with just moments before. She rubbed small circles into my cheek with her thumb, her eyes narrowed, and she seemed to search for something within me that she couldn't find. "I know that you came to look for some piece of her that she might've stashed here, with us, that will lead you to something that feels like the truth. But I'm telling you what the others won't: We don't have it. Whatever it is you're looking for, whatever you hope to find, it's not here with us."

"Then where is it?" I demanded, in tears now, my voice thick with them. "How do I heal from this if I don't even know the truth?"

Naomi's mouth softened with sympathy. "Maybe this is something you're not meant to heal from. Maybe the pain, the grief, is that piece of her that you've been searching for."

Chapter 15

We left the RV camp the following morning, turned out onto a featureless highway that stretched through the deserts of rural Nevada. Our first kill of that day occurred at a small and dumpy nursing home in the suburb of some bigger city that I don't remember the name of. All of us girls spilled into the nursing home, splitting off into various wings to do Death's work.

"Won't it look suspicious that so many people die at once?" I asked Iona in a whisper, edging around a nurse pushing a patient down the hall in a wheelchair with squeaky hinges.

"It's not uncommon." Iona kept a brisk pace. "It often happens like that in places like this. People die in twos and threes. At least, that's what my mom told me. She was a receptionist at a nursing home. When residents died one after the other, she'd say the angel of death had visited on her shift. If she only knew just how right she was."

The rest was a blur, us moving through the various wings of the nursing home, Iona killing as we went, me watching on, awed by her poise. It was as if nothing—not the grief or the pain nor the horror of death—could touch her at all.

It went on like that, death after death, as we edged closer to the deadline in Las Vegas. We spent a week descending on a series of rural towns in the desert, visiting hospitals and hospices—or houses, for the victims that were lucky enough to die in their homes. I learned, in those grim days on the road, that each of the girls had their own signature. Skye liked to pretend that the deaths weren't happening. Her demeanor was so disarmingly casual that none of her marks seemed to know they were dying until their hearts stopped in their chests.

Iona's targets leaned religious. She seemed to meet them at the crossroads of their faith and whatever it was that she believed in. Sometimes she prayed with the people whose lives she took, an easy recitation of Catholic last rites. Once or twice, she'd sung a hymn.

As for Shiloh, I didn't know much about the way she killed. In fact, I'd never seen her kill before. I knew, though, that she often disappeared into the night to meet with Death or else carry out his business. All those poor people who died in the dark.

Chloe was irreverent and lighthearted, which worked well for those who shared her dark sense of humor, like the man with the broken back we found lying in the gutter after being struck by a car in the darkness while walking along the side of the road, drunk.

"Ain't life a bitch," Chloe had said to him, clucking her tongue. She was good—eerily good—at staying stoic, even during the hardest dispatches (the cancer kids and the stillborn babies lying blue in their plastic hospital bassinets). I'd never once seen her clear green eyes so much as mist up. They didn't then, as she stared down at the dying man, his spine snapped, gasping for air on the side of the road.

The dying man smiled at her, which seemed like a small feat in itself. An act of defiance, to grin in the face of death herself. "You know, when my mom said I was gonna end up dead in a ditch if I didn't stop fucking around and start studying . . . I imagined it going differently."

Chloe had smiled back, and she put a hand to the man's chest. "Sorry to prove her right."

He died then, and later that same night, I'd caught her scratching his name into the little diary she wrote in every night before bed. A death diary, filled with the names of everyone whose life she'd taken.

"Why do you do that?" I'd asked her one night, watching her add another name to her list. It was long, several dozen strong.

"I want to remember them; why else?" She chewed on the end of her pen for a moment, then scribbled down another name, a cashier she'd struck down with a heart attack when she'd handed over the cash for our groceries.

"But doesn't it make the guilt worse?"

Chloe had looked at me then, some anger in her eyes. "Guilt is part of the bargain we made. We take lives every day; the least we can do is sit with that."

The next day, I had started a journal of my own.

Stewart Gavin.
Jasmine Wu.

Then I added the RV woman, *Elizabeth Paulson*. I recalled her name from the sticker on the pill bottle.

I stared down at my short list of dispatches, feeling shame and something worse . . . the gut feeling that three wasn't enough. I'd need more to appease Death and, in doing so, find out what happened to Adeline. I would have to find my footing, a way of killing as efficiently as the others did, with that special flair that made the work seem almost easy. Close to art, even, as if death could be something beautiful.

I wanted to be like Naomi, who was gentle and mothering, good with the children, which was probably why Shiloh assigned most of them to her. She took her time when it came to dispatches, answering questions, quieting concerns, never rushing things along, always making the moments at the end of a life feel somehow sacred.

In contrast, Riley preferred to make things quick. So quick, in fact, that most of the people she killed didn't know that they were dying at all. Most of the time, she never said a word to her victims, never even made eye contact with them. At a gas station off the highway—where we stopped one evening, cobbling together a dinner of bagged chips and beef jerky—I watched Riley brush her fingers along the nape of a man's neck a moment before he succumbed to a massive stroke. He dropped so hard and fast he didn't have a chance to catch himself, clipping his nose on the curb between the sidewalk and parking lot. Blood spattered the asphalt, and the man thrashed and struggled, but Riley kept on walking.

"It's for the best," she said, tearing open a bag of Doritos. She'd caught me staring, both aghast at her callousness and impressed by it. "They don't have the chance to worry about anything if you do it fast. Trust me, it's a good death. It's what I'd want for myself. That's all I can give them."

ONE WEEK FROM Death's deadline, I killed entirely on my own for the first time. Without Shiloh or Naomi there to talk me through it. It was a bright and early morning, but the rush hour traffic was thick. After just a few minutes on the road, the caravan crawled to a complete standstill. I smelled the accident before I saw it, burnt rubber and gasoline. And then, above the roofs of cars, in the narrow glimpses between gridlocked semis, a rising plume of black smoke. I knew, on instinct, that there was a life to claim among the wreckage.

One of the cell phones rang. Riley answered, then handed it back to me. "It's for you."

I pressed the phone to my ear. Shiloh's voice came clear over the line: "This one's yours."

I froze.

"You're ready," said Shiloh, as if she could see me.

Out the window of the RV, I watched as her truck turned left, into the lane along the shoulder of the road. Riley followed suit, slotting the RV into a break in traffic, a risky maneuver that could've resulted in a car wreck of our own. Iona trailed behind in the station wagon, cutting in front of a large oil tanker in pursuit of the wreck. I caught a glimpse of her through the windshield, her face a mask of pain, fingers twisting tight around the steering wheel. I wondered if she was reliving the crash that had very nearly claimed her own life, would have if Death hadn't intervened.

The wreck was a bad one. A small red car—mangled like a Coke can someone had stomped on—stood burning in the middle of the road a few yards from the semi that struck it. Large columns of smoke erupted from the car's hood and blackened the air. There was someone inside the car, legs pinned down by the crushed hood, face half-obscured by the smoke. Unmoving.

Riley met my gaze in the rearview mirror, a dare in her eyes. "Well? What are you waiting for?"

I stood up, made for the door of the RV, and stepped out onto the highway. There were the faint screams of distant sirens. I walked toward the burning wreck even as the smoke charred my throat and made my eyes water.

I knew that the person in the car was going to die. The fire was spreading too fast, and the hood of the car was thoroughly crushed, pinning them to their seat, so they'd have to cut themselves free of their own legs to escape.

I leaned down to look into the shattered window. The smoke was so thick I could barely see the bleeding man in the driver's seat. His eyes were swollen, almost shut, and there was a horrible gash along his forehead. He looked very afraid.

"It hurts," he said.

"I know. I'll make it better." I leaned closer. The flames rippled from the crushed hood of the car, close enough to burn me, but I didn't feel any heat. Death was making good on his promise to protect me. "What's your name?"

"Corbin." He cut it through gritted teeth as the flames chewed their way toward him. "I want my mom."

I had been told by the other girls that this was a common response. Some people had the luxury of seeing their relatives in the moments before their death, but most simply asked for them, reverting back to a purer time when we still believed our parents could save us from anything.

But Corbin would not be saved by his mother or by anyone else, except for perhaps me. Though I knew the kind of saving I was here to do was not the saving that he wanted.

The passenger door was held shut by a bent stretch of guardrail, so I had to climb into the ruined car through the broken window. The empty seat was littered with bluish shards of glass, but none of them cut me as I lowered myself into the burning vehicle, sat cross-legged beside him even as the air blackened with smoke and the fire roared under the crushed hood.

I was careful not to touch him. I didn't want to take him before his time. Corbin was fading fast, but I sensed that there was still a little more he had left to say and do in this world. I wanted to give it to him, even though I knew I was expected to be efficient, composed.

Up close, I saw that he wasn't far from my own age. "Am I going to die?"

I saw no reason to lie to him. I felt like the least I could give him was honesty. Later, I would wonder if that made me cruel. If I should've said something else, given him a bit of hope to cling to in his final moments, even if it was just a lie.

"Yes," I heard myself say. "You're going to die."

Through the shattered windshield and the bright plumes of fire, I saw the dark suggestions of people. I could hear their voices, but their words and faces were distorted by the roaring flames. This, I suspected, was by design. Corbin and I had gone to a place that few others could follow.

In this liminal slip of nothingness between life and death, we were alone.

"I didn't have the chance to say goodbye to anyone," said Corbin. He was crying now, and there was blood collecting in the shell of his ear, more of it dribbling from his nostrils. He was choking on it, struggling to breathe. His chest, crushed inward by the force of the crash, rose and fell faster and faster. He was suffering, and I was letting him.

The pain in my hand built until it felt like a knife was splitting through my palm. I clenched it into a fist, tears stinging my eyes—tears of pain and grief and frustration.

I didn't want to be the person who had to do this.

But if I didn't, I would become the person who let him suffer, which seemed even worse.

"Help me," said Corbin, and my god was he young. We were all so young. Him and Adeline, Jasmine, even Stewart and Elizabeth. No amount of time was enough, I realized. It seemed like a cruel cosmic mistake that we could be so full of life and hope, that our minds could expand and consume so much knowledge, that our hearts could hold so much for so many people . . . and then one day just stop.

"It hurts," said Corbin again, and the flames were starting on him now, though they left me untouched. "It hurts so bad."

That was the push I needed. "I'll make it stop."

My hand shifted across the center console, brushing past the shattered glass. Corbin's hand, burnt and sticky with blood, rested on his knee. I touched it, and when I did, my vision went dark, and I felt myself fall through time, through the remnants of memories half-formed until I found my way to something vivid, my soul fitting into a body, a life that didn't belong to me.

I stood on the edge of a beach, looking out over a sun-licked ocean. The waves were gentle, and when they rushed my feet, I felt like I was moving down the shore. I turned to look behind me, saw a woman whose name I didn't know. But her face was as familiar to me as my own.

My mother.

She was sitting on a makeshift picnic blanket, just a fleece throw stretched out on the shore, weighted down with buckets of sand and a couple of beer cans. There was a little girl in her lap, my sister. She had fat cheeks, legs like stubby little sausages, round feet stuffed into plastic sandals. I turned to go to them when a big wave broke and snatched my legs out from under me. The water crested over my head. I saw black.

When I surfaced, I was older, sitting in my car. The windshield wasn't broken. There was no fire or smoke. No sirens screaming. The night was quiet.

Someone had rolled the windows down, and I could hear crickets humming in the nearby bushes. In the passenger seat was a boy peering at me through dark lashes. He looked . . . tentative, like he was standing on a precipice, deciding whether or not he wanted to jump. His mouth was parted open, and I touched it, my thumb trembling a little as I ran it back and forth along his lower lip. I leaned into him and fell into complete and utter oblivion.

I woke a moment later, lying on the side of the highway, to the sound of distant sirens. I sat up, and the world spun and blurred before my eyes. I felt heat and saw that the car was completely engulfed in flames, blazing as bright as a star. A harsh scent, burnt rubber and gas, filled my lungs and made my eyes water. I saw the remnants of Corbin, a dark figure wrapped in fire. I screamed and reached for him, but Riley caught hold of my shoulders and shook me so hard it hurt. The pain was enough to bring me back to myself.

Shiloh materialized in front of me, brushing Riley aside as she did. She took me by the chin, forced me to look at her instead of the burning car.

Her eyes were wide with . . . was that *fear*? "Roslyn, we need to get out of here. Now."

I nodded and stood up, a little surprised that my legs were firm enough to carry my weight. Shiloh guided me to her pickup truck, through the stagnant traffic, and buckled me into the passenger seat. I tried to turn back, to get one final look at Corbin, but all I saw was a storm of bright and hungry flames.

Chapter 16

After Corbin, time seemed to compress. There was never enough of it to go around. The girls scrambled to prove their worth as Death's deadline drew near, killing more and more, until our dispatches climbed up into the dozens. I wrote down my own contributions over and over, making myself remember.

Stewart Gavin.
Jasmine Wu.
Elizabeth Paulson.
Corbin.

One night, with three days left before the deadline, I stared down at the names, the shadows of the campfire dancing over the paper, wondering how many more names I still needed to add to appease Death and earn the truth about what happened to Adeline. I still had the final task ahead of me, a dispatch I suspected would be worse than any other so far.

On the other side of the fire, Shiloh stood up.

"Off to see him again?" Riley asked her, eyes narrowed against the smoke. The hot dog she held into the fire was charred and blackened, but she didn't seem to notice. Her gaze was on Shiloh, sharp and accusing.

"I'll only be gone for a few hours." She walked to her pickup, impervious to Riley, no excuses or attempts to explain where she was going or what she would discuss with Death. It didn't take hours for him to give her a handful of names and addresses. There had to be more they discussed, but whatever it was, she was unwilling to share it. "Stay out of trouble while I'm gone."

For the past week, Shiloh had taken off before sunset and didn't return until the wee hours of the morning. I'd hear her truck pulling in, but she wouldn't come into the RV. No one knew where she went, how she spent the rest of her nights when she wasn't away with Death.

That night, I stayed awake staring at the ceiling of the RV until, four hours after she left, I heard the familiar growl of her engine. I waited a little while, and then, with my quilt wrapped around me like a shawl, went out to greet her. But what I found was Shiloh dead asleep in her truck bed, curled fetal against the cold. She was breathing heavily, eyes screwed shut. With a pit in my stomach, I saw her hands were rusty with dried blood.

The stains of a dispatch. A bad one.

I dropped the quilt from around my shoulders, and I leaned over the side of the truck, draped it over her. I was making my way back to the RV when I heard my name: "Roslyn?"

I stopped, turned back to her. "Yes?"

Shiloh was sitting up, bleary eyed. She was more than two years older than me, but in that moment, she looked younger. "Stay?"

"Okay," I said, and redoubled, climbing up into the truck bed with her. I sat there cross-legged at first, but when Shiloh lifted the corner of the blanket, I slid in beside her, facing her, our bodies slotting together. "Why do you sleep alone out here? There's room in the RV."

Shiloh stifled a yawn. "I don't want to wake you guys."

"Don't worry about that. The girls are knocked out."

"But I woke you up."

"You didn't. I stayed awake."

Shiloh frowned. "You were waiting for me." It wasn't a question.

I rolled onto my back so I didn't have to face her. Overhead, tattered clouds obscured the stars. "I wanted to know what you do out here. Where you go when the rest of us are asleep."

I regretted the words almost immediately, because Shiloh went dark when I said them. I turned to her again and watched it happen, her mouth firming up, the joy leaving her eyes like a light flicked off.

I don't know why I took her by the hand, why I felt bold enough to do it. We hadn't touched each other that way since the night of Jasmine's death, which felt like forever ago. A strange pocket of the past, complete unto itself.

She flinched when I touched her, turning her palm over in my hand, running my fingers along the bloodstains, so dried and faded they looked almost like bruises. "You're going on dispatches. Aren't you?"

Shiloh stole her hand away, closed it into a tight fist. "He expects it from one of us."

"Then pass off some of the work to the others. Any of us would help you."

But Shiloh shook her head, wouldn't hear it. "You need your rest."

"So do you."

Shiloh's eyes fell closed. I sensed I was losing her a bit, but to what I didn't know. "Some of the worst dispatches happen at night. I don't want you guys to see that."

"It's not fair that you have to shoulder this alone."

Shiloh parted her lips to speak but faltered and wet them instead. "I'm all right, okay? I go out on these dispatches because I prefer it. I speak to Death so he doesn't have to speak to you. And I sleep outside because the cold air is nice and I don't mind it. I'm not doing anything I don't want to."

"I don't believe you. None of us want this. None of us would choose to kill if we didn't have to. No good person would ever want to do any of this."

Shiloh opened her eyes, her gaze searching, that same question in them. "How do you know that I'm good?"

The truth was I hadn't thought much about whether or not Shiloh was a good person. If any of us were. I wasn't sure if goodness was a thing that could be retained in such close proximity to Death, with all the horror and violence that came with that.

"You are good," I said, trying to convince her and myself. "I can just feel it."

"Your feelings haven't led you astray before?"

They had. They would continue to as long as I was with her.

I could feel the pull even then, to draw near to her at the risk of everything else.

To lose myself in her.

I swallowed dry. "What are you exactly?"

I could tell I caught her by surprise from the way her eyebrows knit together. "What do you mean?"

"I mean, why did Death choose you?" I said, propping myself up on one elbow, needing to put some space between us. "There are a million girls in the world. How did he land on you?"

I asked the question like I couldn't fathom the answer when, in truth, I suspected that Death had selected Shiloh for the same reason I found it difficult not to look at her. That strange quality she possessed, a kind of dark charisma that made the world seem to shrink around her as if everything and everyone else were suddenly less important.

Shiloh rolled onto her back and pulled off the blanket, like she needed air. "I don't know. I guess there's always been something... wrong with me."

"What do you mean by wrong?"

Shiloh chewed on the inside of her lip, considering whether or not she wanted to answer that question. "When I was little... my parents thought I was the devil."

I choked out a laugh. "I mean, don't all parents think that about their kids at some point?"

"No, I mean literally..." She grasped for a way to explain it, and I could tell she was frustrated, not with me, but with herself for failing to find the words. I was surprised to hear her stutter when she spoke again, voice breaking a little, the tip of her tongue catching on her top teeth. "I—I was . . . odd. I talked to myself constantly, always in a whisper. I didn't play with toys the way that other kids did, just wasn't really interested in them. And I wore my clothes inside out so the tags wouldn't scratch me, and if my mom made me wear them the right way, I'd just . . . break. Couldn't move. Couldn't focus on anything else. I got so agitated, you know? All this anger and energy in me that I didn't know how to express. I think I was overwhelmed."

"That just sounds like normal kid stuff. Everyone has their quirks."

But Shiloh shook her head. "It wasn't just that. There were other things too. Worse things. I had a temper—a bad one. I'd break things when I couldn't find more productive ways to express myself, and that was often, because . . ." She paused, considering. "The world just felt like it was moving fast, you know? Everyone speaking so quickly, on some wavelength that I just couldn't tune in to no matter how hard I tried. And I did try. All the time. I never stopped trying, and I think that was the frustrating part. That I tried harder than anyone I knew and I was still always behind."

I knew what she meant. I'd felt something similar after Adeline died. Everyone carrying on and me left behind with Adeline and the rest of the dead, or near-dead, as if frozen in time.

"When things got really bad, I had these outbursts, I guess you can call them. I'd lash out at people . . . and myself. I'd have bruises all the way up my arms just from—" She stopped short, shook her head. "I scared her—my mom, I mean. I scared her so badly that she started trying to find ways to fix me. She went to the doctors first, but that didn't help, so she turned to the church for answers that medicine didn't offer."

"And what kind of answers did they have?"

"Prayers and snake oil," said Shiloh bitterly. "We lived in this small town in rural Georgia, and the chapel was right down the road. Sometimes she'd walk me there in the summer heat and she'd make me stay on my knees for hours, praying in the aisle, right in front of the altar."

"Good god. Shiloh, I'm sorry."

She didn't hear me, and I watched as she slipped away from me again, into her memories. "The first time she tried to drown me in the bathtub, my dad was on this long work trip. He traveled a lot, and when he did, my mom got meaner and more devout. Anyway, she held me under, said she was baptizing me. Making me pure. When I passed out, she let me go. But that wasn't the end of it. There were more . . . baptisms to follow. And one night—a bad one, just before my tenth birthday—she drowned me. That was when Death showed up."

I didn't want to let myself imagine it, but I did: Shiloh in that tub, thrashing, her mother pinning her down to the bottom. I'd known my share of grief, but this was . . . horror. A mother turned against her own child, drowning her. Shiloh powerless to stop it.

"So he saved you," I whispered as the pieces slotted together.

She nodded. "He brought me back to life on the bathroom floor while my mom was praying in the kitchen. He struck a bargain with me. He told me he'd make sure I got to grow up safe. That my mom wouldn't take my life so long as I agreed that, on my fifteenth birthday, I would belong to him. He'd spared my life just to take it from me." She smiled, but with anger. Like after all the years, she still couldn't believe what was stolen from her, couldn't bring herself to accept it. "I was scared, but I agreed to it. I wanted to live."

"What about your mom? Did she know he came for you?"

Shiloh shook her head. "But things did get better after Death left. I crawled out of the bathroom to see my mom on the phone. My dad had been in a bad accident. Almost lost his life. He recovered but stopped working as a lineman and was home all the time, disabled but alive. My mom got a job as a secretary in town, and she never did warm up to me, but the baptisms stopped. I was safe, if not happy, just like Death promised that I would be. I sort of forgot about the bargain I'd struck with him, started wondering if I'd imagined it. But on the eve of my fifteenth birthday, I went to sleep and woke up to him sitting on the edge of my bed. He'd come to make good on his deal."

It seemed like Shiloh intended to end the story there, but I prompted her to continue. "What did he say?"

"Not much. He gave me simple instructions. Told me to steal my parents' truck. I knew how to drive—kids where I lived learned early—but I didn't have a license. Death told me I wouldn't have to worry about details like that anymore—homework, jobs, GED—all that stuff was in the past. All I needed to do was pack up and hit the road. So I did. Death had me drive north until I reached the home of a woman whose name I don't remember. Maybe I never knew it. As we stood over her, Death took me by the hand and put his power right through my palm. Then he had me kill her. We left, and then, a day later, I killed again."

"Was it hard for you?" I asked, wanting to know if she'd struggled the way I had, the way I was still struggling then. Shiloh seemed like she was born to be Death's servant; it was hard for me to imagine her doing or being anyone else.

"Not really." Shiloh sat up, slid out of the truck like she needed to move, to get something out of her system. She started to pace a bit. "I think I just . . . I felt bad about how easy it was for me. In the beginning, Death only gave me these quiet departures. People who died the way we all hope to. Painless, bloodless, peaceful passings. Of course, I knew there were worse ways to go, but he didn't show me any of that at first. He really protected me, and in those early days . . . I don't know. He was almost like family to me—as close to a parent as I ever had. I know a part of me loved him for that, and I hate myself for it."

"You shouldn't," I whispered, and climbed out of the truck after her. When I put a hand to her arm, she stopped pacing, stood beside me. "You have nothing to be ashamed of."

"But I do," said Shiloh, peering down at me. I was tall, but she had me by a good few inches. "I knew that he was what he was, Roslyn. That he was trapping me and that I had let him. So when he asked me to drive west to St. Louis and find Naomi, I knew exactly what I was dragging her into. But he told me that it would be okay. And you know what? I believed him. Over time, I came to love this life, and I didn't want anything different. Even when the deaths became more violent, gruesome. I didn't mind much, or if I did, I found a way to get over it. At least, that's what I told myself back then."

"What about now?"

Shiloh's eyes glazed over, and she shut them, shook her head. "Now . . . I know that it catches up to you eventually. All of this—the group, this fucked-up family that Death brought together—it's just a bunch of scared girls fleeing the inevitable, and I'm just the go-between. Riley isn't wrong about that . . . She's not wrong not to trust me."

"I trust you," I said, so soft my voice was almost lost to the night.

Shiloh turned to look at me, and I became aware then of the space between us. There wasn't much of it to begin with, but she leaned closer still. "Why?"

It wasn't what I was expecting her to say. "Why . . . ?"

"Do you trust me?"

We were so close our foreheads very nearly touched. My gaze dropped to her mouth, and I had this strange urge to drag my thumb along her lower lip, trace the shape of it so that when all of this was over, I would remember her properly. But I didn't move, except to draw back, my hand limp at my side. "Why wouldn't I trust you? Adeline did, and her instincts were always better than mine."

Something passed over Shiloh's face at the mention of my sister's name, a kind of contamination ruining whatever nameless thing had been building between us.

She leaned back, smiled. "Why do you always do that?"

"Do what?"

"Withdraw into the memory of her every time I try to . . ."

"Try to what?"

Shiloh dragged a hand through her hair, frustrated, grasping for the words. "Every time I try to . . . get close to you."

I faltered, trying to process what she had just said. "You're trying to get close to me?"

Shiloh made as though she hadn't heard me. "You use Adeline like a lifeline. Every time you're presented with the possibility of something beyond her—something that could be good—you retreat back into her shadow like it's the only place you feel safe."

"No, I don't." It was a lie, and I knew it.

"Yes. You do. What are you so afraid to face without her, Roslyn?"

"I'm not afraid of anything, Shiloh. My worst nightmare already came true. I lost her already. What is there left to be afraid of, really?"

Shiloh looked at me with pity. "You tell me."

I flinched, nodded. First to her and then to myself. Then I stepped past her, heading back to the RV. "I should get some sleep—"

"Roslyn, wait."

I stopped, turned back to her, hoping she would say something. An apology or an excuse that would make up for what we'd said to each other, take us back to those quiet moments before the mention of Adeline ruined everything. "What?"

Shiloh didn't look at me, spoke with her gaze on the ground. "There's something terrible waiting for us in Las Vegas. You need to be ready for it."

"How am I supposed to be ready when you won't tell me what's coming?"

"It's not that I won't tell you. It's that I don't know exactly—"

"Bullshit. You know something more than that or else you wouldn't have told me. It's Death, isn't it? Something he said."

"Look, Roslyn, I'm just trying to do you a solid—"

"Then tell me the truth, Shiloh." My voice wavered. "What's waiting for us in Vegas?"

"I said I don't know," she whispered. "But you shouldn't need me to tell you. People die in terrible ways every single day. And you haven't been made to accept that as a physical reality. You haven't been on any truly horrible dispatches—"

"That's not true," I said, affronted, feeling like she was calling me weak. After everything I'd been through? After the people I'd killed? After Death had drilled his power into the very palm of my hand. After I'd watched my sister be carried out of the woods behind our house in a body bag. "I watched a man burn alive in his car. I stopped the heart of a girl my own age. What do you mean I haven't seen anything horrible?"

Shiloh went dark in the eyes. "There is tragedy, and then there is horror. The two overlap, but they're not the same."

I swallowed dry, feeling sick and wondering how a night that felt so perfect had suddenly turned into this. "Is this some kind of punishment?" I asked. "Is Death trying to get me to break?"

She shook her head. "When a new girl enters our group, there's always this... culmination at the end of her first kills. That's what's waiting for you in Vegas, but if you can't manage it—"

"I can," I said. "I'm stronger than you think I am."

Shiloh merely nodded, expressionless. "For your sake, I hope that's true."

Chapter 17

In the morning, two days before Death's deadline, we entered Las Vegas proper. The girls were in a foul mood, everyone sullen and edgy, bickering among themselves about the stupidest things, like who'd used the last of the tampons without telling anyone or who left their clothes in a heap on the floor of the bathroom the night before. Whatever Death's final task was, it was casting a long shadow, and I wondered if that had been the intent all along. If he wanted us to feel so jumpy and afraid. On the verge of breaking.

Spirits lifted when we arrived at our hotel. Shiloh, perhaps sensing that we needed a boost, had rented a penthouse suite on the top floor of a massive casino hotel. It was one of those places where the bath towels are folded into the shapes of swans and the robes hanging in the wardrobes are embroidered with the names of each person staying in the room. The suite came with several amenities:

a hot tub and sauna, a balcony overlooking the Strip, and access to the sprawling breakfast buffet on the first floor of the hotel.

We let the valet park the caravan for us—Shiloh tipping generously for the hassle of maneuvering the RV—and the girls entered the hotel lobby, which was eye-achingly gaudy, like a Cheesecake Factory on steroids. To the left was a casino, which legally none of us was allowed to enter, though that didn't stop Skye from trying.

"I'm so good at slot machines," she said. "Once, when I was six, my mom smuggled me into this casino, and I won a jackpot of three thousand dollars on my first spin. Four diamonds, I'll never forget it."

"Your mom smuggled you into a casino?" Iona asked, stunned.

"Only when she was drunk," said Skye, and I couldn't tell whether or not she was lying. "She's bolder when she drinks and more charming. It makes it easier for her to flirt her way into things, which is how she got me into the casino in the first place." She sighed, smiling and dreamy. "Those were the good times."

Iona's expression screwed into a frown. "That sounds . . . a little messed up."

Skye continued on as though she hadn't heard her. "I can't wait for you guys to meet her someday. You're going to love her, and she'll love you. When we finally make it to California, we can stay with her. I know she'd love to have us."

The lobby had looming arches taller than my house, frescoed ceilings, and a huge tiered fountain complete with motorized fake swans that swam in wide circles. We hauled the last of our bags through the doors, refusing help from the bellhops, who repeatedly attempted to take them anyway, though I suspected they were driven less by obligation than their own keen desires to be near the girls. I couldn't blame them. Even in a place as bright and gaudy as the Vegas Strip, the girls stood out, drawing gazes as they made their way through the lobby and up to the top floor.

My jaw dropped the moment I stepped into the penthouse. It was two stories tall, with four bedrooms and enough beds so that every girl could sleep alone for once. After the rigors of the road—the nights I'd spent on the floor of the RV in sleeping bags or squished into a twin bunk with Iona—it was almost hard to comprehend this level of luxury.

The girls abandoned their bags in a heap on the floor and immediately began to explore our new lodgings. Every cabinet was opened, every drink and snack in the mini fridge was sampled. Miniature glass bottles of soap and shower oil were opened and smelled. Skye phoned for room service and ordered a feast.

Shiloh—tired to the point of looking almost sick—watched the theatrics with a weak smile.

"You did good," I said, the first words I'd spoken since our near-fight the night before. "They needed this. But I hope you take some time to enjoy this too. You need the rest, and they need you, so you'd better start taking care of yourself."

I knew it wasn't my place to nag her, but Shiloh didn't seem to mind. She raised a hand and gently nudged my cheek with her knuckles. "I'll be all right," she said, and sidestepped, busying herself with the many bags the girls had hauled into the foyer of the suite.

I'd been craving a hot shower for days. Not the lukewarm five-minute affairs in the RV shower-toilet combo, but a real, proper shower, and I got one that night, scrubbing myself clean as the showerheads embedded in the walls blasted me from all directions. I felt reborn. We all did.

By the time I emerged from the shower, I found the other girls in the living room gorging on a spread of room service: chicken fingers, mac-and-cheese kids' meals, tinned caviar and filet mignon, charred bananas Foster topped with hills of melting ice cream.

I settled myself between Chloe and Iona, the latter leaning into my shoulder. There was a black-and-white film playing on the TV, a moon with a man's face jabbering at the camera. It was weird and nonsensical, but the girls seemed charmed by it, erupting into fits of giggles when two men started fighting on-screen.

I decided that this was how I wanted to remember them when the worst was over. When I had my answers about what happened to Adeline and I returned to my life in Michigan, I would hold this memory as close as I could, revisit it often to make sure it remained clear in my mind as the years passed and I learned to live without them.

"Roslyn?"

I blinked rapidly, a few tears falling down my cheek when I did.

I was surprised to see Riley staring at me, expectant. "You all right?"

Riley had never seemed remotely interested in how I was or what I was thinking. From what I gathered, she'd never quite gotten over the fact that I hadn't earned my way into the group the way the other girls had, by being hand-selected by Death. She'd made it clear that she saw me as nothing more than an unwanted appendage.

"I'm fine," I said, immediately defensive, but as it turned out, I had no reason to be.

Riley offered me something I never once expected to receive from her: a compliment. "You know, it's pretty impressive that you weren't even picked by Death and you've still managed to make it this far. I didn't think you had it in you."

"I know," I said. "I heard you and Chloe talking on my first night."

Chloe's face went white. "How much did you hear, exactly?"

"Enough to know you didn't want me to join. That you thought I'd make a mess of things."

"I mean, in our defense, verdict's still out." Riley sucked caviar off a mother-of-pearl spoon and closed her eyes, savoring. "We'll see what Death has in store for you tomorrow. I'm sure he'll have some twisted test up his sleeve."

I faltered. "Wait, a test? What kind of test?"

"Can't say. Could be anything. I had to kill a kid from one of my classes. RIP, Toby."

"For me, it was my grandma," said Skye, shaking her head. "Poor Bernice."

"I thought she was your great-aunt?" Naomi asked.

"Whatever. She was a relative, all right? It was hard. My mom was so mad—"

"Your mom knew what you did?" I asked, flabbergasted, but all at once, everyone was talking over each other, going on and on about the cruel and twisted ways Death had tested their resolve.

What would Death demand from me? What did I have that he hadn't already taken? My thoughts immediately went to my parents. They'd had us in their late thirties, and they were only getting older, slower, and Adeline's death had aged them faster. They were pushing toward their fifties, and people died all the time at that age, with blood clots lodged in their lungs or from stress-induced heart arrythmias.

I was on my feet in an instant.

Riley glanced at me, eyebrows raised. "You all right?"

"I—I need to call my parents."

Chloe and Skye exchanged a knowing look, but it was Riley who said, "Calling isn't going to change shit. If Death wants them dead, they're dead. It's—"

"Riley, shut up." It was as harsh as I'd ever heard Naomi be. She turned to me, forcing a smile. "The box of phones is in the main suite, but only a few are charged. Take all the time you need."

I nodded, and went to the bedroom. The hatbox full of cell phones was on the desk, charging cords snaking out from beneath the top. I sorted through them and found mine, but it was long dead. So I grabbed the one beside it, a palm-sized iPhone several generations old in a furry green case. It was one of the few in the box that was charged enough to use right away. I dialed my mom's number, pressed it to my ear. She didn't pick up the first time, but I left a message and called again. This time, she answered on the first ring. "Roslyn?"

"Are you okay?"

"What? Why?"

"And what about Dad?"

"He's fine too. We're both okay. Roslyn, what's going on? Are you all right?"

I faltered, realizing how crazy I must've sounded calling in a panic. "Yeah, I just . . . I had a bad dream about you and Dad. I wanted to make sure you were okay."

"Well we're just fine. How are things at the lake?"

"The lake—oh, right, the lake. Yeah, things are great here. The girls are wonderful, and it's been good to get away. I miss you, though."

"I miss you, too, sweetheart. Are you coming home soon?"

I was shocked that it was a request and not a mandate. And the way she said it, so soft and earnest, she didn't even sound like herself. It was as if someone was . . . suppressing her, almost. Maybe Death. "You're sure you and Dad are okay?"

"Better than okay. We're just fine."

We said our goodbyes. I lowered the phone back into the box, and when I did, I noticed another. Unlike the others, it was relatively nondescript, in just a clear acrylic case. The only adornment was a fortune taped to the inside. It read: *The future is a lie.*

I knew at once it was Adeline's. The fortune was a dead giveaway. I remembered the day she cracked open the cookie that contained it. It was her first meal after being discharged from the hospital. My mom was superstitious—hanging dried garlic up in the kitchen, forbidding horror movies for fear of welcoming demons into our house—and when Adeline read her fortune, Mom had immediately told her to burn it and pray. But Adeline had just smiled, said that if the future was a lie, that meant she could make it whatever she wanted it to be.

With shaking hands, I took one of the tangled chargers from the bottom of the box and sat breathlessly on the edge of the bed waiting for it to charge enough to turn on. After a few minutes, it did. I knew the code, and unlocked it. There were no apps on the home page, apart from the ones you couldn't delete. But the background was what gave me pause: It was a photo of Adeline and Shiloh.

In it, Shiloh had her arm slung around Adeline's bare shoulders, eyes narrowed against the sun so that I couldn't tell exactly what she was looking at. Adeline was turned away from the camera, a smile half-hidden in Shiloh's neck. There were more photos like that one in albums, sorted by day. Shiloh and Adeline hand in hand, standing on the edge of a canyon like they were trying to decide if they wanted to jump together. A photo of Shiloh, taken from behind, from the shoulders up, her collarbones bare, her hair fallen across her face.

I scrolled through it all—a montage of the two of them—until I couldn't stomach it any longer, until my hands shook so badly I could barely even hold the phone. I don't know how long I sat there, frozen on the bed. But it was long enough to prompt Naomi to come in and check on me. She rapped her knuckles on the doorframe. "Roslyn? You okay?"

I didn't turn to look at her. "Where's Shiloh?"

"She went out—"

"Out where?"

"There was a dispatch she needed to handle."

I turned to look at her over my shoulder, tears streaming down my face. "You don't know where she went?"

Naomi's eyes flashed wide. "Roslyn, what's going on—"

"I need to talk to her *now*."

"I don't think that's a good—"

"Where the hell is she, Naomi?" It was almost a shout, but my voice cracked.

Naomi flinched, and then gave me the address, stumbling over her words in her haste to get them out, like she was afraid of what would happen if she didn't. Maybe she was right to be.

I got dressed, stripping out of my robe in favor of a denim jacket that belonged to one of the girls, or maybe all of them. I slipped Adeline's phone into my pocket and set out, taking a mirrored elevator down to the lobby. The casino was swarming with people. I shouldered through the crowds and out onto the Strip. Shiloh's dispatch was remarkably nearby, which I realized was probably by Death's design. We never happened upon a place by accident. There was always some dispatch that led us there.

The address Naomi had given me led me a few blocks away, to a concrete slab of an apartment building with tiny windows. I took the stairs up to the third floor. The door of the unit was open, and I smelled blood the moment I stepped inside that cramped little living room. It was dark; the only light came from the TV, which was playing silently through a series of commercials. The screen, I noticed, was badly cracked.

"Shiloh? Are you here?"

I stepped into a small dining room and saw her on the floor in the kitchen, sitting slumped against the fridge like she'd been shot. Her left cheek was spattered with blood. When I stepped into her line of vision, she didn't blink.

I forgot myself for a moment—why I was there, the betrayal of what I'd found on Adeline's cell phone, all that she'd hidden from me. I rushed to her like she'd die if I didn't, pressed a hand flat against her heaving chest. "Shiloh, look at me. Are you hurt?"

Shiloh blinked slowly, came to. Her eyes were slow to focus, but when they did, when she saw it was me, she slapped my hand away and scrambled to her feet. "What the hell are you doing here?"

With Shiloh on her feet, I saw it, in the hallway off the kitchen: a small bloodied hand. Stiff fingers with long nails painted pink. A small wrist ringed black with bruises, bent at the wrong angle as if someone had gripped her tight and twisted it. The rest of the body was, thankfully, concealed by the wall.

I heard myself speak. My voice thin and shaking. "I-is that a—"

Shiloh didn't look at me. "Yes."

"And is she—"

"Yes."

"Who did this?"

"Doesn't matter," said Shiloh. "He's gone too."

I felt like I was going to be sick. I'd seen my share of death, but this was something different, something worse. I knew murders happened, of course, that people did gruesome and terrible things to each other all the time. But seeing it firsthand was different.

Shiloh's gaze slid toward me. She looked annoyed and exhausted, utterly wrung out. "Why are you here, Roslyn?"

I held up Adeline's cell phone.

Shiloh's face went blank for a moment, but she recovered herself fast.

"We need to talk," I said.

"Not here." Shiloh made for the door, leaving me alone in the kitchen. I spared a last look at that hand in the hall.

Shiloh was waiting for me down in the courtyard, fumbling with her vape, her hands shaking.

"Look, Shiloh, you're not okay—"

Shiloh pulled on the mouthpiece, exhaled hard. "I'm fine."

"If you need a moment—"

"I said I'm fucking fine, Roslyn." I'd never seen her so angry, and it frightened me, how much she looked like Death. "You wanted to talk, so let's have it out."

My chin quivered, but I fought the tears. I wouldn't give her the satisfaction of letting her see me cry. "Why didn't you tell me sooner?"

Shiloh dragged a hand through her hair, not looking at me. "I didn't think it would be like this. I felt drawn to you from the beginning, and I thought it would pass, and when it didn't, things just happened so quickly that I couldn't find the right moment to tell you the truth."

It wasn't enough, and she knew it.

I could feel the tears coming, and my voice strained with the effort of holding them back. "I don't know what you had with Adeline or if it was real or what it meant to her, but I don't understand why you didn't just tell me the truth."

Shiloh reached out to me. "Roslyn, I wanted to—"

"Don't touch me."

Her hand fell.

"You led me on. I was starting to like you, and you knew that. You made me think that there was some chance of something between us when all you wanted was her."

"You know that's not true."

"It is," I said, cementing it as reality because it hurt too much to consider another alternative. "I know that now. We were both just trying to find the ghost of her through each other."

Shiloh shook her head. "That might be true for you. But not for me. What I feel for you is different from what happened before, with her. I don't expect you to believe that now, but it's true just the same."

"You're right. I don't believe it. I don't believe anything you say." I stepped around her, heading back to the hotel.

But Shiloh called after me. "You're more than just your sister. You deserve to live and love and experience things that are more than just an extension of her. I wish you would accept that. I wish you could just see yourself the way everyone else does. The way Adeline did."

"You say that like you know me, but you don't. Not really. You know this"—I gestured to myself with a pass of my hand—"but it's just grief. That's all I am now: the loss of her."

"That's a lie."

"It's not." It came out in a hoarse whisper. "When she died, she took the best of me with her. I'm just remnants now of the person I was before, with her."

"You could be more than that if you would just let yourself."

I turned then, left her alone in the courtyard. "Maybe I don't want to be."

Chapter 18

The next morning, the eve of Death's deadline, I woke early to the smell of bacon, the hiss and crackle of it frying in a pan. The bedroom I'd fallen asleep in—a large one with a king-size bed and a private bathroom—was empty, making it the first time I'd woken up alone since I'd started traveling with the girls. I fumbled for one of those white terry cloth bathrobes and stumbled into the hall, disoriented—only half-sure where I was or why I was even there. I rounded the corner into the kitchen to see a man bent over the stove.

"Happy three weeks, Roslyn." Death turned to look at me, beaming. "Hungry?"

I froze, reeling. I wasn't expecting him until tomorrow, on the day of the deadline. What was he doing here? "I—I don't eat pork."

"It's turkey bacon," he said, and gestured to the barstools by the island. "Please sit. I could use the company."

I started forward, stunned, and tugged the barstool out from under the island. I folded my hands to keep them from shaking so he wouldn't know how afraid I really was.

"You like your eggs scrambled soft, right?" he asked, turning back to the stove.

"How do you know how I like my eggs?"

"Don't worry. I'm not omniscient, just inevitable," he said. "We've met before. At your diner. I circled through a few times, wearing a different face than the one I'm wearing now."

"You can do that?"

"I can do a great many things," said Death. "But what I can't do is read minds. That's why I'm so curious to know how your experience has been these past few weeks."

Was there a wrong way to answer that question? Would he still tell me the truth about Adeline if he was displeased with my performance? Something told me the answer was no. "It's been good. Eye-opening."

"Oh? In what way?"

I paused, considering. "I guess . . . I just didn't know what it was to live until I witnessed a bunch of people die."

"How poetic. I do envy you."

It seemed like such a strange thing to say. What could I have that Death didn't? "Envy? Envy what?" I asked, and he turned to me again, his face a younger, softer version of itself.

"Living." Out in the hotel hallway, a door slammed, and there was yelling. A lover's spat, from the sound of it. "You know, I love hotels. Apartments and trailer parks too. Any place where people live packed together. It gives you a glimpse of all these lives so tightly contained, condensed into the same small place. Listen."

He closed his eyes, and the voices in the hall grew louder. It was, in fact, a couple arguing. From the sound of it, a girl had caught her boyfriend texting an ex she didn't know she still needed to worry about.

"So much verve," said Death, beaming. He layered more bacon into a sizzling pan, and I realized he was cooking enough for the other girls too. "So much energy in them."

I fell quiet, waiting with a pit in my stomach for him to get to the point, explain why he was here the day before his deadline. He didn't seem to be in a hurry.

"You've done well with the girls these past few weeks," he said, and it surprised me just how much those words meant to me, how proud I felt when he praised me, like I'd actually done something good. "I hope you know how important it is, the work that you all do."

"Just how many of us are there? Doing your work?"

"Quite a few." He took the frying pan off the heat, using a fork to pick up the slices of bacon and lower them to a plate lined with paper towels.

"So everyone who dies encounters someone like the girls? Or someone else that you hire to do your dirty work?"

He frowned at my wording but didn't correct it. "No. I do most of the work myself. Invisibly, for the most part. Believe it or not, mine is not the face most people hope to see on their deathbeds. So I often adopt the form of a family member, or a dream; occasionally I'm a nightmare. But I'm always there in one way or another."

"How do you choose who to send for what death?"

He took a carton of eggs from the fridge, cracked ten into the pan, and scrambled them with a fork. "I believe you'd call it . . . a gut feeling."

"And that gut feeling led you to assemble a group of teenage girls to do your work for you?"

"Not exactly."

"Then why did you choose us? I mean them," I quickly corrected myself, remembering with a small pang that Death had never really chosen me at all.

"I chose the girls because I like their intensity," he said, pushing the eggs around in the pan. "Teenage girls are like a bottled scream, or the charged quality of the air just before lightning strikes. All this potential and possibility condensed into such a frail human body. There's real power in that. A power I very much like to observe when I have the chance. And our agreement gives me the opportunity to do just that. It's been a great highlight of my service."

I noted his word choice. A highlight of his *service*, not his *life*, because Death wasn't alive or dead. He was just . . . himself. Whatever that meant. I realized then that it might be my last chance to ask. "Who are you, really?"

Here, Death deflected a bit. I could tell that he was choosing his next words with care, like he was afraid of saying the wrong thing. His self-consciousness surprised me, me being a teenage girl and him being a god of Death with the power to do what he pleased. But it felt nice to be taken so seriously, as if my opinion mattered to him. "I've walked through many ages and worn many skins."

"So you mean you've been many people?"

He nodded, then faltered and shook his head. "I haven't been anyone in particular. I've adopted various human forms, but that doesn't make me human. And as a . . . *not-human*, I don't experience the passage of time in the linear way that you do. For me, past, present, and future happen simultaneously."

"So, in your eyes . . . I'm already dead."

"Dead, alive, immortal, unborn." He spooned the scrambled eggs out of the pan and into a serving bowl. "That's the charm of you humans. You can be many things at once. Not me, though. I'm just the one thing. I always have been and always will be. It gets tedious after a while, which is why I relish the connections I make with inquisitive characters, like you."

This came as something of a surprise to me, given how very unlike the rest of the girls I considered myself to be. They were objects of fascination. Easy to love and obsess over. Filled with verve and energy, as Death had put it just moments before. Once—back when Adeline was alive—I was more similar to them. I was the moon to Adeline's sun, and I took on a little of her light, so I seemed to glow all on my own. But now, in the wake of Adeline's death, I didn't shine like that anymore. Grief had dimmed me, made me small and forgettable.

"You have your own assets," Death said. "You've already proved yourself a valuable addition to the group."

I hated myself for the way my cheeks flushed with pride, the way my rounded shoulders squared just a little. I don't think I was aware, until that moment, just how much I wanted to hear him say that. How much I needed him to.

"If I'm such a valuable asset, then why didn't you choose me to begin with? The way you did all the other girls." It sounded more bitter than I intended it to, but Death took it in stride. In fact, I cringed a little at the way he regarded me then, with a gentle smile, overly gracious—a clear attempt to coddle me as if I were a child in need of consoling. I felt my cheeks warm.

"I had my reasons." He fixed me a plate: three strips of turkey bacon and a fluffy heap of eggs layered with a slice of melting cheddar, the same way Conny served it at the diner. He gestured for me to take a bite, and I did. The eggs were perfect, creamy and salty like he'd cooked them in butter. The sliced cheese had a sharp and expensive taste. "I suppose we should get down to the business that brought me here."

I swallowed wrong. Almost choked but recovered myself. "You mean the final test?"

"A favor," he said, but nodded. "It's been weighing on me for some time. Are you still willing to help me?"

I felt fear like a fist clench around my stomach, making it hard to keep the food down. "Why ask when you could just force me? You're the one holding all the cards."

Death leaned forward, took a tray of toast—thick-sliced brioche that smelled almost as sweet as cake—from the oven. "You're still capable of surprising me. Any request I make can be denied by you if you see fit. That's what makes this real."

"But there have to be consequences, right?"

He took butter from the fridge, sliced it into pats, and layered several of them onto each slice of brioche. "We'll get to those in a moment. But first, the task itself: I need you to choose one of the girls. To kill."

I felt like I couldn't breathe, as though someone had turned my lungs inside out. I almost slid out of my seat and gripped the corner of the countertop to keep my balance, my hands shaking so badly I could barely catch hold of it. When I spoke, I didn't even register my voice as my own. It sounded so far off, foreign to my own ears. "What? Why?"

"It's time." He fiddled with the toast slices, arranging them in an artful little stack on a dinner plate. "For one, they've grown cocky. Puffed up by their own self-importance, as demonstrated by their inviting you into the fold without my consent or permission. I fear, if they're not humbled, made to remember me, something will . . . *give*. And I can't have that."

I squeezed my eyes shut, trying to make sense of what he was saying as my mind reeled. The pressure of tears building in my throat made it almost hard to speak. "B-but you made a promise. You had a deal with them—"

"One they broke by allowing you into the group."

I struggled to grasp the implications of what he was saying. This was *my* fault?

"Don't be so hard on yourself." Death turned and poured me a glass of orange juice. "There were other instances too. You weren't the first time the girls disobeyed. I've given them grace in the past, pointedly ignored certain missteps. But I can't afford to keep doing that. It's time for them to remember what I am, and I hope that you'll have a hand in showing them. If you do, if you take this on, I'll tell you what you want to know about your sister." Death reached across the countertop, touched my hand, and I caught a flash of Adeline, alive in the playhouse, gazing at me. "You see?"

He drew away, severing the vision, leaving Adeline alone to die.

"No, wait—" I lunged for him, desperate to return to her, but Death pulled back.

"Not yet," he said. "Not until the dispatch is complete. You choose a girl, and I'll give you what it is that you're looking for."

"But I—I can't kill one of my friends." It came out in a broken sob. "There has to be another way. What if I take myself out of the equation? What if I offer myself up?"

"How very noble." He gave a pinched little smile. "But I'd rather you not. You're a good asset to this group, humble and talented. One might even call you a stabilizing force. You set an example that the other girls could stand to learn from. I feel the same about Shiloh. I'm quite fond of her, as you know. But ultimately, the choice is yours. You won't be punished for your sacrifice if you do decide to make it. As long as someone dies, I'm satisfied."

Death wiped his hands on a tea towel, then nodded to himself. "You have a day to deliberate. I'll return tomorrow at midnight to see that the task is done." He smiled with a warmth that felt genuine. "Good luck, Roslyn. I've not made it easy for you, but I know you'll rise to the occasion. You haven't failed me yet."

Chapter 19

I sat alone in the living room long after Death's departure, watching the sun pull clear of the Las Vegas skyline. Gradually, the other girls woke up and stumbled into the kitchen. None of them seemed to notice anything was wrong at first. They thanked me for the breakfast I hadn't made, eating the cold eggs and chewing on strips of bacon, devouring the thick slices of brioche, their cheeks fat with it.

It was Shiloh who first noticed something was wrong. She was one of the last girls to emerge, rubbing raw eyes with her fist as she entered the kitchen. She took one look at me and just . . . knew, as if I'd told her everything. "Family meeting," she said.

Confused, the other girls brought their plates from the kitchen to the living room, settled themselves on the couches. Shiloh sat among them, and I wondered when Death had told her about his plan. Was it the night I'd seen them together across the Walmart parking lot when everyone else was asleep? Or had this been set in motion well before? Had she always known and kept it secret, like the relationship with Adeline she'd kept hidden from me?

Skye bit a limp strip of bacon. "So? What's up?"

Shiloh's eyes remained on me. "Roslyn has something to say."

"No," I said, shaking my head. "You tell them yourself."

Shiloh's expression remained even, her eyes dark and unblinking. And that was all the confirmation I needed, of a betrayal so great it staggered me.

Riley's eyes narrowed. Her gaze carved toward Shiloh. "Tell us what?"

When Shiloh didn't answer, and I couldn't contain myself any longer—couldn't justify holding the girls in suspense—I blurted out the truth: "Death says that one of us has to die."

The girls remained remarkably, almost eerily calm. Skye put the rest of the bacon in her mouth and chewed in solemn silence. Chloe's lips pressed into a thin and bloodless line. Naomi carefully set a slice of toast on the plate, wiped the butter off her fingers on a napkin, and crumpled it.

Riley was the only one who cracked. She kept shaking her head, muttering, "I fucking knew it. All this time, I fucking knew—"

"Why would he do that?" said Iona, her voice small and throttled, the question landing like a plea. "We've killed for him. We've been good. We've kept up our end of the bargain—"

"You're a fucking traitor," said Riley in a hoarse whisper, looking at Shiloh with utter disgust. "All this time, you've known this was coming. Haven't you?"

"I tried to talk him out of it," said Shiloh, and her expression reminded me of the salt plains surrounding the festival where we killed Jasmine Wu. Empty desolation. "I tried to do more than my part. I spent half my nights killing just to satisfy his bloodlust, but it's not enough."

So that was what she'd been doing on those long nights away. Trying to appease him, to stave off what I then knew was inevitable: One of us was going to die.

"How long do we have?" Naomi asked. She sounded calm. Clinical, almost.

"He'll give us until midnight," I said.

"We can't go through with this," said Skye, her hands clutched into tight fists, her cheeks flushed. She seemed more angry than afraid.

Chloe sucked her teeth. "If we don't, we're all goners. I mean, what choice do we really have?"

"We could run," said Skye, hopeful even after everything, all the people she'd killed and the things she'd seen. Somehow she'd still managed to retain the innocence of a child, the earnest belief that everything would be okay. But I knew better, and so did the other girls.

"We need to choose someone." Shiloh seemed almost despondent. "And I want to put forward my own name."

"I don't know if that's a good idea," I whispered. "Death . . . doesn't want it to be you."

"You spoke to Death?" Iona asked.

I nodded. "This morning. He told me it has to be someone, but he'd prefer that I didn't pick Shiloh. I mean, he said he'd respect my decision either way, but . . . I don't know. It felt like a threat almost. Like something bad would happen if we chose her."

"Of course," said Riley, bitter and spiteful. "He always protects his favorite."

"Riley—"

"What, Naomi? You know it's true." Riley shoved to her feet. "Shiloh here has been dealing with Death behind our backs. Sitting on this for fuck knows how long. We can't trust her." Riley then turned to me. "Or you."

"What did I do?"

Riley pointed to Shiloh and me, waving her finger in the air. "You two were gone a long time last night. What were you talking about? Hm? Deciding which of us to offer up to Death?"

"We talked, we fought about my sister and the fact that she and Shiloh were together last summer. Something that not a single one of you bothered to tell me. Even when you knew that I was starting to—" I didn't finish that. I couldn't, for the shame of it. "You all should've told me."

None of them denied it, but it hurt the way they wouldn't look at me after I said it: Naomi dropping her gaze to the floor, Iona staring out the window with glazed eyes, Skye pushing eggs around on her plate. I wondered how much they knew, why they didn't say anything. I knew they were loyal to Shiloh, but I'd thought that I could trust them enough to have my back.

But Riley made no apologies. "What else did Death say to you? Did he tell you who to kill and how?"

I debated telling them the truth. I hadn't yet confessed that Death had charged me alone with the task of choosing a girl to kill, and I knew that, if I did, I'd have an even bigger target on my back, just like Shiloh. But so far, keeping secrets from each other had only brought about chaos. "He said it was my choice."

"*Your* choice?" Riley laughed, looking to Shiloh. "Better watch out. Looks like Death has a new favorite."

Shiloh turned to me then. "Did you tell him how you planned to choose?"

"Of course not," I said, shocked that she'd even ask the question. "I—I told him I couldn't. I'm not going to kill one of you guys. I can't do that."

"So it's just up in the air, then?" Iona looked on the verge of panic, her hands shaking in her lap. "I mean, what are we even supposed to do with that?"

"I say we vote," said Riley. "It's only fair. So far, we've got two votes for Shiloh. Her vote and mine."

"Just stop it," said Naomi, looking to Riley. "We can't afford to turn on each other. If there's a way out of this, now's our time to seize it. Skye is right; there has to be something else we can do."

Skye reached for her hand across the coffee table and held on to her.

Riley sneered, visibly disgusted by the optimism, by all of us, really. "All right, if Skye's got some brilliant plan to outwit Death, let's fucking hear it."

"We could go to my mom," said Skye, and she popped to her feet, triumphant. "She's a psychic. She can help us."

"Here we go again." Riley rolled her eyes. "Look, Skye, I hate to tell you this, but a D-list actress turned Hollywood psychic can't and won't spare us from Death incarnate."

"You haven't met my mom," said Skye with a sudden fierceness. "She's not just any psychic. She negotiated with Death and lived to tell the tale, which is more than you can say for yourself."

"What do you mean she negotiated with Death?" I asked, stunned that she hadn't mentioned this before. When Death said there were others who'd made pacts with him, I'd imagined them as far-off and shadowy figures. No one as immediate as someone's mother.

Skye looked, for the first time since I had ever met her, a little shy. "When my mom was young, she was diagnosed with brain cancer. Brain cancer, as you probably know, is bad to begin with, but this one was really bad. Inoperable, treatment-resistant, fast-growing. The worst kind, basically. She was in hospice when Death appeared at the foot of her bed. Somehow she cut a deal with him, talked her way out of her own death sentence."

It was far-fetched, but it was better than drawing straws, deciding who should die at random. "How did she bargain with him?"

"I don't know," said Skye. "She never told me, but whatever it was, it worked."

Riley seemed unconvinced. "You'd think, if she'd found an effective way to cheat Death, everyone would do it."

"My mom isn't everyone," said Skye. "You'll see when you meet her. She's different, like us. I'm telling you, if anyone can help us, she can."

There was a long pause as the girls considered this, deliberating silently.

"I think it's worth a try," said Shiloh, and just like that, it was decided. "Let's go."

We packed our things as quickly as possible, overcome with panic, stuffing clothes into bags without zipping them up, leaving what we couldn't carry behind. No one spoke of Death, or spoke at all, really, and I don't think I'd ever felt so cut off from the other girls or seen them so cut off from each other, moving around the suite in silence like they were strangers.

We checked out of the hotel, the valet retrieving our vehicles with some difficulty. It was just over a four-hour drive from Vegas to Palm Springs, but the traffic was thick that day, stretching the trip to the six-hour mark. It was late afternoon by the time we reached Palm Springs proper. The place looked a lot like the set of a movie. Softly lit buildings, tall and skinny palms swaying gently in a weak breeze.

We pulled into an almost disturbingly well-manicured neighborhood. Skye's childhood home was all sharp angles, with glass walls and a sloping tin roof. It looked aerodynamic, like if you put it on wheels and pushed it down the driveway, it might just catch the wind and fly.

There was a woman on the stoop, standing barefoot in a blue silk robe cinched tightly at the waist. Her hair was silver blond, long, and parted neatly down the middle. She was older than I'd expected, by a good twenty years, and she looked like an elderly member of the Manson cult. When the wind caught the sleeves of her robe, I saw that her forearms were stacked up to the elbows with carved wooden bangles. Skye kicked open the door of the truck before we'd even slowed to a full stop and ran into the open arms of her mother.

Chapter 20

Monica Love was famous, but softly, in the way TV presenters and news anchors are. I couldn't quite place her face, but I knew with certainty that I'd seen her before, maybe in the supporting role of a movie I'd liked as a kid or on one of those late-night infomercials that play on repeat in the wee hours of the morning. A face you only half remember but never quite forget.

Monica's home was filled with old Hollywood memorabilia. There was a large and glossy poster for some off-Broadway musical I'd never heard of featuring a younger Monica dressed as a flapper. Beside it, in a frame no bigger than my hand, was a receipt with some scribbled writing on it.

"Marlon Brando wrote his number on that," said Monica when she caught me looking.

Monica led us into a large living room with gleaming floor-to-ceiling windows that overlooked the pool out back. All the furniture was sleek, with the same aerodynamic dimensions of the house itself. A cowhide rug stretched across the floor, layered with Persian tapestries and sheepskins. In the far corner of the room sat an acrylic baby grand piano beside what appeared to be some kind of altar, complete with melting candles and crystal balls, burnt bundles of sage. In what seemed like something of a Palm Springs cliché, there were also plastic flamingos everywhere.

"God, I want your life," said Chloe, gazing around the room. The other girls—apart from Shiloh and Naomi—seemed similarly awed.

I had always been scared of getting old. It's vain, and I feel bad admitting it, but the idea of gray hairs and liver spots, wrinkles bracketing my mouth, had always filled me with fear. I just couldn't imagine who I would be at that age, when all my youth was gone. But Monica was a living hope of something more than that. I'd be lucky to grow old the way she had, in her glamorous house with the suave velvet sofa and a record player whirling in the corner, its speaker blasting a twangy folk song.

Monica ducked into the kitchen, and all the girls, even Shiloh, followed her like ducklings. She took two trays of muffins out of the oven, steam trailing off them.

We hadn't had anything to eat since breakfast, so we finished two dozen muffins, slathered with jam and vegan butter, in a matter of minutes. Monica made mocktails—with lime, lavender syrup, and tonic water so bitter and bubbly it burned my throat when I swallowed. We drank from chilled cocktail glasses and sat around the kitchen, snacking on olives and crackers and other tidbits served in plastic dishes patterned with cartoon flamingos and other tacky designs.

Skye watched all of us, looking proud and content despite the grim circumstances that brought us here. I wondered if this was something she'd wanted for some time, her two worlds brought together into a kind of harmony. Sad that it had only happened then, as we stood on the precipice of tragedy.

After we ate our fill, Monica led us back to the living room. Skye claimed a furry beanbag chair, while Naomi and Iona settled on a curved love seat opposite the couch. The rest of the girls sat on the couch or floor.

But Monica loomed over us, frail arms folded across her chest. "So, what's happened now, love?"

"Trouble with Death," said Skye. "He wants us to kill one of our own. Someone in this group. We have until midnight to decide, but we can't go through with it. We need your help."

Monica's expression remained neutral, totally composed. "Well, there's no help to be had here. You've got to do as he says. Appease him."

"But Skye told us you negotiated with him," said Shiloh.

"That was a long time ago."

"And yet you're still here," said Shiloh.

Monica's eyes narrowed. "I am for now." She moved to sit down on the edge of the couch, fumbled with a pack of cigarettes and a lighter, her hands shaking so badly she could barely get the flame to catch. She finally lit up and spoke in an exhale of smoke. "At a certain age, you come to accept the harsh reality of your own mortal life. You hear your cue, and if you have any dignity at all, you heed it and step offstage, so to speak."

"Are you telling us to go belly-up?" Riley asked. I could tell she was incredulous, pissed that we'd come all this way just for Monica to tell us to give up.

Monica shrugged. "Death gets what he wants in the end, so you might as well save yourself the time and give it to him. After all, it doesn't take long to die. For most of us, it's a few bad moments if we're lucky. Or a few bad years if we're not. In the scheme of things, it's really a rather short process. But we spend our whole lives waiting for it. Trying and mostly failing to come to terms with the inevitable. I must admit I don't see the point of it anymore."

"So you just . . . accept it?" said Skye, gazing at her mother. She looked like she was on the verge of tears. "Mom, he's telling us that one of us has to die. That's not something we can stomach."

Monica plucked a tissue from a box shaped like a topless woman. She dabbed at Skye's eyes. "Sweetheart, don't cry. It's going to be okay, I—"

Skye slapped her hand away. "It's not okay. We're not going to let this happen. I'm not just going to sit here and watch him kill off one of my friends."

Monica stared at the floor. "It's not so bad, unless you make it that way. There's that old saying, right? The lucky ones die young."

I thought of Adeline, alone in the playhouse. "You're wrong," I said.

Monica's gaze shifted to me for the first time. Her eyes reminded me of Death's. Eyes that had seen so much, eyes that held so much of what they'd seen. "Your name?"

"Roslyn."

"Pretty name for a pretty girl. Let me guess: You're new to all of this?"

"Not very," I said, a bit defensive. "I've had my dealings with Death before."

"You lost someone." It wasn't a question, but I had no idea how she knew. Why was it so easy for her to see right through me? "Who was it?"

"My sister."

"Older or younger?"

"Older."

She gave a low whistle. "That's a hard thing. In my experience, sisters always hate each other a little bit. That's the way it was with me and my sister. Our hatred for each other would've ruined everything if the love between us wasn't that much bigger."

"I didn't hate my sister," I said, fast and too defensive.

Monica gave me a gracious and knowing smile, as if to let me win. "Tell me, what are you doing with these girls?"

I froze, feeling singled out. Exposed. Was it really so obvious that I didn't fit among them? Was I really that different? "They're my friends."

"Are they? Can you have friends in your line of work?"

I could tell Naomi was growing uncomfortable, but she kept her gaze level, firmly fixed on Monica. She might've lacked the steel of some of the other girls in the group, but she knew how to fake it. "We can and do. Roslyn is one of us. Just like anyone else here."

"Hm." Monica looked unconvinced. I was relieved when her gaze finally shifted away from me. "Sometimes it's better not to fight. You do know that, right?"

"How about you let us make that choice?" said Shiloh. "Tell us how you cut a deal with Death. How did you convince him?"

"I offered him something he wanted," said Monica, mumbling around the filter of a cigarette. "There was nothing more to it than that."

I didn't believe her. Not fully, anyway. It wasn't what she said, exactly, so much as the way she said it. Intentionally casual, composed. But the longer I watched her, the easier it was to see the girl hiding behind that facade. She was one of us, maybe the very first of us, and perhaps that was why Death had really chosen to spare her. Not because she begged or bargained well, but because she was different in a way that piqued his interest.

"Please," said Shiloh, a broken whisper, like a knife's edge dragged across concrete. "We're running out of time. We only have until midnight."

Skye leaned into her mother, shoulders rounded, chest bone caving inward, looking even younger than she usually did. "Just tell us what you did, Mom. How did you best him?"

"Oh, baby . . . I didn't." Monica cupped a hand to Skye's cheek. "I did the same thing he wants you to do now. I offered someone up in my stead. Someone I loved very much so the sacrifice was great enough."

"Who?" Skye asked, squeezing her mother's hand. "Was it Grandma? It's okay if it was, she was kind of a bitch—"

Iona's eyes flashed wide. "Jesus, Skye."

"Could we do something like that?" Skye looked to her mother again. "Like, is there some sort of ritual or sacrifice we could make—"

"No." Shiloh and I said it in unison. But the girls, I noticed, looked to me for an answer.

I shifted in my chair, uncomfortable with the idea of standing in as Death's proxy. "Death said it has to be one of you. He thinks you've grown . . . complacent. Rebellious." I hated the idea that I was speaking for him like Shiloh usually did.

Chloe's hands tightened to fists. "So this is a punishment?"

Shiloh nodded.

Monica leaned forward, her chest pressed nearly to her knees. When she spoke, her voice was a stern and scathing whisper, like she feared Death was eavesdropping. "Listen, girls, very carefully. There is no way to work around him. To get what you want, you have to decide among yourselves who to give up. That's the only choice you have now, and you'd be fools to squander it. You care for each other, don't you?"

Skye nodded vehemently. "Of course we do."

"We're all we have," said Iona, her voice breaking a little. "We just want to protect each other."

"Then find someone to give to him," said Monica. "Make your sacrifice so that the rest of you can carry on somehow. That's the way it was for me. I made the tough decision, and . . . it wasn't so bad after that. He let me be."

"So that's it, then?" Riley looked crestfallen. I hadn't realized that she'd been allowing herself to hope until I saw the disappointment written across her face. "We came all this way, wasting time we didn't have, just to give up on ourselves?"

Monica pressed to her feet. "I'm sorry. I'm afraid that's the only choice you have now. And you'd better make it quick." She extended a hand to Skye. "Come on. Let the big girls talk."

But Skye didn't move. "I'm staying with them. I—I . . . I want to put my own name in the ring."

"*No*," we all said in unison, horrified by the idea of it.

"Not you, Skye. You're the youngest," said Naomi. "Whoever we choose, it won't be you. It can't be."

She looked to the other girls for confirmation, and we all nodded. Even Riley. At fourteen, Skye was the baby of the group. None of us were willing to lose her, and it felt good that we could all agree on that when everything else was so uncertain.

But Skye remained defiant. "You don't get to make that choice for me no matter how young I am. I'm in this group too—"

"No one's forgetting that, kid." Shiloh mussed her hair. "Whatever comes next, we'll meet it together. I promise you that."

Chapter 21

With just a few hours left until Death's deadline, we gathered out back by the pool to talk, needing the fresh air. Monica, after several failed attempts to lure Skye away, retired to her room. At first, no one really had much to say. It was almost awkwardly silent. A few false starts at conversation dwindling off. The sound of water lapping gently at the walls of the pool. In the distance, the mountains of Joshua Tree loomed over us like a threat.

We were running out of time.

"It should be me," said Naomi. "I'm the oldest, so—"

"No chance in hell," Shiloh cut her off. "I was the one who brought this group together. I eat the consequences. You guys can continue on without me."

"Out of the question." Naomi shook her head, and Iona nodded in agreement. "You lead us. We don't have a group without you. You're the last one who should be offered up. Death will tear us apart after you're gone. You're the only one who knows how to reason with him."

"We could still fight back." Skye sounded timid and terribly afraid, though she was probably the only girl in the group who had complete immunity.

"Fighting back will only result in all of us dying." I knew on gut instinct that Naomi was right. "Better one dies than all of us."

"Couldn't agree more." Riley picked at her nails. "But that doesn't change the fact that we need a name. We have to give up someone, and soon."

But no one wanted to give up the name of the girl they thought should die. People had their favorites, of course. To pretend that we were all equally close was a farce that we usually liked to ignore, but that night, it became painfully obvious where the respective loyalties lay.

Shiloh, as the leader of the group, had ties to everyone. We relied on her guidance, and for that reason alone, she was probably safe. None of the other girls, except Riley, would allow her to sacrifice herself. And even if we did agree on that, something told me that Death wouldn't have it.

Shiloh was his first girl, after all. His favorite.

Skye was also immune, due to her young age; that was one thing all of us could agree on. Naomi was the oldest, and she'd been a mother to all of us. She kept track of medications and made sure the RV was stocked with enough toilet paper and food. Shiloh had brought us together, but Naomi had made us a family, or something close to one, at least.

She was the best of us, and we knew it. I couldn't imagine anyone voting for her.

There was Riley, whose bluntness—and at times cruelty—had created friction in the group. As far as I could tell, none of the girls were particularly fond of her. Chloe was the only one who really seemed to like her.

But Riley had her assets. She was the only girl in the group who could drive the RV reliably, maneuvering through tight streets and winding roads, even parallel parking it in a pinch. She was also good at dispatches, especially the violent ones—the murders and dismemberments, the particularly gruesome car wrecks, worse even than Corbin's. Everyone respected her for that, myself included. To lose her would mean that we'd have to shoulder the grim burden that she'd been bearing in silence all these months.

Then there were Iona and Chloe, who weren't leaders like the older girls, and yet I couldn't imagine the group without them. They filled our days with laughter and color. After the darkest dispatches, they always found a way to make us smile, and as a result, they were both well-liked by everyone. No, it couldn't be one of them.

Then there was me, the newest addition and, by proxy, the one with the weakest ties. I wasn't supposed to be an official part of the group anyway. Shiloh had chosen to spare me out of guilt over what had happened to Adeline. Riley, and perhaps some of the other girls, too, had never really wanted me to be a part of their caravan in the first place. And sure, I'd taken to the work of Death well enough. I did my part. Death seemed pleased with me, and in time, I'd come to count myself as a competent asset to the group. I considered myself close to the girls, but because I was so new, I wasn't sure how much those bonds counted.

The fact remained: I was the newest girl and the only one who hadn't been chosen by Death. It would make sense to pick me.

"We need to vote," I said. "It's the only way. The easiest way."

Shiloh nodded and looked to Skye. "Grab us some pens, paper, and some kind of bowl or pot."

Skye nodded, pale and drawn, and disappeared into the house. She returned with a mixing bowl, paper, some pens and colored pencils, and a pair of kitchen scissors. Her hands shook as she began to cut up the paper into little strips, equally sized. Naomi distributed them.

"We'll write down the name of the girl we think should die, and whoever has the most votes is the one we offer up," said Shiloh, remarkably calm given the circumstances.

"What if we have a tie?" Chloe asked. Her face had drained of all color; she looked like she was on the verge of passing out. And she wasn't the only one. I glanced around the group and saw that every single girl looked similarly stricken.

I realized, with a start, that every one of them thought it would be them.

Shiloh took a pencil and slip of paper from Naomi. "If two girls get the same number of votes, we'll vote again and again until the matter is settled."

Riley tore the cap off her pen with her teeth. "This is bullshit."

"I agree." Skye looked down at her pencil and paper, her face contorting. She snatched the paper and crumpled it. "We don't have to do this. We can still fight back—"

Shiloh's eyes were on her paper. "There's no fighting Death."

"Well, I'm not going to vote on which of my friends should die."

"That's your right," said Shiloh. "But it'll still have to be someone. He'll make us choose or else we all go. Is that what you want?"

Skye's chin wrinkled with the effort of holding back tears. "That would be better than betraying my friends."

Naomi sat down beside her, rubbed circles into her back. When she looked to Shiloh, her eyes were filled with something I can only describe as grief. She took a fresh piece of paper and placed it into Skye's hand. "Let's just get this over with."

I clutched my pencil so tightly I feared it would snap in my hand. I thought of abstaining from the vote, the way that Skye suggested we should, but it didn't sit right with me. I could almost hear Adeline's voice in the back of my mind telling me to suck it up, not to be a coward. I knew that, if she were here, she would've found a name to write down. She could be cold that way, if the situation demanded it. I tried to channel her, tried to think of a girl to give up, but the only name that surfaced was my own.

And that scared me.

It scared me because it wasn't the first time I'd allowed myself to consider the idea of following my sister. I didn't believe in heaven or hell. But I knew that whatever was on the other side of death was where Adeline had gone, and in the moment, that felt like . . . peace to me.

I didn't want to die, but I wanted to be close to her. I had wanted that since I'd lost her.

So I wrote down my own name on the paper, got up, and put it in the bowl.

I was the first girl to vote. Skye went next, looking self-assured despite her vehement objections to the vote. Naomi voted after her. Shiloh followed Chloe, and Iona voted next.

Riley was the last to put her slip in the bowl. I was surprised to see her fighting tears as she scrawled down a name on the paper, crumpled it in a closed fist like trash, and tossed it cleanly into the bowl from where she sat. She scrubbed furiously at her bloodshot eyes, wouldn't look at any of us. I wondered why she felt so guilty when she'd made it obvious she was going to vote for Shiloh, that we all should.

With all the votes cast, Shiloh got up stiffly and walked to the bowl. She selected the first piece of paper and read the name aloud. "Skye."

Everyone froze, except Skye, whose eyes were trained on the dark and distant mountains.

Shiloh pulled another slip of paper. "Iona."

A chill raced up my spine.

She read the next vote. "Chloe."

Chloe, like Skye, remained expressionless.

Shiloh plucked another piece of paper from the bowl. Frowned. "Roslyn."

I stopped breathing for a moment, my hands shaking in my lap.

Shiloh pulled another slip of paper. "Naomi."

I went rigid at the mention of Naomi's name. I hadn't expected that anyone would vote for her. As far as I knew, she was beloved by all the girls in the group.

Shiloh read the last two names. "Shiloh and Riley."

I froze, realizing the implications of what had just occurred. There was one vote for each of us.

Was it possible that every girl in the group, even Riley, had voted for themselves just like I had? I guessed that Shiloh had also done that, and I suspected that Naomi had too. Then there was Skye, who despite her moral qualms had voted without hesitation, which didn't make any sense unless she—like me—had offered up herself. I looked to the other girls in the group, the frightened smiles, the relief.

Even Riley was laughing in disbelief, head hung, shoulders shaking. "We're screwed," she kept saying it over and over, but with this wry, slightly crazed smile. "We're fucking screwed."

"You all voted for yourselves, didn't you?" I asked, looking at the girls.

Every one of them nodded.

THERE WAS SOME deliberation about what to do next, in the three hours before the midnight deadline. We silently agreed that we wouldn't vote again, choose a girl at will or at random. Ultimately, we chose to force his hand, leave the decision up to him. Opting to suffer his wrath and die together before giving up one of our own.

An hour before the deadline, we retreated inside, piling ourselves onto the couch. Skye procured pillows and blankets, and we tucked ourselves in, nestled together so tightly that we seemed like one body, breathing together, our hearts beating as one. I lost track of my own limbs, whose hands belonged to who. And I remembered thinking, as I drifted off to sleep, that this was what I had been searching for my entire life—in Adeline and within myself—a completeness that had always seemed so elusive until now.

"Roslyn?" I heard Skye whisper. She was sleeping closest to me, and I could feel her warm breath blooming against my cheek. "Are you awake?"

"Yes," I whispered. "What is it?"

"I just . . . Thank you. For coming to the pool party. For being my friend. I'm sorry that it turned into this. I wanted things to be good for you."

"Come here," I said, and shifted to face her, wanting to look her in the eye one last time. But Skye fit her head into the crook of my shoulder before I could. She was so small, and I felt an almost painful urge to protect her, from Death, from everything and everyone that could possibly hurt her. I wondered if this was what Adeline felt like on the rare occasions when she'd held me. "You don't have anything to apologize for. We'll figure this out somehow. It's going to be okay."

"I know," said Skye, and I could tell that she really believed it.

Chapter 22

I woke to screaming and sunlight flooding in through the windows. It wasn't a normal scream, more of a bellow, really. A round sound that came from the belly and seemed to swell, filling the whole house. I sat up, the rest of the girls along with me, bleary eyed and confused.

Shiloh and Naomi were the first on their feet. Riley and I scrambled after them to the pool.

I saw Monica on her hands and knees by the back door.

And there, just beyond her, was Skye floating in the pool.

If she hadn't been facedown, I might've thought she'd just fallen asleep in the middle of a morning swim. But her fingers had gone blue, and her hair fanned out behind her, moving like a living thing on the surface of the water.

I moved with the tide of the other girls, through the living room and out onto the back patio. But it was Naomi who first waded in to retrieve her, fully dressed, stepping stiffly down the stairs and into the cold water. With all the tenderness of a mother—as Skye's real mother lay heaving on the patio—Naomi turned Skye over. Her eyes, wide open, were a raw red from the chlorine. Her lips were just parted, as if she had something she wanted to say but died before she could get the words out.

Shiloh waded into the pool, helped Naomi drag Skye from the water. They laid her down on the pool's edge, combed the hair back from her face.

Someone called 911. I don't know why. It was too late, and we knew it.

That was when I saw him: Death, standing on a jagged ridge more than half a mile from the house. He was motionless, facing us; perhaps he'd been there the whole time to watch the scene unfold. But the moment I registered him—a black mote against the bright morning sky—he turned and began to walk away.

I felt a rage in me. Something horrible. A crack or a break, like the sickening crunch of a rolled ankle, a beat of shock, and then white pain after it.

I let myself out through the back gate of the house, stepped barefoot into the desert. The sand was hot beneath my feet, studded with sharp rocks and bristling cacti. I started running anyway, a sudden burst, like I'd launched myself off a starting block. I didn't feel the pain at first, but by the time I caught up to Death, my lungs were on fire and my feet were throbbing, my soles cut deep and bleeding. I caught him by the back of his shirt, clawing at a fistful of fabric, dragging him back.

"You're a coward," I said. "Come back and look at what you've done. Look at what you've taken and explain it. You don't just get to walk away from this. Not this time. Not with her."

I pulled hard again, but Death kept his back to me, his head turned so that I couldn't see his face. But he rolled his shoulders, seemed too thin before my eyes. His chest caved in, bones and ligaments and muscles snapping, a sound like a chorus of knuckles cracking. He seized up, as though his body was struggling to contain the stuff of his soul. When he finally turned to look at me, he was wearing Skye's face. "There's nothing to see."

I blacked out. I must've, because I don't remember him leaving or anything between the moment I saw Skye's face and when I woke up in the dust. Eyes wide open, I stared up at the sun-bleached sky, black spots—like the charred circles of cigarette burns—obscuring the periphery of my vision. My eyes stung like they had sand in them. I squeezed them shut, scrubbed at them with a closed fist, afraid I might've blinded myself staring at the sun.

Shiloh dropped to the ground beside me, breathless, catching me by both shoulders. She spoke to me, but her voice was warped and tinny, slow at first and then altogether too fast, everything coming in garbled spurts of syllables and broken words.

"She's gone," I said, over and over again. "She's gone. He took Skye."

Chapter 23

Shiloh carried me back to the house, cradled to her chest. There were paramedics on the scene when we returned, attempting to pump life back into Skye. Her body looked so frail and small, splayed out on the poolside. I couldn't bear to look and closed my eyes. When I opened them again, I saw Shiloh looming over me, drawing a blanket up to my chin.

"I'm going to fix this," she said. "I promise."

It was the last thing I heard before sleep pulled me under.

When I woke, I didn't know what day it was or how much time had passed. It was blue dark in the bedroom, so I thought it might've been early morning or just after sunset, on the cusp of night. There was no clock, and I got up, disoriented, and wandered into the living room, which was packed to near capacity, both with the girls and a number of well-dressed celebrity types, some vaguely familiar, some not. Monica sat among them, dressed in the same billowy robe she'd been wearing when she found Skye.

Her hair hung tangled down her back, and her eyes were raw, swollen almost shut.

Seeing me, Shiloh got up and led me back to the other girls. They were sitting in the far corner of the living room, huddled around the baby grand piano, clinging to each other as if for warmth. None of them had changed clothes since the night before, and their flowing cotton skirts, bright florals, and ragged vintage denim clashed wildly with the black attire of the other mourners.

"What is all of this?" I asked in a whisper. "Who are all these people?"

"Friends of Monica's," said Shiloh. "Here for the wake."

"The *wake*? How long was I out?"

"Eleven-ish hours?" said Iona, to my shock. "You seemed like you needed the sleep."

What I needed was a tranquilizer to black me out so that I could wake up from this mess back in my own bed in Michigan, where things at least somewhat made sense. It was the first time I'd missed home since joining the girls. The first time I'd ever really wanted to go back.

"What now?" I asked.

"Now we get the fuck out of here," said Riley. "We can't stay."

"But where will we even go?" Naomi demanded, despondent. Her cheeks were crusted with rivulets of dry mascara. Her lips were badly chapped and bleeding. "He took one girl, but he's going to make us choose someone else. He'll come for us no matter what. So I'm not running anymore. I'm going to stay here for Skye, to see her off."

Chloe and Iona nodded in agreement.

"I'm starting to think that you all don't quite grasp the concept of a bargain," Riley snapped, angry now. "We stay here keeping vigil over Skye's body and we'll end up just like her."

Shiloh cut her eyes narrow. "Riley, have some respect—"

"It's true, and you know it—"

"Shut up," said Shiloh, a low threat. The girls were already drawing stares from the rest of those gathered, and their raised voices only made things worse. We didn't belong here. We were the youngest in the room, obvious misfits. Without Skye, it was clear that we weren't wanted.

I could see it in the way Monica stared at us, wide bloodshot eyes wavering with tears. She looked like she wanted to spit or curse at us, but all she did was twist her head away. I realized she must've believed we'd voted for Skye, that we did this to her daughter. And in a way . . . we had.

"I'm with Riley," I said, surprising myself. "I think we should go. We're not wanted here."

"Skye would've wanted us here, and that's enough for me," said Naomi. "We were—*are* family. I'm not just going to leave her now." The girls looked to Naomi, and Naomi looked to Shiloh. "What's it going to be?"

Shiloh stared at the pool as if Skye were still out there, floating. "We can stay for the wake. But the moment it's over, we hit the road."

Skye's wake was a star-studded affair, the way she would've wanted it. A number of C- and even B-list stars drove up from LA for the occasion, pulling into the cracked parking lot of the Palm Springs crematorium in their black SUVs with tinted, paparazzi-proof windows. We did our best to dress for the occasion, wearing long skirts and gowns that we'd procured from antique shops and garage sales during our journey west. The girls who were more comfortable in suits—Shiloh and Riley—opted for tailored dress pants and button-downs with starched collars.

We entered this tacky little chapel off the crematorium—with a dusty red carpet and gold leaf candelabras—to see Skye at the end of its short aisle. She looked like a doll lying in the casket, a rental that was sized too big for her, made to contain someone both older and taller. I was surprised that the casket was open at all. It seemed mawkish to me, somehow wrong. I wondered if Skye would've wanted to be displayed or if these theatrics would've felt as perverted to her as they did to me. All these people gawking over the body of a little girl.

But then, that's the way of these things.

Whether they want to admit it or not, people love dead little girls. Sometimes I wonder if they love them better than living ones.

We sat in the back row of the chapel. There were hymnbooks stuffed into the backs of the pews, and Chloe thumbed through one to busy her shaking hands. Shiloh stared openly at the casket, as if she felt obligated to look. Naomi did the same, weeping in silence. Riley and Iona kept their gazes pinned to the floor.

It was strange to me that a single dead body could make us all so squeamish after everything we'd seen, everything we'd done. But it was different when you knew the person. And that thing in the casket—waxen and swollen—was not our Skye anymore.

The service began with a hymn on an electric organ. We only got three chords into the song before Naomi, racked with sobs, sprang to her feet and fled. We all got up as one and followed her, streaming out of the chapel, leaving Skye behind.

The fight broke out as soon as the last of us stepped outside. Riley turned to Shiloh and said something so nasty it ripped the air right out of my lungs. "Why are you so upset when *you* did this? You put her in that casket."

Naomi stepped forward. "Enough."

But Riley wasn't to be quieted. Not this time. Her upper lip peeled away from her teeth as she stared at Shiloh, disgusted. "Your hands are sticky with blood. But you love it. You love all of this just as much as he does, and that's why he picked you. Because there is nothing you want more than to do this, and you think we all can't see it."

Shiloh didn't defend herself. Didn't argue. She just laughed, dark and disbelieving, as if at the punch line of some horrible cosmic joke.

I'm not sure who threw the first punch. I'm not sure that it mattered. Riley shoved Shiloh so hard her head struck the bricks of the chapel, a gashing blow.

Shiloh's eyes began to roll back into her head. Her eyes fell closed. Somehow she stayed on her feet, clinging to consciousness, and smiled. Blood bubbled from her nostrils, and she wiped her nose clean on the back of her hand, a bright smear. When she spit, red spattered the tops of Riley's boots. "That all you've got?"

No one came between them when they started fighting again. No one dared. Riley dragged Shiloh off the wall, and Shiloh crashed on top of her, throwing punches as Riley thrashed and struggled, pinned to the ground beneath her.

At some point, Riley stopped struggling.

But the blows kept coming.

And then Riley's eyes were closed, and I was half on top of Shiloh, dragging her away. We both hit the ground, sprawling. Shiloh turned to me, and I flinched away as if waiting for her to strike, but the resolve went out of her as she came to, registered what she'd done. She deflated.

"Stop it right now," Naomi pleaded, fresh tears streaming down her cheeks. "You're acting like children."

But they weren't. Their cruelty was well beyond that, and we all knew it. They'd fought like they wanted to kill each other.

Riley managed to push to her feet, hunched over, hands braced on her kneecaps. She, like Shiloh, looked utterly spent. Her face was a mask of contempt as she gazed at Shiloh. "Why don't you just tell her the truth about what really happened to Adeline?"

I froze. My heart pulsed hard—a sharp punch to the backs of my ribs—and then seemed to beat almost in reverse. I looked to Shiloh, who very pointedly did not look at me. "What does she mean?"

When Shiloh didn't answer, Riley wheeled on me, laughing. The tears streamed freely down her cheeks now. She didn't hide them. "You might be the only one who doesn't see, which is ironic because she's screwed you over more than she has anyone else."

"If this is about her and Adeline, I already know," I said, bristling at the implication. I was tired of being treated like a useless appendage, like I didn't know anything about the girls or the group when I'd been traveling with them, becoming a part of them, for weeks.

"Then you know your role in all of this?" Riley asked, a threat in her tone. But she was holding back, baiting me to ask for more. I didn't want to give her the satisfaction, didn't want to believe there was still a chance that I was in the dark. "It was you."

Shiloh froze, face pale. "Riley, please. Don't."

But Riley wouldn't hear her. She kept her gaze on me, malice in her eyes, as if I had caused all of this. Like the one she was really angry at was me and she'd only just realized. "She was set on you before you ever met."

I knew she meant Shiloh without her having to say it. But I wasn't ready to hear it, to believe what I had suspected to be true. I turned to Shiloh, waiting for her to say it, wanting to hear it from her mouth before I was forced to believe it. "What is she talking about? What did you do?"

Shiloh deflated, all the fight gone out of her. If Riley had held a knife to her neck, then and there, I don't think she would've fought back or even flinched.

"Adeline talked about you all the time," said Shiloh. "Listening to her . . . I got curious. That's all it was at first. I looked you up, found your Instagram, before. Before Adeline died, you used to write these captions about your life and running and the way you saw the world, which was strange to me at first, and then it was intriguing, and then . . . I don't know. I guess I didn't want to stop seeing through your eyes. I liked the world as you saw it, and I don't know when that stopped being enough for me, but one day, I realized it wasn't that I wanted to see the world as you. I just . . . wanted you."

Shiloh's voice gave out, and she seemed so small and broken then that, in spite of everything, I wanted to go to her. Comfort her. But in my anger, I didn't move. "The things you said and the way you said them made me feel like someone understood what was going on in my mind. Like someone saw me. I don't know if I've ever felt that way before, about anyone. But it still took me a long time to admit to myself that you were the one I was supposed to be with. Or at least that I was supposed to be with someone who made me feel the way I did when I thought about you, when I read those captions, when I saw your face. I realized that what I felt for Adeline—what I thought I liked most about her—was just the traces of you."

It was a terrible thing to say. Cruel enough to crush someone. To kill them, even.

Chloe clasped a hand tight over her mouth. Iona squeezed her arm, her eyes pinned to the ground like it was too painful to watch this scene unfold. Naomi choked back tears. I wondered if they knew, if it was just Shiloh who'd betrayed me or if it was all of them too.

"Y-you broke her heart," I whispered, understanding fully now. The shock dulled my emotions so that I felt almost blank, like this was happening to someone else, a stranger that I didn't know. "You broke her by choosing *me*?"

"I didn't mean to," said Shiloh, and her voice broke. "I swear it. But one night, she caught me on one of the phones. Saw me looking at your posts, and she just . . . knew. Maybe she had for some time; I don't know. But that night, she processed it. It hit her, I guess."

"What hit her, Shiloh?"

"That I wasn't meant for her. I was meant for you."

I felt like the breath had been ripped out of my lungs. "You didn't even *know* me."

"But I did. At least, I knew enough, through your writings and through her. Adeline talked about you all the time, Roslyn, and the way she talked about you—I don't know . . ."

I didn't care about that anymore. I didn't want to hear it. "What did she say when she found out?" I asked. In the moment, it was the only question that mattered. The only thing that I cared about was my sister and the way I'd broken her heart without ever really realizing it.

Shiloh drew a hand through her hair. She looked like a ruin of the girl I'd first met weeks before. "She told us that she was going to leave. And then she did."

As she said this, for the first time, I saw the truth: I had killed my own sister, whether I'd intended to or not.

And she'd hated me for it.

My legs gave out, and I scraped the skin off the bottom of my palms trying to catch myself on the concrete. The girls rushed forward, calling my name, the sound warped and garbled like we were all underwater.

They shook my shoulders, tried to bring me back to myself, but I was beyond them now. Beyond everyone and everything, except for maybe Death. I could feel him, closer to me than the girls were, and more real. But he didn't show himself. He didn't need to. In that moment, we were one and the same. I had killed my sister just as surely as he had.

Chapter 24

We drove back to the house in total silence. All the mourners were gone, so it was just us and Monica. I was glad she wasn't alone, but I couldn't help but wonder if she even wanted the company, especially if that company took the form of the very girls who were, more or less, responsible for her daughter's death.

But Monica had softened in the aftermath of the wake. To my surprise, she welcomed us back just as she had that first night when Skye was still with us. We ate from whatever was in the fridge and pantry—boiled eggs, stale crackers, brown bananas mashed with a fork and smeared across slices of gluten-free freezer bread. None of it tasted like anything much. All my senses were still dampened, my ears ringing faintly, my hands numb, my vision prone to spirals of vertigo whenever I turned my head.

I realized, in a kind of distant way, that I was having a panic attack. Not the kind that Adeline had suffered—violent affairs with a lot of crying and hyperventilating, puking sometimes if things got bad enough. No, what I was experiencing was something more muted, removed. Like I was being pulled slowly out of my body.

"Come sit with me," said Monica, and I felt her hand at my back, a soft pressure.

I came to and saw that she was standing over me, all the rest of the girls looking on with concern. I scraped back from the kitchen table and stood up, letting Monica guide me to the living room. I settled on the couch, and Monica limped across the room to the piano bench, her knees giving a little beneath the weight of her, which, frankly, wasn't much. She was so small that it almost scared me. I hadn't noticed until that moment how frail she really was under all those layers of shawls and scarves and silk.

"Are you all right?" Her gaze was searching, her eyes raw and swollen from crying; the dried tears had formed crusting tracks down her hollow cheeks.

I realized that I should have been the one comforting her. She was the one who had lost a daughter, and I'd had almost a year to come to terms with my own sister's death. But I knew full well, from my own experience grappling with grief, that there was nothing a person could say to ease a pain like that. Nothing anyone said to me had ever helped.

I decided it was best to stay quiet, thinking Monica would do the same. But then she spoke in a scraping whisper. "I hope she felt it all, in the end. She would've wanted that. You only die once, after all. She would've wanted to make the most of it, to witness every moment. To relish it, even. Skye was always so curious that way. Even about bad things. Especially about the bad things. Maybe that's why she found her footing with the girls."

It was a grim hope, maybe a cruel one. Skye was young, and I couldn't imagine what she felt in those final moments—the terror of the water filling her lungs, sinking alone to the bottom of the pool, to her death. What kind of mother would want their child to experience that? But then, Monica was no normal mother, and Skye was not a normal daughter.

Monica raised her gaze to me, searching. "Why are you with them? You're not like them. Not made of the same stuff. I know you try to hide it, but it's obvious. You don't belong. I saw it the moment you first walked through the door."

"People keep telling me that," I said, with no real defensiveness this time. I didn't have anything to prove to anyone anymore. I knew the truth of what I was. And the truth was terrible. "But you're right. I'm not like them. They're full of life. Skye was full of life. But not me. I'm less like the girls than I am like Death. All I do is bring pain and chaos wherever I go, sometimes without even realizing it. I did it to my sister—I see that now, and I know that's why she's gone."

Monica stared down at her hands, her expression pained. "I promised Death my first child, but I never actually expected to have one. I was your age, or thereabouts, and sick when I made my bargain with him. Really sick. The kind of sickness you don't recover from. I had stopped fighting it, and all the strength I had left to spare was channeled into this *anger*. I was so mad my life had been stolen from me, and when Death came . . . that anger turned to desperation. I think I would've sold out the world to live."

My mind scrambled to process what she'd just confessed. That Skye had been the collateral, the person she'd offered up to Death to spare her own life.

"I took precautions, of course. All these medications to keep me from having a child. I even tried to find a surgeon who would take my womb, but no one wanted to do it. They couldn't understand why a young girl with her whole life ahead of her would want to do something like that to herself. They didn't want to be responsible for my mistake. If they only knew." Monica shook her head with disgust. "Anyway. I met a boy. Death took him, too, years ago now, and even if I'd known that back then, I think I still would've fallen for him, been with him. We didn't mean to have Skye. I'd told him under no circumstances would I ever have a child. But she just . . . happened, despite all my precautions. Skye was a miracle. I didn't know I was pregnant with her until I was laboring in the bathtub alone. I delivered her myself. Pulled her out with my own two hands."

The idea of that, of Monica giving birth alone in a bathtub, was both gruesome and fitting. It made sense that a girl like Skye was dragged into the world that way. "Jesus."

Monica only smiled. "I know it sounds crazy, but I was happy. And that happiness was dangerous, because it blinded me to reality. Deluded me into believing that it would last forever. I forced myself to forget the deal I'd struck with Death so that I could cling to that joy for a little bit longer. I thought things would be okay, and for a while, they were. They were better than okay, actually. My career started taking off. I wed the man I loved. We'd created this perfect little girl. Everything felt like it was going to be okay until the day my husband took his life, leaving me alone with Skye. And I thought surely that was sacrifice enough, surely Death would be satisfied. But, of course, he wasn't. He never is. He didn't show himself to me again until the night that Skye went into anaphylactic shock just before her third birthday. She'd developed an allergy to nuts, which I found out as she was suffocating.

"I rushed her to the hospital, where she very nearly died. They managed to stop the reaction just in time. As soon as she was stabilized, Death appeared at the foot of her hospital bed. He told me that he would take her soon, though he wouldn't say when, even though I begged to know how much time I had left with her. I wanted him to at least give me that. But, as you well know, he's not particularly accommodating. He left that night, and afterward . . ." Monica shook her head. Whatever she was going to say, she couldn't bring herself to. "When Shiloh and Naomi showed up years later, I knew that it was time for me to let her go, knew that Death was making good on his promise to take her from me. I was relieved, to be honest. I'd thought that, when he did come for her, it would be final, the end of her life. And it was, in a way. I knew the moment I gave her over to the girls that she would never be mine again. Our life together, as I knew it, was over. So I let her go. Sometimes that's all you can do."

"You're wrong," I heard myself say. "You're her mom. You should've fought for her. Even if it was pointless. That's what she would've done for you."

Monica hung her head in shame. I couldn't believe she was the same bold and glamorous woman I'd envied just days before. I saw that all of it—the clothes and the money—was just a distraction, really, a front for her cowardice. "It wouldn't have made a difference either way."

"Skye said otherwise," I whispered. "She said that, if we came here, you would teach us how to fight back. That you had answers."

"She was mistaken."

"Then why did she sound so convinced?"

Monica dragged a hand back through her hair. "Because I only told her half the truth. I never told her that she was what I traded for my own life. I didn't want her to hate me."

"She wouldn't have. Skye was all love."

Just then, there was a sharp cry; both Monica and I startled at the sound. Chloe burst into the living room, panicked.

"What's going on?" I asked, springing to my feet, certain that Death had returned to finish off the rest of us. A part of me was almost relieved, if only because I was so ready for it to be over, for the dread to end. "Is he here?"

Chloe shook her head. "Shiloh's locked herself in the bathroom, and we can't get her to come out."

The room reeled. I rushed forward, catching myself on the wall to stay on my feet, sprinting through the living room and shouldering my way past the girls and down the hall to the guest bathroom at its end. Naomi and Riley were there, taking turns banging on the door. No sound came from the other side, even when I shouted Shiloh's name, begged her to let us in.

I felt like the floor dropped beneath me, and all at once, I was back in Michigan, ripped through time to the day that Adeline first disappeared. I was back in that hallway, banging on the door, crying out for my sister who was already dead. "Open the door. Please open the door. Please—"

Riley—her bruised eye screwed shut from the fight at the wake—gave the door a vicious kick. Then another. It burst open and struck the wall with a sound like a gunshot. And there was Shiloh, curled fetal on the floor. There were open pill packets strewn about her, plastic bottles with the tops pried off. Froth collected at the corners of her mouth. Her eyes were closed.

I screamed.

Chapter 25

We kept vigil in the waiting room of the hospital. They gave us just two updates throughout the night—one to tell us Shiloh was alive, and then a second, hours later, to let us know she was stable. The rest we gathered from conjecture. I knew from past experiences with Adeline that hospitals tended to keep you for some time when they had reason to believe you were a threat to yourself. Most likely, Shiloh would be transferred to some psych ward for further observation and care. I didn't know what that meant for us or our deal with Death. But I had a bad feeling. We knew that Death still expected us to choose someone. He was strict that way, unrelenting. Skye's drowning, as horrible as it was, was just a warning shot really. But we still needed to fulfill our task—our most terrible and important dispatch—by killing one of our own.

Death was near. I could feel it in the bathroom when I forced my fingers down Shiloh's throat, made her bring up the pills she'd swallowed down. I could feel it when I got in the ambulance with her, and we all rode to the Palm Springs hospital. I felt it in the waiting room too. A kind of certainty that this journey we'd been on with Death was nearing its end.

At daybreak, when most of the girls were eating breakfast in the cafeteria, one of the nurses ducked into the waiting room to tell us that Shiloh was awake and ready to take visitors. Riley, still bitter from the fight the day before, deferred to me. I got up stiffly and followed the nurse back into the ward, feeling like the last person that should be by her side. I had barely looked her in the eye since I found Adeline's phone, unable to wrap my mind around the betrayal or even be near her without feeling like I was coming undone. As I walked to her hospital room, trailing the nurse, I didn't know how to comfort her, or if I even could.

Shiloh was sitting upright in bed when I entered, and when she gazed up at me, I saw her as I had that first night we'd met across the pool as if dragged back through time. I'd known then, from that first moment, that she had the power to break me if she'd wanted to. And now here we were.

I came to stand by the bed. Shiloh's wrists weren't cuffed to the guardrails, but I noticed that there was a nurse in the room, sitting in a chair by the bathroom.

"You can go now," said Shiloh, nodding to her.

The nurse frowned but got up anyway, told me to ring for her before I left the room.

In her absence, Shiloh was quiet for a long time, like she was expecting me to speak. But I didn't have anything to say to her. It felt like all my words were spent. I had nothing else to give except my presence there by her bed.

"They're trying to keep me," she said at last, peering at me, tentative almost, every word a careful test like she was afraid, if she said the wrong thing, she'd chase me off.

"Why did you do it?"

"I had to. If I didn't, if I *don't*, it'll be one of you guys. Death took Skye already. I'm not going to watch you be plucked off one by one until there's no one left. It's my responsibility to end this."

"You were overdosing. You were going to die, Shiloh—"

"I don't think he would've allowed that. He wants me, maybe even needs me. I thought I could force his hand. If I'd died, I'd have fulfilled his demand even if he brought me back. But if he called my bluff and I did die as a result, then at least you all would've been safe. I would've protected you the way I should have Skye." Her voice cracked. She scrubbed at her eyes before the tears could fall.

In another life, one less cruel than this one, I would've taken her hand. I would've cradled her face, brushed her tears away. I would've told her that I was less afraid of Death than I was of losing her. But I knew that Shiloh wasn't mine to keep. That whatever existed between us was less than love . . . It had to be, because if this was love, why did it hurt so much?

I swallowed my own tears, drew a hand through my hair. I couldn't remember the last time I had been this tired. "You can't just strike out on your own without telling anyone, all right? We're a group. A family. And last night, you turned your back on all of that. For too long you've been icing people out, doing things on your own. Keeping me in the dark, especially. That whole thing with Adeline and you and me. You should've told me, Shiloh. Why didn't you say something?" I could barely get the words out, my throat so tight and swollen with the tears I was holding back.

"I didn't want you to have to carry it," said Shiloh, looking sick with herself. "I thought you were dealing with enough. I didn't want to add guilt to the mix. I don't think that Adeline would've wanted that either. I mean, if she had, she would've told you before she died—"

"Adeline doesn't get to decide what I can handle, and neither do you. You know, I'm not half as weak as either of you think I am. I already lost the person I loved most in the world. Do you think that anything else could break me? I watched them carry my sister's corpse out of the woods, rotting in that body bag. Then I went to the morgue and—" I cut myself short. "I saw it all, and it wasn't enough, because I still don't know what happened to her that night in the woods. I need the truth so I can finally let go of this. I feel like I've earned it."

"You have," said Shiloh. "You deserve better."

I knew she was talking about more than just Adeline and Death.

A nurse stepped into the room then, clutching a clipboard to her chest. "Shiloh, your father is here. Should I show him up?"

"My . . . *father*—" Shiloh's eyes flashed wide with horror.

I sprang to my feet, shouldered past the nurse and into the hall even as Shiloh called me back. I pressed the elevator button, but there was no cabin, so I took the stairs down to the first floor, taking the steps three or even four at a time, tripping over the tops of my own sneakers.

I burst into the waiting room, but he wasn't there. In fact, none of the girls were, and the sight of those empty chairs seized me with panic. I backtracked so fast I almost fell, pushed down the hall, and went to the cafeteria. But a quick scan of the mostly empty tables was enough for me to confirm that the girls weren't there either. I turned back, began to retrace my steps, when I saw him standing at the end of that empty ward.

"How about we have a chat?"

Chapter 26

I don't know why I followed Death into the chapel. Maybe because I knew deep down that I didn't have a choice. That no matter what I did or where I went, he would always haunt and hunt me.

The chapel itself was small. Empty benches were arranged in short rows on either side of a narrow aisle. There was a small altar at the front of the room beneath a little stained glass window that offered a glimpse of a courtyard garden. The air smelled very faintly of incense.

Death claimed the bench nearest the altar. I sat down beside him on the opposite side of the aisle. I wondered, in passing, if I had come in here just to die.

The thought didn't raise as much fear as I expected it to. I was more ready for this than I'd realized, to make a sacrifice, to see my sister on the other side.

"Where are they?" I asked. "Where are the rest of the girls?"

"They're alive and well." Death flexed the fingers of his right hand slowly, watching in apparent fascination as the tendons pulled taut. "Though they did get into something of a spat, I think. The hospital nurses had them take their fight out to the parking lot. Apparently, there was a lot of yelling involved. They were so absorbed that they didn't see me come in, which is for the best, I think. I wanted the opportunity to talk to Shiloh alone. But now that you're here, I think you'll do just fine."

"What do you want to discuss?"

Death steepled his fingers, aligning them very carefully and with some awkwardness. He had an almost childlike demeanor, the clumsiness of someone who hadn't resided within his body for very long.

"You resent me," said Death. "More than the other girls do."

It was strange to hear him put words to what I had felt for so long. This despise of him, for what he'd done and taken from me. For the ways I'd been changed by him without my will or consent. It was evil.

"The other girls didn't lose a sister to you recently. They didn't have to work for the person—"

He cut me short. "I'm not a person."

"Fine, the *thing* that took her."

Death didn't like being called a thing. I could tell from the way his eyebrows pinched together in a frown that seemed more petulant than truly frightening. "Is that how you really feel?"

"That's the reality," I whispered. "You know that. You said it yourself. I didn't want to live enough to do this, to kill people on your behalf. The only reason I'm here is because of what you promised me if I did."

"But is that still true?" Death narrowed his eyes. "Once I tell you the truth, will you really be content to turn your back on all of this, live a normal life?"

I faltered. I'd mostly avoided thinking about what would happen to me after fulfilling my end of the deal with Death. I had been so focused on finding out what happened to Adeline. Her, her death, and my grief were like a fog too thick to see through. I'd forgotten there was a horizon on the other side of it. "I—I don't know."

"They came to love you, you know. The girls." Was it jealousy I sensed when he said it? "It was beautiful to watch."

I didn't like how he spoke in the past tense, as if it was a thing that had been and not something that was now.

"Human beings are so fascinating to me. You have these instincts coded into the intrinsic makeup of your being: the drive to live, and to live well, at that. You're all so loyal to your dreams, no matter how far they are out of reach. But there's an error in your makeup. A desire that supersedes your survival instinct. Do you know what that is?"

I shook my head.

"It's freedom. I put immortality in the palm of your hand, and you turn up your nose at it. Why? Because you'd rather live a short, free life than live forever under my care."

"Under your boot, you mean."

Death allowed for this insult with a smile.

"We don't want to be bound to you any longer. And you're right, I think some of us, maybe most of us, would rather find freedom in death than continue on as participants in this sick experiment."

"A sick experiment that *you* agreed to."

"You coerced us."

"I gave you all a choice." His eyes grew bright with sudden anger, motes of fire burning in the dark of his irises where his pupils should've been. "One that others would *gladly* kill for. Do you know how rare this is? What exists between me and you? Do you think it's a normal thing, to converse with your own demise? What all of you fail to see is that there is no greater freedom than that which I've given to you already."

I knew he expected me to cower, to shrink in the wake of his anger. But I refused to give ground. I had already seen the worst of him, in the cold corpse of my dead sister. "Don't pretend this is charity. You didn't give us anything. We suffer to do your work. We're not like you. We have feelings and souls. We carry guilt with us always, and it's heavy."

"Then put it down," he said, and the light in his eyes dimmed to black. "I'm not making you carry it any longer. Put it down and forgo the truth about your sister. Let her go, and you're free of me. For now, at least."

"And what about the others?" I asked, but I knew the answer. They were bound to him in a way that I wasn't. I could turn my back on this, but they couldn't, not without sacrificing their lives. "They deserve the chance to live their own lives, free of you."

"The girls have to make their own choices. Hopefully, they're not as foolish as you are. I suspect that most will come around.

They're kind girls deep down. But even kind girls can be selfish. If they know what's good for them, they'll choose well, and they'll be safe with me for as long as they're in my service. That much I can promise you."

Someone spoke from behind us. "That's not enough."

I turned to see Shiloh standing in the doorway of the chapel. And she wasn't alone. The rest of the girls were behind her. Iona stepped forward first to take Shiloh by the hand. Then Chloe, gazing at Death as she had at those men across the parking lot, like she was ready to tear him apart with her teeth if need be. Even Riley stood her ground, hands locked into fists at her sides.

Then Naomi shouldered to the front of the ranks, making a shield out of her own body. "I would die a thousand painful deaths before I'd let you take another one of these girls."

I could've sworn that Death looked almost . . . afraid.

He stood up, and he was taller than he was when he'd first sat down. The harsh cut of his figure seemed to blot out the light cast in through the window, darkening the room. "I'll give you twelve hours to reconsider. If you fail to change your minds, then you all will die tonight. Well, not all of you." He turned to me. "You'll remain." He put a hand on my shoulder, and when he did, the room emptied, all the other girls gone, just him and me alone.

I tore away from him, terrified, and the vision ended. "N-no—"

"Twelve hours." It was as close as he'd come to yelling; his voice seemed to suck all the air from the room. "If you haven't come around by then, you live, and they die."

The girls froze, breathless. I waited for them to recant, to plead for their lives or else beg for forgiveness, but they didn't. They stood silent, with tears streaming down their faces. Even in the wake of Death himself, they refused to cower.

He could have killed us all. In the moment, I half expected him to.

But instead, he just lowered his head. A father disappointed by his daughters.

"We'll talk again soon," he said, stepped into the hallway, and was gone.

Chapter 27

As soon as Death left, the girls came undone. Riley kicked one of the benches hard enough to topple it. Chloe sat down on the floor, pulled her knees to her chest, and cried. Iona rubbed circles into her back, murmuring the sort of nothing promises that people make when things are bad enough, little lies to fill the silence ... take the edge off the fear.

"What now?" Naomi asked Shiloh, her eyes brimming with tears. A few of them spilled, and blue eyeshadow bled down her cheeks. "There has to be something else we can do."

Shiloh dragged a hand through her hair. She shook her head. "I—I don't know."

A message played over the intercom about a missing patient.

"We need to get out of here," I said, turning to Shiloh. "They're looking for you, and they're sure to transfer you to a psych ward if they find you. We need to go. *Now.*"

We managed to navigate out of the hospital, bursting through a fire exit to a chorus of sirens. We sprinted to the pickup truck, which the girls had driven last night, chasing after the ambulance. There wasn't room for all of us, so Chloe and Iona rode in the bed. Riley told everyone to hold on and peeled out of the parking lot so fast the tires burned.

And then we were on the road again, back to Monica's. The front door was unlocked, but the house was dark. She wasn't home. A note left on the kitchen island explained that she'd gone to visit a friend.

"Well," said Riley, sitting hard on the couch, "I guess this is as good a place to die as any. And who knows, maybe we'll have an audience. Skye? Can you hear us? If you're not haunting this place, you should. You'll get quite a show when Death comes to slaughter us all tonight."

"So we're just giving up?" Iona looked to Shiloh for answers, but there were none to be found with her. She turned to me next. "This is the end?"

I racked my brain for an answer, some hope to cling to.

And then . . . I found it.

"When Death touched me that first time—to give me his power—I felt like . . . I was falling through time," I said, whispering, afraid that Death could hear me. And maybe he could. Maybe we would all drop dead the moment the words fell from my mouth, and that would be it for all of us.

I found the bravery to speak anyway, determined to say this even if it was the last thing I ever did. "I saw Adeline when he touched me. I saw her dying in the playhouse, almost like I was there. The vision of her was just as vivid and real as you all are standing before me now."

"I had a vision like that too," said Iona. "I got dragged into the past, to my grandmother's death."

"I saw my cat dying," said Naomi in a little whisper. "When he put the touch of Death in my hand, it was like I was there with her, under the house where we found her. It didn't make sense to me. It was years ago, but it was so real—"

"What of it?" said Riley. She didn't mean to be unkind, but we were running out of time, and she was impatient. I couldn't blame her for it. "What difference does a bunch of visions make, and how are they going to save us?"

"What if they weren't just visions?" I asked. "What if they were real?"

A quiet fell over the girls as they considered my idea.

Shiloh spoke, her voice thin and ragged. I could tell she was weak from the overdose, tapping the last of her energy just to speak. "What are you trying to say?"

I thought back to that first night with Death, when he put the power of his touch in my palm, showed me Adeline in the playhouse. "Death told me that he doesn't experience time in the linear way that we do. He's lived through many eons—out of order or simultaneously, I don't know. The point is he's not a thing of flesh but spirit. He can be where he wants when he wants to be there. When everyone meets the same inevitable end, how you get there or when stops mattering."

Naomi's eyebrows knit together. She reached for me and faltered, her hand trembling in the air. "Roslyn, look, you're tired. Maybe—"

"Hear me out." I wheeled to face them all. "I saw Adeline when he touched me, in that playhouse where she died. If I touch him again and go back to that moment, what if . . . what if I'm the one who kills her? And when I do—"

"You fulfill his demand," said Shiloh, nodding as the realization came to her. "He wanted us to kill one of our own."

The girls went wide eyed as they processed what she was saying.

"You want to go back in time with Death and *kill* your own sister?" Riley asked, skeptical. "That's your grand plan?"

"You really think you could do that?" Naomi asked, eyeing me. "You think you can kill your own sister?"

I couldn't answer that question. The reality was that I didn't know. I would never know until the moment I met her there, at the scene of her death. Part of me felt like I was still there with her, like I always would be. Unless . . . I found a way to set us both free.

Shiloh shook her head. "And what if he refuses? What if he just kills you with his touch?"

"Then you all live. Right?" I managed a weak smile even though I felt like crying. "If I die when I touch him, then I've sacrificed myself. Fulfilled the final dispatch."

"I'm not going to let you do this," said Shiloh.

"Well, you don't have a choice." I sat down beside her, made sure our gazes were level. "This is my life, Shiloh. I'll do what I want with it."

Tears stood in her eyes, threatening to spill over. "Roslyn. Please just—"

But I wouldn't hear her. "No, you don't get to choose for me anymore."

And I meant it. I was done letting others chart the course of my life. If it was going to end, it would happen on my terms. No one, not Shiloh or Adeline or even Death himself, could take that from me. I wouldn't let them.

"She's right." I turned to see Riley standing behind me. "If she wants to do it, we should let her. The way I see it, this is the best way forward." Riley turned to me now, resolute despite the fact that she was shaking. I don't think I had ever really noticed just how afraid she was, how young she looked when she wasn't hiding behind her near-perpetual scowl. "I've got your back. I'll make sure you can reach her if it's the last thing I do."

"You realize that it might be, right?" I asked, wanting to be sure she knew what she was getting into. What this might mean for her.

"I'm ready," said Riley, and the other girls followed suit, offering their assurances and promises. They were ready to fight back, tired of waiting for their futures to be decided for them.

Death was right about them, about all of us. We would rather die free than live under his shadow.

Shiloh drew forward, conflicted. I could tell that she hated this, that she wanted to drag us back from the brink. That she blamed herself. I wanted so badly to take the guilt away from her, but I knew that I couldn't.

"So, what, we just wait for him here?" Chloe asked.

"No," I said. "No more waiting. I'm sick of being a sitting duck. Death said that he'd give us twelve hours, so let's make the most of the time we have left. So that, even if we die tomorrow, we'll have lived well today."

"And what does that look like?" Naomi asked, the idea so distant to her, to all of us. We'd had our fun on the road, sure. But we had always been riding the swift tides of Death's agenda, going from one dispatch to the next. We were free from that now, and the idea was almost startling. What was there to do with a day that might well be your last one?

"I want to go to the ocean," I said, and then, a little embarrassed, "I've never actually seen it. Not for real, anyway. I'd always planned to go with Adeline; she promised me this big cross-country road trip, from the East Coast all the way out to LA and then back again. An eighteenth-birthday trip and gift for me. But, of course, that won't be happening. I'd still like to see it, though. I know it's a bit of a hike—"

"It's about two hours down the highway," said Shiloh. "Three if there's traffic. But we can manage it."

And just like that, it was decided.

Chapter 28

We made the most of our last day. As soon as we'd decided on a plan, we wrote a brief note to say goodbye to Monica and hit the road, taking just the RV and truck, leaving the station wagon behind in the driveway. There was some debate about what beach to go to, but ultimately, we decided to push west toward Newport Beach, one of the closest to Palm Springs. We'd only made it halfway there when one of the tires on the RV blew out.

I was inside when it happened. We were on the highway, and there was a horrible sound—the painful scream of metal on metal—and then a sharp jolt that threw us out of our seats.

Riley cried out, struggling to regain control of the RV. "Holy shit!"

There was a steep drop-off on the side of the highway, a wide gully between us and a large construction site. The yellow dirt blurred past the windows as the RV drifted right, careening toward the guardrail, and for a sick moment, I was certain we'd plunge straight through it. There was a spray of sparks, and Riley wrenched the emergency brake, and we all snapped forward. I crashed into the kitchen cabinets, cups and bowls raining down around me. Chloe lurched forward, slamming her head on the countertop as the RV ground to a wheezing stop.

I thought we would die, thought the guardrail would give and we'd wreck in the gully. I thought that Death would appear a split moment before the RV imploded into a ball of raging flames and we would all burn, like Corbin, in a gruesome tragedy of his design.

The door of the RV burst open. I froze in terror, but it was just Shiloh. She went to me first and then the others, checking to make sure everyone was okay. By some miracle, Chloe was the only one injured. There was an ugly bruise forming on her forehead where she'd struck the countertop, and we debated among ourselves whether or not we should take her to the hospital. Her pupils were the same size, and she knew what month it was, so it didn't seem like she was concussed. But we were all on edge, with Death's threat hanging over our heads. What if he planned to pluck us off one by one? What if Chloe was bleeding out from the brain right now—a deadly hemorrhage?

"You're paranoid," she said, holding a pack of frozen spinach to her swelling temple. "I'm fine. We don't have time for a hospital detour. We need to get to that beach. Let's go."

We took her word for it. But when Riley attempted to fit a new tire on the RV, we realized that the damage was more extensive than we'd thought. A bit of metal had twisted itself around the axel when we'd run over it, gashing the underside of the RV, making it undriveable even if we changed the back tire.

"She's done for," said Riley, wiping sweat from her brow. It was brutally hot, even with the wind from the cars streaking past us on the highway.

So we piled into the pickup and set off. Abandoning the RV on the side of the road felt a lot like leaving one of our own behind, and I turned to watch as it shrank into the distance and disappeared.

Shiloh rerouted us off the highway and onto a small exit off the road. We were still about forty minutes away from the beach and decided to get off the highway to avoid the traffic. I sat shotgun in the pickup truck, Shiloh behind the wheel; despite our protests, she'd been determined to drive. The space between us felt charged and narrow, and even after everything, a part of me wanted to lean into her, forget the rest. But I refused to let my own body betray me.

We pulled around a tight turn, and there it was. The ocean, dark and glistening, white-capped waves almost as tall as I was breaking against the shoreline with a roar. I'd seen big water before, spent my share of spring breaks on the coast of Lake Michigan, but the ocean was different. Hungrier and more frightening. The sight of it—the vastness and power—stole the breath from my lungs.

Before the truck pulled to a full stop, we got out and ran for the water, kicking off our shoes and stripping out of our clothes as we ran down the beach. The bravest girls—Chloe and Iona—plunged into the surf headfirst in nothing but their underwear. I ran with them but stopped just short of the waves to take it all in. The view was sweeping, and I felt pulled by it, as if I were sliding down the shore as the waves rushed and swirled at my ankles.

Shiloh came to stand beside me, sliding her hands into the pockets of her jeans. She looked out over the ocean, eyes narrowed against the sun. "So? Is it everything you thought it would be?"

"It's all right. As good a place to die as any."

"You know, we had a beach day when Adeline was traveling with us. We went south, toward Florida, to the prettiest beach you've ever seen. Better even than this one. The waters were clear blue; you could see straight down to the bottom. It was stunning."

I smiled, imagining Adeline in the water with Iona and Chloe, the rolling waves lifting her off her feet. How she would've laughed, even in the wake of the biggest ones that charged the shore with a roar. "I bet she loved it."

"She would've if she'd come with us. But Adeline wouldn't go, wouldn't even get near it. She told us to drop her off at a mall in town, and she stayed there all day until we came back for her."

"What? Why? She always wanted to see the ocean."

"She was waiting for you." Shiloh kept her eyes on the water when she said it. "She said she didn't want to experience it for the first time with anyone but you."

I felt the tears coming then, a pressure in my throat that I tried and failed to choke back. Adeline was never one to deny herself any pleasure, certainly not on my behalf. It didn't matter what she wanted or if I stood in the way of it. She'd always gotten what she wanted. Or at least, that's what I'd thought. "Did she really say that?"

Shiloh nodded. "She was adamant. We tried to get her to come with us, but she refused. She always had this space for you that she held close. There was no future she imagined for herself that didn't have you in it, and I think she wanted you to know that, even if she couldn't say it, if she didn't know exactly how."

I was crying now in a way I hadn't for some time, the tears hot and angry, streaking my cheeks, dripping off my chin and into the ocean.

Shiloh turned to me then, a hand raised to my face. But she faltered, thought better of it. "Are you okay?"

I nodded, wiped my tears on my arm, but it was no use. They kept coming. "We just took so much from each other, and we were so jealous and so resentful, especially at the end. Sometimes I think I hated her as much as I loved her, and I loved her a lot."

"You did the best you could."

"I want that to be true. I really do. But I could've given more. That night before she left, we had a fight. Our worst one. Ever. I don't even know how it started, really. It was stupid at first, or it seemed that way until we were screaming at each other. Saying the sort of things you can't take back."

"Like what?"

I considered ignoring that question. I had never been able to bring myself to say or even think the things I had spit at Adeline that night in the midst of my anger and hurt. "I told her that I was tired of her being so sick. I said that there was no one, not even me, who could love her out of the misery of being who and what she was and that I was tired of trying. That wasn't even the worst of it."

With her eyes narrowed against the glare of the sun, Shiloh looked almost pained. "What was?"

I let myself remember for the first time since Adeline disappeared, the words coming back to me so clearly, like a past version of me was speaking them aloud: *Why do you take so much from me? Every single day, you drain everyone in this house of their time and their concern and their energy. And then you just sit here, useless, watching all of us live and suffer in your stead because you're too weak, or maybe just too fucking selfish, to take accountability for your own misery.*

And then Adeline's sobs, broken little sounds, small and animal.

I couldn't bear to listen then, had left her alone on the floor of her bedroom coming undone. But I heard her now, made myself listen, until the memories faded into the rush and pull of the waves.

I closed my eyes for a moment, and when I opened them again, I turned back to Shiloh. "I made sure she knew all the ways she'd failed me. I think, as screwed up as it was, I wanted to punish her in that moment. I wanted to hurt her, and I did. I wish I'd known then that those were the last words I'd ever say to her. I'd give anything to take them back."

The wind blew my hair in front of my eyes. This time, Shiloh let herself touch me, pulling my curls out of my face, tucking them carefully behind the shell of my ear. She held me for a moment, a hand at my cheek so that I couldn't turn away. "You need to forgive yourself."

"I can't," I said, frustrated that she didn't, couldn't understand. "I can't, because the guilt and grief are all tied up together. I can't untangle the two, and even if I could, I don't want to, because that's all I have left of her now, and if I let that go, then she's gone. Really gone, and there's nothing I can do to get her back. So I'd rather keep it. Even if it hurts. Even if it kills me."

Shiloh dropped her hand. She was quiet for a long time, watching the waves roll. "If you want to punish yourself, that's your choice. But don't delude yourself into believing that you're doing it for her. I might not have known Adeline as well as you did, but I know that she wanted you happy. She wanted it so badly that, even when she was staring down her own death, she begged me to make sure you were okay. It was her dying wish. Are you really going to deny her, Roslyn?"

In the distance, the sun hung above the water like a charm. In its light, the other girls seemed to glow. It was so easy to imagine Adeline among them, where she belonged. But she wasn't here today.

I was.

So I made a choice. Not for myself, but for Adeline. I decided to make the most of the time I had left.

For a few hours, everything felt good and right and perfect. We swam and made pitiful sandcastles. We told jokes and recounted the best stories from our travels thus far. There was a diner just down the coast, less than a mile away, and Riley returned with milkshakes so thick we couldn't suck them through our straws and greasy paper bags full of fried seafood—scallops and fish, clam strips and shrimp, skinny little smelt fried whole—which we ate while the ocean licked at our toes.

The sun carved its path across the sky, sinking low to the water, disappearing, and just like that, our last day was over. In the darkness that followed, we waited for Death.

And Death came. We saw him walking down the beach, a black figure wrapped in a storm of sand.

He stopped just short of us. The sand went still. His expression was placid, the corners of his lips slightly upturned into a smile that seemed cruel in the moment, but there was no real venom in it.

The girls all scrambled to their feet, but I shouldered my way to the front, standing beside Shiloh. I reached out to give her hand a small squeeze, but it felt cold and dead in my grasp. When I looked at her, I saw her expression, blank with grief . . . and hopelessness. And I realized that she thought this was the end, my last day—maybe hers too.

Taking that first step toward Death was one of the bravest things I'd ever done. I took a second one and felt a sharp tug—Shiloh's fingers grasping onto mine, attempting to drag me back. I turned to her. "Let me do this. It's the only thing I want."

I meant it.

The way I saw it then, the distance between me and Death was the distance between me and my sister. He might as well have been wearing her face. He could've been her in the flesh, for all it mattered to me in that moment. I knew that I had to go, that whatever was on the other side of this would be closer to her, and that was enough for me.

I needed to put this to rest. Even if the cost was my life.

I tore free of Shiloh's grasp, and Death cocked his head, perplexed.

I stepped forward. "The first time you touched me, you sent me back to the night my sister died. I want you to take me back so I can take her life and fulfill your request that we kill one of our own."

There was a long beat as Death considered my sacrifice. I didn't breathe as I waited, watching, staring into the swirling black of his irises, that pinprick of light in the center of them.

I braced myself for the worst. Waited to die. And when I was certain it would happen, when I said my silent goodbyes, Death's mouth curved into a smile. I knew then that I had him, that I'd baited him with a scenario too intriguing, too twisted to refuse.

"Very well," he said.

I didn't see him step forward, but my fingers seared with pain as his hand locked around mine. And then it was as though we were ripped backward down the beach and through time itself, the ocean blurring, the sand shifting beneath our feet, kicking up into burning sheets and torrents, blinding me.

I heard the distant shouts of my friends, Shiloh screaming my name, as I left my body behind.

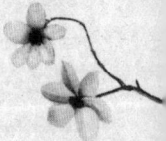

Chapter 29

We fell through a hundred thousand deaths. Children sucked from their beds by storm winds, soldiers with arrows between their ribs, suicides and car wrecks, strokes and seizures, felons thrashing in electric chairs, starved men with swollen bellies, mothers bleeding out in their birthing beds, houses burning in the night, missiles falling from the sky with screams, knifepoints splitting flesh. I saw Skye floating facedown, limbs loose and weightless, hair fanning out behind her head, a kind of halo. For a moment, she appeared to be flying.

And then she was gone. Or I was, falling through time again until I slammed back into my own body with a strangled cry. I was standing at the edge of my own backyard, on the cusp of the forest. Death stood beside me; his face was washed in shadow.

I flexed my fingers, lifted a foot, testing the limits of my own body, which felt unfamiliar to me. As if I'd been torn from it for some time. I looked around at the surrounding pine forest, which I recognized, even in the dark. I was home, back in Michigan. "Is this—"

"Yes," he said softly.

"The same night? The night she—"

"Yes."

I'd done it. I'd really done it. I'd made it back to her.

Death started forward into the deep thicket, moving through the forest like a deer or a ghost. Something that belonged there. I followed after him.

"You know, you're braver than I took you for," he said, turning to look at me over his shoulder.

I ducked under a low-slung branch. "I'm not brave. Just desperate."

"One and the same."

We walked for some time before the playhouse took shape, at the heart of a small clearing, lit by a sharp slant of moonlight. The plastic shutters on the windows were closed, so I couldn't see Adeline within. But I knew that she was there, could feel it, as if she'd called my name.

"You should go to her," said Death, stopping a few yards short of the playhouse. "She's been waiting."

"What will I say?"

"You'll know when the time comes. Go on, then. I'll wait."

But I didn't move. "What will become of the others after this? Are you going to cling to them forever?"

He frowned at my phrasing. "I'll cut them loose someday."

"When?" I needed an answer while I still had some leverage left.

He considered the question, a shadow falling over his face. "When . . . the story is over."

"And when will it be over?"

"I don't know. I haven't decided yet."

I turned to face him in full. There, in the deep of the forest, he looked more human than I'd ever seen him. Maybe he'd settled into that body of his during his time with the girls. "They love you; you know that, right? In their own way. As much as souls as small as ours can love an idea as big as you."

He narrowed his eyes, uncertain—mistrustful, even—like he wanted to hope but wouldn't let himself. "Do you really think that's true?"

"I wouldn't lie to you. Not here." I paused a beat, torn between Death and the playhouse, wanting to go to Adeline but knowing I had work left unfinished in life. I didn't know what was on the other side of this, if I would live to leave this night. But Death was still with me, and somewhere—through time, in the future, back on that beach—the girls were still alive, and I still had a chance to save them. Set them free.

"You should cut them loose. Not for their sake, but for yours. If you hold on to them any longer, they might destroy you. That's what happens to things we humans love in the end. I should know." I stepped closer to him, raised a hand to his cheek. I was surprised by its warmth. "All this time, I thought that we were becoming like you. But really, you were becoming like us. Living through us. That's why you're so scared to let us go."

Death's expression went blank for the briefest moment, but he recovered himself quickly, his eyes turning soft and fond, gentling. When he clasped his hand over mine, I thought he would kill me. For my insolence and honesty, for daring to see him as he truly was. "I'm not afraid of losing you."

"Then prove it," I said, playing a game of my own. "Set them free."

I slipped my hand from his before he had the chance to answer and took six long strides across the forest floor to the door of the playhouse. I could feel Adeline on the other side of it. But it took a moment to work up the courage I needed to crouch down, grasp the plastic knob, and tug it open.

And there she was, slumped against the far wall. Alive.

My sister was blinking slowly, like she'd only just woken up. Seeing her for the first time, I expected to feel the full weight of my grief—months and months of it bearing down on me at once—but instead, I felt lighter, like the pain had been taken from me, like I'd reverted back to the girl I was before: Adeline's little sister. I was hers again.

I stalled in the doorway on my hands and knees, my resolve failing as I looked at her. I didn't want to go in, and in this reality, on this quiet night, she was alive as long as I didn't. Nothing and no one could take her from me. I could stop time if I just stayed there, frozen.

But then Adeline raised her head. "Roslyn?"

I sprang forward with a little cry, the door falling closed behind me. I half expected her to disappear when I hugged her, evaporate in my arms. But she was there, just as real and alive as I was. "You're here. You're really here."

"I've been waiting for you," she said, and her voice was weak. "I knew you would come."

Every intention I'd had—to kill her, to save the girls, to fulfill my bargain with Death—dissipated in that quiet moment. I couldn't think of anything beyond her.

Adeline looked up at me, her eyes slow to focus. "Did he bring you here?"

I knew she meant Death. "I chose to come."

"Good. I always wanted it to be you in the end."

"Don't say that." I could barely speak for the tears.

"Why not?" said Adeline. "You know what you're here to do, and so do I."

"I haven't decided yet."

"You will," she said. "You were destined to be the death of me, and I wouldn't have it any other way. You're the best of both of us. I'm glad that, in the end, you're the one to make it through."

"You're wrong. You're going to die tonight, and I'm going to be nothing without you because that's all I am apart from you."

"That's not true." Her words came in a ragged gasp. "And I wish I could make you see that. I wish that I hadn't—" Whatever she'd wanted to say, she couldn't. Her voice seemed to snag, her eyes flashing wide like she'd seen something on the other side, beyond me, beyond life itself.

We were running out of time.

"I know about Shiloh," I said, because I needed to. I couldn't bear it, the idea that she would die without knowing how sorry I was.

Adeline's brows knit with confusion. "How do you—"

"Memories of the future," I said, and then, when she began to ask a follow-up question, I waved her off. "Never mind. It doesn't matter how I know. I just do. And I need you to know how sorry I am—"

"Roslyn—"

"Not just for the stuff with Shiloh, but all of it. Everything that I said when we fought. The jealousy. The anger. The things I said to you that night—last night, I mean. I apologize for all of it, and I've spent every day since then wishing I could take it all back."

"You don't owe me any apologies," said Adeline, in tears. "I'm the one who should be apologizing to you. I should have been there for you, and all I did was make things worse—"

"You didn't—"

"But I did," she said. "I was your older sister, and I was supposed to protect you."

"You did. In your own way."

"I did for a while," she said. "But I . . . Roslyn, I cracked. I broke. And when I did, I think I broke you with me. No, I know that I did. I just couldn't keep it up. I wanted to do better, to be better for you, but I just couldn't do it. I would see all these sisters who shielded their younger siblings from the worst of the world, the worst of themselves. And I so badly wanted to be that for you, but I couldn't. Instead, I became the thing that I should've been protecting you from."

"That's not true."

But she couldn't hear; she was lost to herself, as if the playhouse were empty. "I resented you. I wanted what you had. I always have."

I laughed aloud at that.

Adeline's face screwed into a pinched frown, the same look she always gave when she felt someone was belittling or talking down to her. "What's so funny?"

"Nothing. It's just absurd to me that you even think that. I mean, what could I possibly have that you don't?"

The question startled her; she looked at me, shocked. "What do you mean?"

"Exactly what I said. I'm just trying to catch up to you. I always have been."

Adeline blinked rapidly, shook her head with disbelief. "Roslyn, you have *everything*. The grades, track, and that weirdly loyal boyfriend—"

"I broke up with him, by the way." I knew she'd be glad to hear it. It was a small thing, but I wanted to give her as many good moments as I could before the end.

"I'm glad, because he's an idiot. But that's the thing; even idiots like him like you. Everyone does. You don't have to do anything to be seen or heard except be yourself. I've always known that, but it was only after Shiloh that I started to resent you for it."

"Adeline, please. I'm so sorry—"

"You don't have anything to apologize for. Neither does she. It wasn't her that screwed me over. I did it to myself. Because I was so jealous of what you had—and so miserable over what I lacked—that it broke me. But it's been that way for a while, before Shiloh ever came into the picture. She was just a living confirmation of what I've always known."

I didn't want to ask the question, but I forced myself to anyway. "What have you always known?"

Adeline spoke so softly I barely heard her. "That I don't measure up to you."

I couldn't have been more surprised if she'd leaned over and slapped me. "Tha-that's not true, and if you'd just come to me and told me that you were thinking that, I could've . . . helped you. Or *something*. We could've talked. Made things right."

"I was too ashamed," said Adeline. "I felt pathetic, and I hated myself for resenting the person I love more than anyone else. I didn't know how to face you, so I just stopped trying. I got sicker and sicker and angrier and angrier until you hated me too."

"I never hated you, I—"

"Don't lie to me, Roslyn. Not now."

I clamped my mouth shut. She was right, and we both knew it. Sometimes I'd even wondered if it was impossible for me to love her so fiercely, to know her as well as I did without that hatred. As if it was a price I had to pay for the proximity. "Adeline, I'm so sorry."

"Will you stop fucking apologizing?" It was more a plea than a demand, no anger in it, only desperation.

"But I have to, because I don't want you to—" I couldn't bear to say the word *die*. "I don't want to leave here without being sure that you know the truth. You say you didn't measure up to me, but that's not true. I have only ever existed in your shadow, and I don't know who or what I am without you. All I've done is fill the spaces you've left behind, but I'm no substitute."

Adeline shook her head. "You're wrong, Roslyn—"

"I'm not. I've taken everything from you because I wanted so badly to be who you are. To have what you have. You're so full of fire and life, and everyone knows it. I'm nothing in comparison."

Adeline was quiet for a long time. Not looking at me. "What I have is artificial. Put on. It has to be, because I'm so weak beneath it all. But you're not like that. You're stronger than you seem. You always have been. That's why you'll walk away from this. You're going to have a good, long life—"

"Stop—"

"You're going to find someone who really cares about you. Someone who really deserves you—"

"Adeline, shut *up*—"

"And I'll watch on, from my place in forever. And I'll be happy for you. Really happy this time. There's nothing I'll want to take from you or be jealous of. No way for us to hurt each other anymore. Just the good things left."

I was crying too hard to speak. I crawled across the playhouse, tucked myself into her the way I used to when we were kids. She'd hated it when I'd done that. Adeline was never a touchy person, always squirming her way out of hugs, the first to pull away. But when I leaned against her then, she tipped her head to mine, her cheek pressing into the top of my skull.

"I know what you're here to do," said Adeline, and her voice was weaker now. "I'm ready for it. I've known for some time that it was coming, and I'm tired of fighting it. I'm tired of just about everything."

"Even me?"

I felt her shake her head. "No. Not you. You're the hardest part of all of this, but . . . you've got to let me go."

"Why?"

"I was never yours to keep," she said, a fact so simple I couldn't challenge it. Because a part of me had always known that it would come down to this. I had spent my whole life preparing to lose her, fearing the day she'd cast me off or just disappear. I knew I couldn't hold on to her any more than I could grasp a fistful of fog. But despite all the years I'd had to prepare for her inevitable loss—I still wasn't ready to let her go.

"Promise me you'll stay with me?" I whispered. "In whatever way you can?"

"I will," she said, and nodded to herself. "That's a goal of mine."

I laughed aloud at the stubborn absurdity of it. Only Adeline would have a list of goals to accomplish in death. But I believed she'd be able to do it.

"You're not scared?" I asked her, still stalling, trying to prepare for the moment. My hand, the one cursed with the touch of Death, gave a dull throb. A warning. It was almost time.

"Of course I'm scared. I've been scared my whole life." Her expression suddenly changed, her mouth pulling taut at the edges. Her heart fluttered up to her sternum and trembled there, like a leaf in the wind.

I grabbed her, harder than I intended, my fingers clenching around her wrist like I was free-falling and she was the last thing I had to hold on to. "No. I'm not ready."

"You never will be," said Adeline, and when she took me by the hand, I felt a flash of white pain, sharp and momentarily blinding. My vision seemed to reverse for a split moment so that, instead of looking into her face, I was staring at my own.

I looked broken.

I blinked, returning to myself. Adeline guided my hand to her sternum, and I could feel her heart.

"There's no hospital that can save me now," she whispered, smiling as she said it.

I tried to pull my hand away, but Adeline held it fast, even as her strength began to fail her. Her eyes went out of focus, threatening to roll back into her head as she fought to stay conscious.

It couldn't have been easy, what with her heart barely beating in her chest.

"Come on," she said again. "I can't do this without you. It has to be a choice, and I want it to be yours, not his. It's the last thing I'll ever ask. Don't say no."

I felt the pressure of tears in my throat, like a stone that I couldn't choke down. I had more that I wanted to say to her. More that I wanted to ask—about what I should do in the future without her, the kind of person I should be, how best to mourn her, where she wanted me to spread her ashes, when and with whom. But the time for questions was over.

"Goodbye," she said, and her chest gave beneath my hand. I fell through her, into free fall, through memories—hers or mine, I didn't know. I saw our house in Michigan, in the middle of summer. I ran toward it, the asphalt so hot I had to pick my feet up quick, run faster, throwing myself forward with abandon to keep them from burning.

I grew older, slower. My feet turned heavy, like stones I could barely lift. The sadness came down like a smothering blanket, settled around my shoulders, until I could barely think beyond it. I lay in bed with my sister, our bodies fitted together, and I told her that I was going to get better someday and that, when I did, we'd go to the sea.

It was a promise I couldn't keep. One of many.

My sadness festered, turned to anger. Then the anger turned to rage. The sessions with the therapists stopped helping. Pills were offered that I couldn't bring myself to take.

That same summer, I went north with my aunt, to a little cabin in the woods near the lake. At night, when I was supposed to be sleeping, the water called to me. And when the rage hooked its claws between my ribs, when the blanket of my sadness grew so heavy I felt like I'd die beneath it, I answered.

I left the house in the middle of the night, barefoot, in a T-shirt, and walked two miles through the trees, sliding down the dunes to the lake's edge. It was cold, and the wind tossed the water into whitecaps that wrecked themselves on the shore. I stepped into the dark water. It was so cold I could barely breathe, but I managed to get three words out, a pinched whisper: "Here I am."

I waded deeper, until the water came up to my chest, until I couldn't feel the bottom anymore. Then I went farther still, let the currents take me. The black waves broke over my head, and then I was falling, weightless, sucked down into the deep.

When I woke, the morning sun was pulling clear of the dunes and there were six girls standing over me. Shiloh and Naomi, Iona and Chloe, Riley and Skye. Though I didn't know their names yet. Behind them was the dark cut of a man, Death.

A bargain was made. A deal struck.

Roslyn.

The memories fractured. I saw Shiloh with her back to the stars. I saw a playhouse in the middle of the woods. I saw myself—no, my sister. Her dark eyes filled with tears. She was screaming at me, pleading, almost. I wanted to tell her that everything would be okay, because I would make it that way. Because I loved her. Because she was the best of me, and I'd always known it. Even then, at the end, I knew. I wanted to tell her, but the words were gone. I was losing her.

Stay with us.

New memories surfaced. The forest in the dead of night. A city of lights, music pulsing through me. Then, all at once, I was in the back of a pickup truck, Shiloh's, wind ripping at my hair.

I fell, through time and memories, reeling through a thousand stolen moments, shrinking into the distance, into the pinpricks of stars, the whorls of the galaxies cycling around me. I closed my eyes, and when I opened them again, the spinning had stopped, and she was there with me, at the end.

Roslyn.

I took her by the hand. Pressed it to my chest. And in that moment, she was everything.

Come back to me.

I OPENED MY eyes, found myself back in my own body, staring up at a black sky spangled with stars. The girls encircled me, their faces backlit by moonlight. "She's alive. She made it."

I sat up, and they parted so that I had a clear view down the shore to the black figure of Death, wrapped in a storm of sand.

There was a sound coming off him, the voices of the dead forming a kind of windswept chorus. I don't know if I imagined it, but I thought I heard Adeline and Skye, their voices on the wind. I didn't know what they were saying, but it felt like goodbye.

"He's setting us free," said Shiloh, tears streaming down her cheeks. And it wasn't just her. All of them were crying as we watched him slip away.

All at once, I was on my feet. I ran—fast as I ever have—but Death, walking slowly, kept pulling ahead, leaving me behind. He shrank into the distance, so small I could barely see him. Wind rolled down the beach, throwing sand between us. When it settled, he was gone.

Chapter 30

We traveled together through the last of that summer, both relishing our newfound freedom and completely and profoundly lost. From the beach, we doubled back to retrieve the RV. We sold the station wagon at a car lot and forked over the cash from the sale to get the RV fixed, Riley presiding over the mechanics like an anxious mother watching surgeons operate on her child.

The RV pulled through, and we resumed our road trip to nowhere in particular. We pored over maps and scrolled through internet forums to find the places we wanted to see. We were almost out of money, so we lived as true nomads. No checking into hotels or impromptu shopping trips. We bought only what we needed, and what we couldn't afford was paid for by cobbling together odd jobs—painting houses, cleaning up yards, washing cars, babysitting, and other gigs.

It was hard but good, and we knew it wouldn't last forever. But

I don't think any of us expected things to dissolve as quickly as they did, on that brisk morning at the tail end of August, at a gas station in the middle of Utah.

"It's time," said Shiloh. She was sitting on a picnic bench, watching the sun rise over the distant hills. No one asked what she meant. We all knew.

Death's experiment—our role in it—was over. It was time to disband.

We decided to pool the last of our funds into gas and food, to drive all the girls back to their homes or someplace where they could crash for a while until they decided who and what they wanted to be next.

Riley was the first to come to a decision. We drove with her to Montana, where the sky seemed bigger than it did in any place I'd ever been before. We left her at a rural hunting cabin where her grandfather spent his summers.

"I could use the quiet," she said as she dragged her bags from the belly of the RV. "It'll be nice for a change."

Riley hugged me for the first and final time, a tight embrace, her shoulder cutting so deeply into my throat she choked me a bit. "You're the best of us," she said, and then she was gone, stepping into her new life.

We sold the RV just after that, for the gas money we'd need for the rest of the journey. It was a tearful goodbye at a car lot in the middle of North Dakota.

Chloe was the next to leave. She decided to go to Chicago to live with her godmother, a sculptor with an artist's loft in the heart of the city.

"You know," she said to me, just before leaving, "you could stay here if you want. We never did get your wardrobe figured out."

I laughed aloud, but part of me was tempted. I liked the city; it felt like it was a place where I could remake myself. But as much as I dreaded the return to Michigan—and I did dread it, with a growing pit in my stomach—I knew that I needed to go home. Not forever. But for now. There were loose ends to be tied up, parents I missed, and a plastic playhouse in the middle of the forest that I needed to see just one more time.

We left Chloe in Chicago and drove up to Michigan the next day, all of us packed into Shiloh's truck. I choked back tears at the sight of my own house. The windows all aglow from the light of the TV. The same sun-stained patio furniture cluttered together on the front porch.

"Here we are again," said Iona. She would be leaving after me. She'd picked a town in upstate New York where she thought she could make a life. Naomi—still in the worst of her grief after losing Skye—had decided to go with her. "Are you ready, Roslyn?"

I shook my head, holding back tears. "No."

In the rearview mirror, Shiloh's eyes met mine for the briefest moment, then she cast her gaze sharply away, her hand tightening around the steering wheel.

I got out of the truck and said my goodbyes, feeling half out of my own body. I gave Naomi a fierce hug, and Iona clutched onto me so tight our cheeks smashed together. There were tears and apologies and promises that we wouldn't be able to keep, and we knew it and made them anyway.

Things came into focus again when I turned to Shiloh. She

wiped my tears on the sleeve of her jacket and dragged me into a hard hug.

"It's pretty down in Texas this time of year," she said, murmuring into my hair. "You'd like it there."

"I know I would," I whispered. "But I can't go with you this time."

Iona and Naomi looked very pointedly at their shoes, giving us some privacy. Shiloh tipped her forehead to mine, our lips just apart, eyes closed. I could've stayed in that moment forever, but Shiloh pulled away, faster than I expected her to, and I had the urge to catch her by the arm, drag her back. But instead, I let her leave me. I watched as she climbed back into the truck, Naomi and Iona following her.

They pulled around the cul-de-sac slowly. I watched them trail down the street and disappear around a bend.

I stood in the driveway for some time, waiting to see if they'd come back.

They never did.

Epilogue

In the months that followed, I folded myself back into the confines of my old life with an ease that scared me. My parents welcomed me home with tears and hugs so fierce it was like they were afraid I'd disappear if they didn't hold on tight enough. They didn't ask many questions, but weeks after my return, I would still catch my mom staring at me, trancelike, a furrow in her brow as if she was trying to decide whether I was really there or if her daughter had been replaced with someone she didn't know.

I didn't have the heart to say it was the latter.

We didn't talk much about that summer. I spun a few stories about Lake Michigan, twisting the tales of my time on the road to keep up the ruse, and I told them about the girls, because I missed them so much, and if I didn't share my memories, I worried that they would die with me. My parents listened to my stories without asking any questions. It hurt at first, their lack of interest, but after some time, I realized what was really at work, that my parents had been held in a sort of suspended state of being, a kind of suppression. It was here that my parents had dwelled, in this thin not-reality where my being away was a question that needed no answer.

It was, I realized, the work of Death.

It took me three weeks to summon the courage to go out into the forest. But then, one cool night the first week of October, I did it. I found a flashlight in the basement, put on my dad's rain boots, and trudged out into the thicket, which had grown higher and denser during my time away. I walked for a long time and had begun to suspect I was lost when I saw the clearing in the middle of the woods. Empty.

The playhouse was gone, just a bleached square of grass to mark where it once stood.

I lay down, closed my eyes, and imagined myself dying in the thick of the forest just like my sister had. I thought of my body, bloated and soft, and imagined all the hungry things in the forest floor surfacing to consume me. The vultures that would circle down from the sky to feed on the flesh of me. I would give it to them freely and without complaint.

I would feel no pain.

I opened my eyes, gazed up at the sky studded with stars. Then I got up and left the forest.

I would never return.

After nine months of playing catch-up—of late-night tutoring sessions and extra online classes to make up for the ones I failed in my grief—I graduated. As I climbed up onto the stage in my cap and gown, I turned to look at the crowd, and for a moment, I thought I saw them. The girls, all six of them, sitting in the back row, their faces washed featureless by sunlight. But when I stepped offstage, they were all gone. The seats empty.

I got into a college that was decent enough to make people think I was okay. My life grew to become good in its own way. I made friends and went out with them on Fridays. I talked to a therapist every week. I started running again, not with a team, but in the evenings after my classes, just for the rush of it.

Life fell into its familiar rhythms. Nothing strange or gruesome. No shocks of death or brushes with my own mortality. With time, that summer with the girls faded to a grim and wonderful memory.

So I was surprised when I first saw the two of them walking across campus.

I noticed the girl first. It was bitter cold that day, but all she wore was a thin black cardigan and a matching skirt that stopped short at the middle of her thighs. Her legs, at least, were sheathed in burgundy tights, and her shoes were sensible, loafers so well-worn and soft that they must've been vintage. She was pretty enough to turn heads as she jaywalked across the intersection, seemingly oblivious to the cars that blasted their horns as she cut past.

But it was the man by her side that really startled me. He was tall and wiry, dressed in funeral blacks. A different face, but I would've known him anywhere. Death.

He followed the girl so closely there was no way she could've missed him, but she walked as though she were alone, her fingers shoved into the shallow pockets of her skirt, frail shoulders rounded against the cold. She seemed young—younger than me, maybe. Around Skye's age if she'd survived that summer. In fact, she favored Skye. Something in the set of her mouth, the look in her eyes when she met mine from across the intersection. I expected her to walk out into the traffic again, but she stopped short.

I shifted my gaze over her shoulder to Death. He smiled and I saw that the girl was his, the way I used to be. I had the sudden urge to run from them both, the instinct kicking my heartbeat into a fast and terrible rhythm.

But when the light changed, I stepped out into the intersection anyway.

Not without fear, but in spite of it.

Death's gaze held mine as we moved toward each other, meeting briefly in the middle of the intersection, passing so close that our hands brushed, and when they did, I caught a glimpse—just a flash, really—of us. The girls on the beach as he'd seen us, wide eyed and afraid but brave enough to face him. I heard his voice on the wind, in the sound of so many boots scuffing over concrete, in the rush of the passing traffic: *Until next time.*

I turned to look at him over my shoulder—to say goodbye or something close to it—but he was already gone.

I haven't seen him since, but I know that one day he'll come back for me. Maybe he'll wear Skye's face or my sister's. Or perhaps he'll send the girls, one last dispatch for old times' sake. I think I would like to see them all, just one more time, before the end.

Acknowledgments

I want to start by thanking my editor, Polo Orozco. From our very first conversation, I felt like you had the same heart and vision for Roslyn and the girls as I did. I can't thank you enough for helping me shape their story into everything I hoped it could be. I'm so lucky to have you as my editor.

I also want to thank my publishers, G. P. Putnam's Sons and Penguin Random House Children's across the pond, with special thanks to my UK editor, Amina Parchment-Youssef, for her wonderful insight and contributions to this book. Thank you, Zach Meyer, for illustrating such a beautiful cover, and Kelley Brady for designing it. I also owe a thank-you to Rachel Skelton, who copyedited this book with so much care and consideration, and to Eileen Savage for doing such a great job with the interior design of this book. And thank you, Ilana Jacobs and Madeline Art. I'm so grateful for the contributions you made to this book and all the work you put into it.

I want to thank Jenny Bent for being the best advocate I could ever ask for. You've been with me since this story was just a seed of an idea and worked so hard to help me grow it into the book it is today. I'm incredibly grateful to have you in my corner.

Thank you to my partner, Alice, for reading my drafts and keeping me (somewhat) sane through the process of writing them. I'd also like to thank the rest of my family and friends, with special thanks to my aunt, my little sister, and my beloved cats. And I would be remiss not to thank my mom, who was alive when I first started writing this book and gone by the time I finished it. I'll love and miss you forever.

Finally, I want to thank my readers. It brings me so much comfort and joy to know there are people out there who connect to the stories I've created, or even see some part of themselves in my books. That sense of belonging is really sacred to me, and I'm so grateful for it. Thank you.

Alexis Henderson is a speculative fiction writer with a penchant for dark fantasy, witchcraft and cosmic horror. Growing up in one of America's most haunted cities, Savannah, Georgia, instilled in her a life-long love of ghost stories. When she doesn't have her nose buried in a book, you can find her painting or watching horror movies with her feline familiar. Her acclaimed adult books include *The Year of the Witching*, *House of Hunger* and *An Academy for Liars*. Her debut YA novel, *When I Was Death*, published in March 2026.

@lexish

PRAISE FOR *WHEN I WAS DEATH*

'Atmospheric and achingly lyrical, *When I Was Death* is a tale of untamed girlhood, defiant loyalty and a relentless search for truth.'

Sophie Clark, author of *Cruel is the Light*

'Honest, emotionally raw and brilliant, *When I Was Death* shattered my heart and rebuilt it into something new. Packed with gut-wrenching turns I never saw coming, it's the kind of story I wish I could experience for the first time all over again.'

Angela Montoya, author of *A Cruel Thirst*

'Alexis Henderson's hauntingly beautiful prose explores how girlhood and grief are often intertwined. I savoured every single page.'

Cynthia Murphy, author of *Win Lose Kill Die*

'Hauntingly beautiful and equally heart-wrenching, *When I Was Death* explores love and loss in a way that both hurts and heals. Alexis Henderson has crafted an intimate, powerful and utterly unputdownable tale.'

Channelle Desamours, author of *Needy Little Things*

'A searing portrayal of girlhood, at once sparkling and violently dark. *When I Was Death* is thrilling and wholly original.'

Goldy Moldavsky, author of *The Last Girl*

'This is girlhood at its darkest and most glittering. *When I Was Death* is the culty road trip fantasy of your dreams. It's horror with heart, unafraid to explore the sharp edges of friendship and sisterhood.'

Maria Meservey, author of *The Ironfell Inheritance*

'Henderson's prose glows with honesty, her characters richly textured and utterly alive. The story drifts through the relentless current of love and loss, tracing the sharp-toothed gaps grief leaves behind and the lengths one might go to fill them.'

Abby Dewsnup, author of *Rabbit Heart*

'I couldn't put it down! *When I Was Death* is brilliant from start to finish.'

Abiola Bello, author of *Love in Winter Wonderland*

'A beautiful exploration of grief and girlhood. Five stars. I'll be haunted by this one for a long time.'

Beth Tomlin, author of *To Hell With You*

Also by Alexis Henderson

ADULT NOVELS
An Academy for Liars
House of Hunger
The Year of the Witching